MW00435963

CLOSER THAN YOU THINK

CLOSER THAN YOU THINK

A BROKEN MINDS THRILLER

LEE MAGUIRE

TCK PUBLISHING.COM

Copyright © 2018 by Lee Maguire.

All rights reserved.

No part of this book may be reproduced, stored in retrieval systems, or transmitted by any means, electronic, mechanical, photocopying, recorded or otherwise without written permission from the publisher.

This is a work of fiction. Names, characters, places, and incidents either are the product of the author's imagination or are used fictitiously. Any resemblance to actual persons, living or dead, events, or locales is entirely coincidental.

ISBN: 978-1-63161-060-8

Published by TCK Publishing
www.TCKpublishing.com

Get discounts and special deals on books at
www.TCKpublishing.com/bookdeals

Sign up for Lee's newsletter at
www.leemaguire.ink

CHAPTER ONE

MAX AND I STOOD ON the front porch, listening for signs of life from within. Max looked forlorn, and I wondered if my face mirrored her expression.

I rang the doorbell again.

The porch was pretty much the same as when I lived there not so long ago, apart from a couple of new plants hanging from twisted ropes secured to the ceiling. The deepening sunset gave the front of the house an ethereal glow.

I turned the knob. The door opened a crack.

"Vicki?"

No answer.

I wiped my feet and stepped into the foyer. Max dashed ahead, not bothering to look back.

I took a deep breath and trudged toward the kitchen at the end of the hallway. There, a large bay window provided a view of a lush backyard bordered by a line of lovely pin oaks—one of my favorite spots in the house.

Max disappeared.

There was no sign of Vicki. I did find, however, a note with my name on it on the kitchen table. I picked it up.

Bryce: Had to scoot. If you don't mind, please put Maxie in the room.
Talk soon. V

I closed my eyes to strengthen my resolve. Big mistake: the smell of warm vanilla sugar greeted me, jolting my eyes open. I felt off-kilter. I had to keep moving. "Max!"

I heard her rooting around in the basement. I figured she would heed my call in a minute or two.

I sat down at my kitchen table. And why not? I bought the damn thing, after all. I shook my head.

Vicki predicted—correctly—I would enter the house and wander into the kitchen. I wasn't sure which irritated me more—her absence or her foresight.

"Max!"

"Woof!"

Shared custody of a basset hound isn't always easy.

I stopped staring out the window and glanced at the pile of mail on the table. I reached out, coaxed a few of the top pieces off, and slid them toward me.

I shouldn't be doing this.

I glanced around to check if anyone was watching, then flipped through the envelopes. Bills.

My face flushed, and I put them back. I wanted to snoop some more, but it didn't feel right.

"MAX!"

This time, I heard her short basset legs and antique-bathtub-claw-foot paws pounding up the stairs.

"Hey, don't you know to come when I call?"

Max looked at me and—I swear—she grinned. No remorse at all.

I rubbed Max's head, raced up the stairs with her, and let her into the master bedroom. I shook hands with her and closed the door behind me, although part of me wanted to check things out.

Maybe go through a dresser.

No. Enough snooping for one day. I jogged down the stairs, turned the lock on the front door as I left, and drove home to my townhouse.

My stomach growled, but my eyes were heavy, and every step was an immense effort. I skipped the refrigerator and headed straight upstairs. I stripped off my clothes, hoping hot water would help nudge me toward sleep.

Afterwards, I headed to the bedroom and flopped on the bed. Drowsiness beckoned, opening the portal for fleeting images: Vicki and me playing with Max. Laughter. Max burrowing under our arms, licking our faces. Holding hands with Vicki as we climbed the stairs toward our bedroom. Vicki's soft skin. Pulling me close....

And at that moment, I was struck by the scent of a soft, floral fragrance, foreign in this space. Perfume? I sat bolt-upright.

Was someone in my house?

I sat on the edge of the bed and listened. But I heard only the sound of my heart pounding a rock-drum beat in my ears. I flipped on the lamp on my nightstand and glanced around the room as I tried to slow my breathing.

I scrambled off the bed and pulled the balcony door open. It was unlocked, as was the screen door beyond it.

Hadn't it been locked earlier?

I stepped outside, past the lawn chair awaiting more reflective moments, and stumbled toward the railing.

Nothing. Glancing down, I saw only dark grass and the nearby parking lot. No movement.

Puzzled, I returned to the bedroom. Remembering that discretion is the better part of valor, I picked up a flashlight from the top of my dresser and made my way out the bedroom door into the hallway, snapping on lights as I went.

With each step, I expected someone to leap out, shoot, fling a stiletto, or crank up a chainsaw.

Apprehension sent my heart rate into overdrive. I lurched through the rest of the upstairs rooms but found nothing incriminating. No broken glass, open windows, or dead bodies awaited me.

But I couldn't relax yet. I had more real estate to cover, and I was concerned about my ability to manage my racing pulse.

I crept down the stairs; my flashlight beam cast shadows along the wall. In my mind's eye, I thought I glimpsed a crouched shape. A silhouette of a tall, thin figure wearing a hat, hiding beyond the corner. Sounds of muted breathing. I spun toward the shift in air flow, sensing a hand about to grasp my wrist. My chest was so tight I couldn't draw in a breath. Every shape seemed sinister and foreboding.

Even after I stumbled along and flicked on light after light, my fear remained. But nothing seemed amiss. All entry doors were still locked. I even checked the closet in the laundry room. Only Max's dog food—in the large economy bag—and a broom lay inside. Max's bed was in there, too, for those occasions when I went to work and she was left to guard the house alone.

I closed the closet door as I stepped back. Something under my foot shrieked. I twisted away and tripped, hitting the floor with the palms of my hands, sending jolts of pain up my arms. There on the floor—one of Max's squeaky toys. A goofy yellow furry doll, one of her favorites.

Feeling like a quarterback who'd just been laid out by a pair of linebackers, I got to my feet and leaned against the washing machine. The cold steel against my fingers pushed a chill through me. A shiver forced me to take a breath.

The soft ticking of my living room clock oriented me. How long had I been standing in the laundry room? I took a step forward and reversed my earlier course, returning the downstairs to darkness. I trudged up the stairs to the second floor and returned to the bedroom.

The amber glow of the clock said one-thirty. My body cried out for rest, but I knew sleep wouldn't come. Vicki always called me a night owl, but I never felt it was by choice.

Sometimes, thinking or completing paperwork was easier in the quiet of the night. Most of the time, it was an inability to sleep. Forget meditation and other non-pharmacological sleep aids. They were for garden-variety sleeplessness. What I experienced had a life of its own.

A whisper of floral scent lingered. If it held a special meaning for me, I couldn't place it—yet an olfactory memory stirred deep inside, teasing me. It was a peculiar sensation, like having someone's name on the tip of your tongue.

I sprawled on the bed, turned off the light, and stared at the ceiling. I rolled to the other side and pressed my head against the pillow. The scent tickled my nostrils. There. On the pillow. Not the one I used most often, but the other one that completed the set. A soft, floral perfume, clear as could be.

I turned on the lamp once more, gathered the pillow in my hands, and inspected it. For comparative purposes, I sniffed one pillow and then the other. If this were a *Candid Camera* routine, I was sure going to be embarrassed.

Someone had spritzed perfume on the pillow. I had no idea who, why, or when. I wasn't even sure which question to tackle first. I wouldn't need to worry about succumbing to sleep anytime soon. Nerves on edge, I turned off the light and found myself wishing for someone to talk to.

I recalled the images of Vicki, and for a moment I wondered if perhaps she had been in the house. Perhaps she had hoped to surprise me and had waited for me in the bedroom, but I had returned too late. I realized it wasn't the right answer even before the last thought cooled in my brain. I would have better spent my time pounding my head on a rock. Fear bled into loneliness, and squeezing my eyes shut failed to keep the deepening dread out.

CHAPTER TWO

AT FIVE A.M., I GAVE up and got out of bed. My body was too busy
listening to my head. Nothing made sense. I found my slippers, slid
into them, and shuffled down the hall to the second bedroom/home
office. With the blue banker's lamp glowing, I powered up the
computer and settled into my soft leather desk chair—one of my
vices. Comfort in the workplace.

As the operating system loaded, my attention meandered
from the screen to the rest of the room. Other than the table on
which the computer rested, the room held a smaller table that I used
as a workspace, the desk chair, and a green-and-rust-colored futon
decked out in a Southwest cover. There was one bookcase filled
with a range of treatises. A small but tidy office. Well, small. I
tended to put things into piles until they grew large enough to
dwarf little children, followed by inevitable periodic purges to
manage the clutter.

The piles, I was sure, were genetic. At one time, my father had
labored to build a two-car garage that never housed actual vehicles.
Instead, it became a storage space for all kinds of tools and
mechanical equipment that did nothing but gather dust. Boxes, jars,
and containers holding odds and ends stored over several decades
consumed the rest of the space. A child of the Depression, he saved
everything, no matter how impractical or inconsequential.

My thoughts log-jammed as I remembered my father's garage.
He had died about two years before, succumbing to lung cancer at

the age of eighty while my mother cared for him at home. It was a sad end for a strong man—an ex-Marine gunnery sergeant who'd fixed the roof of his house when he was in his seventies. My wife and I logged many miles in the family car to visit during those final weekends. After he died, we decided to move closer to support my mother. That was eighteen months ago.

And for six long months, I had lived alone in this townhouse.

How the mind wanders in the early morning hours. I shifted my attention to the computer monitor and clicked the email icon. The program prompted me to enter my password. I pulled an index card out from under my mousepad, located the appropriate password, and typed it in. Six messages loaded. There were several from colleagues. A couple ofadvertisements. I clicked on a message with the return address "*ribschild.*" A simple, one-line message sent a shiver through me:

Closer than you think.

Anxiety pressed me against the back of the chair; I folded my arms across my chest for protection. What was this about? I struggled to sort out the message. Maybe it was only junk mail. Perhaps I'd be getting a barrage of graphic adult advertising of some kind. Or someone might be coming out with a tasty new barbecue sauce.

My gut twisted. None of those alternatives felt right. First, the perfume. Now this.

I had dialed the number before I even realized the phone was in my hand.

"H-hello?" Vicki asked, clearing her throat.

"It's me. I, uh, needed to talk with you for a few minutes."

"Huh? What's going on? What time is it? You sound funny."

"It's after five. I don't feel funny. The weirdest thing happened to me tonight, and—"

"Wait, what? You woke me up for this? You couldn't wait to tell me later?"

"Tell you later? Like we have a planned time? Like last night? You weren't even home at the time we agreed to meet."

"Yeah, well, something came up. But I'm tired, here. So tell me about the weird thing, or I'm going to go."

"I'm trying. Thing is, after I got home from your place, when I got to the bedroom, I smelled perfume. Someone had been in my room! It scared the crap out of me!"

"What? Are you sure?"

"Yeah, I'm sure. I won't soon forget the experience." I paused. "I even thought for a second…well, that you had come over."

Crickets. My heart beat in my throat as Vicki's silence lengthened.

"Vi…?"

"Come over? What, like I came over to hang out in your bedroom and spread some pixie dust? Surprise you when you returned home?"

I put down the phone for a moment and took a breath.

"Yeah, that's what I was thinking. I know. It's silly. But there's no denying the perfume. It's on one of my pillows, and *I* certainly didn't put it there! How do you explain that?"

"There's got to be some other rational explanation. Do you really think someone broke into your place just to spritz your pillow?"

"I know it sounds odd. But it happened, and then I got this email message that spooked me." I read the message.

"That's pretty vague. Sounds like random chain mail or an advertisement for antiperspirant or toothpaste. You know, a 'smell-better-so-people-will get-closer' type of thing."

"Maybe, but I'm still shaken up."

"Aw, Christ, Bryce. You get spooked when there's nothing going on. It's your nature. Remember when you accidentally parked in front of a handicapped ramp so you could carry out a box from a neighboring store? And the receptionist ran out and chewed you out? You were on edge for hours because you thought the police were going to come arrest you."

Not one of my best moments.

"Okay, yeah, but this is on an entirely different level," I said.

"If it's not a commercial, there are probably lots of people who would send out crap like that. It's probably a practical joke. Or spam. Don't put yourself through the wringer over this."

"Yeah, of course. I'm sure you're right. It's good to hear your voice, though."

I thought I heard a distant sigh.

"Is that what this is about? You called me at five a.m. just to hear my voice?"

She was irritated. How to recover?

"No, of course not. I was just upset. I needed to connect with someone, and you were the someone I called."

Vicki sighed again. "Next time, unless your place is on fire, wait to call me at a decent time. I need to work in a few hours."

"Right. I know. It's, well…I miss you."

There. I'd said it. Glutton for punishment?

"I realize that. I get that it's hard, but we didn't get to this point overnight. We aren't going to fix it tonight," she said.

It felt like a 10,000-pound weight settled on my chest. I tried to shrug it off.

"How are we going to fix anything if we don't even talk?"

"I need this space from you right now. It's all too…"

"What? Too what?"

"Too intense. Like tonight. Everything all stirred up. I can't save you anymore. You need to find your own way. I can't do it. I won't."

"Save me? What do you mean? Save me from what? I'm not asking to be saved. And you make it sound like you already made a decision and you're not telling me."

"No, it's not…. We can't go on repeating the same pattern. I'm tired. I need to go."

I caught myself frowning.

"What same pattern?"

"I can't get into all that again right now."

"Right. It's early. Can I give you a call tomorrow, er, later today?"

"Let's give it a day or two, okay? *Goodnight.*"

"Right. Goodnight."

As I hung up the phone, I felt a familiar sensation beckon. Like I was being pressed against a long glass wall with no way to navigate upward. No crevices or cracks on which to gain a foothold. And I was sliding toward a dark pit somewhere beneath me, a pit where unknown demons lurked.

CHAPTER THREE

NO TIME LEFT TO SLEEP. I trudged into the bathroom, stripped off my pajamas, and surveyed the face in the mirror. I was a ringer for a refugee from a Las Vegas casino. Beard stubble, circles beneath bloodshot eyes, and sandy brown, unkempt hair. I looked like I'd lost it all on the slot machines and spent the night at the casino bar.

It was an effort to shave off the stubble and step into the shower. I thought I heard my body creak as I adjusted the showerhead. I remembered a time when I was in better shape. However, as I recalled with modest humor, some comic strip character had once stated, *"Round* is a shape."

In the kitchenette, I poured a glass of grape juice and sat down on a barstool. I sipped the juice and stared out the kitchen window at a potted geranium on the windowsill. I never had a green thumb, but I appreciated colors.

The sun crept over the treetops as I climbed into my Toyota Prius. Driving the Prius is a pleasant experience once I cram my six-four frame into the vehicle. It provides both zip and fuel economy — the latter an important feature for me as gasoline prices always seem to be on the increase. Today, however, I experienced little pleasure as I got in and paused to gaze at my townhouse. Images from a few hours earlier revisited without invitation. I headed toward town.

New Alex, Pennsylvania sits in the northwestern part of the Commonwealth. It's an area surrounded by hills and trees, considered by many to be "God's Country." Even in my shitty frame of mind, I agreed. There are several state parks nearby, and lush havens provide outdoorsy types with much to satisfy them.

I glanced at the speedometer and backed off the accelerator. I reminded myself I needed to take it easy. I intended not to rush through these next two days, blocked off to take care of a couple important tasks—driving South to Titan College to prepare for a psych course I was scheduled to teach as an adjunct in the fall, and find office space for a part-time private practice.

CHAPTER FOUR

FRIDAY IS A CONSULTING DAY.

The children's agency nestles in what had once been a huge dog food factory. The sand-colored building spanned half a square block, had several floors, and had been taken over by the city a short time ago, who then began to lease space inside to businesses. The idea took hold, mostly because of the reasonable cost per square foot, and so by now, most spaces in the vast building had been rented out. There are some private physician practices and medical labs clustered together. Also ensconced in the cavernous dwelling is an outpatient behavioral health center for those kids and teens that functioned well in their environments, and, in a separate area, a residential facility which housed the most troubled adolescents — those who could not function in their communities.

The patients in the residential setting are there for up to a year, sometimes longer, having been determined by the legal system to be either delinquent and in need of treatment or rehabilitation, or dependent and needing their emotional and behavioral issues addressed. I consulted with both the outpatient and residential areas.

I parked my car in the lot across the street, crawled out, straightened my tie, grabbed my briefcase, and headed across the road and into the complex. Marge, the receptionist, smiled as I entered the main office to check for messages.

"Dr. Davison, good morning!"

At this point, dressed in my best work persona, I smiled back.

"Good morning to you, Marge. How's it going?"

"Some days can be a challenge. The phone never stops ringing, it seems. But I do enjoy the days that you're here. You have a calming presence about you, and I think everyone benefits from that."

"What a nice thing to say. I appreciate that. What you just described — that's what I hope to bring with me each day."

Marge nodded and handed me several messages. Which reminded me....

"Hey, Marge, I've been meaning to ask. How do you decide which calls warrant paper messages and which go to voicemail?"

Marge tapped a finger on her forehead. "You're the first person to ever ask me that. Not to belie my youth, but I was here before voicemail was a thing. It's a combination of how busy I am at a given moment and if it sounds like the caller might benefit from me talking with them further." She laughed. "At least that's how I think I do it."

"Well, just keep doing what you're doing. And thanks for your ongoing support."

As I left the outer office, I glanced at my watch. I had time to make a cup of tea. I went into the kitchen area where a couple of childcare staff members were talking. Tom and Nancy, if memory didn't fail me. Learning and remembering people's names in an agency with regular turnover was often challenging for me. Regulars like Marge, with whom I interacted every day, were much easier.

"Morning, guys," I said as I found my cup in the cupboard. I wasn't sure if I'd interrupted a casual chat or a work discussion, but I intended to move from the area as soon as my teabag hit the water in my cup.

"Hey, doc," Tom said. "How's it going?"

I had bumped into Tom several times. Stocky, balding, and difficult to pin down, age-wise, although I guessed he was thirtyish. He seemed friendly enough. I had heard from another staff member that Tom had worked in residential treatment prior to receiving his master's degree and enjoyed it enough to continue in a higher-level position with this agency. Now he served as one of several assistant unit directors in the residential treatment center.

"So far, so good," I said as I selected the tea *du jour*. After the late night I had experienced, I was glad to see it was Earl Grey and not Sleepytime.

"Great," Tom replied. "When you're new, finding your way around the corridors of this place is a challenge. Hey, we could do a wicked psychology experiment. Lock the staff in, cut off their food, put a block of cheese in the building somewhere, and let them find their way to it."

"That's wicked all right. But it would never get past an ethics committee. They're a stickler for things like depriving staff members of food."

"Yeah…ethics. Like that Hilgram study with the electric shocks."

"You mean Milgram. *Stanley* Milgram."

"Yeah. Slip of the tongue. Anyway." Tom glanced at Nancy and left the room.

Nancy watched him go and then turned toward me, smiling. She was young. Early twenties? It was getting harder for me to guess people's ages. She was blonde, leggy, and tan. In my interactions with her, she had always been friendly. Like most unit staff members, she had a bachelor's degree in psychology. From snippets of conversation as I met staff members, I believe although Nancy's degree was newly minted, she had worked hard and accumulated human service experience during summer employment.

She touched my forearm. "Dr. D, I have someone I'd like to discuss with you, maybe Monday. If I can, I'll bring him along with me. Your input would be helpful." She glanced at her cell phone. "Shoot, I have a unit meeting. So I'll catch up with you soon. Will that work for you?"

"Sure, stop by any time."

She left, and although she was gone, I continued to feel the touch of her fingers on my arm. Her eye contact was direct. More so than an incidental conversation might require.

Or maybe Vicki was right. My imagination was in overdrive.

Back on track, I followed through with the rest of my game plan. I plunked the teabag into the cup and headed down the hall to my office. Years of practice meant that I was adept at juggling a briefcase and cup of tea, fishing the office key from my pocket, and unlocking my door.

I let the tea steep for a bit while I reviewed the phone messages, putting them in a to-do-later pile. I scrounged through my desk drawer for some sweetener but found none. Time to search the cabinets.

Before I could step away, the phone rang. Marge's extension blinked on the phone panel.

"Dr. Bryce, there's a call for you. May I put it through? I'm sorry, but the caller won't give me any information."

Odd. I debated for a few seconds. I did not, however, want to keep Marge waiting. "Yes, Marge, I'll take it. Thank you."

I cleared my throat, picked up the handset, and in a hesitant voice said, "Hello?"

There was a pause on the line and then a whispered voice. I strained to hear the words....

"Closer than you think, Dr. Davison," informed the whisperer, and the line went dead.

I hung up the phone and rolled my chair back from the desk. Trying to take a full breath, my chest felt too tight. A wave of anxiety washed over me. The caller knew who I was, where I worked. Knew my schedule!

I had an urge to run. But where? Outside? See if anyone was in sight with a cell phone — and do what? Look like an idiot in front of those who turn to me for guidance? What do I do now? My thoughts collided.

I felt as if a wintry wind had pierced my entire body. Shivering, I took a sip of tea. It tasted bitter. Or had my fear altered my perception? Either way, I needed to get a handle on my well-being before it was too late.

One thing was for sure, I thought as I stepped out into the kitchen area to find some sweetener. The place I had found myself was a lonely one.

CHAPTER FIVE

RITUALS AND ROUTINES. I SETTLED into my consulting office Monday morning with a cup of tea, augmented on this occasion by a handful of Advil. Sitting back contemplatively, I glanced at the scenic ocean painting that graced one wall of the office.

Hanging over a corner of the frame was a circle of dead flowers.

I jumped up and snatched them from the picture frame. I wasn't sure what kind they were, but at one time, they may have been pretty. They were tightly woven and had not been preserved in any way. Not dried flowers—just dead ones.

A knock at the door startled me. I looked up to find Dr. Lawrence Jones standing in the doorway. He appeared in his usual form: tie off-kilter, shirt a bit rumpled; a combination of elder statesman and absent-minded professor, gray hair and all.

He nodded toward the flowers. "New hobby, or a new decoration?

"Oh, it's an old thing I was trying to figure out what to do with." I tossed it on an empty chair.

"I wanted to see if you could join us for a staffing in a few minutes," he said. "There is a new patient being admitted today, and we would like to hear your thoughts. Down in my office."

"Sure," I replied. "Be right there."

Dr. Jones vanished—and not a moment too soon. Had he stayed a second longer, he would have noticed my hands shaking.

CHAPTER SIX

DR. JONES'S OFFICE OCCUPIED THE corner of one of the wings on the residential unit, which had rooms on four corridors, pragmatically referred to as the North, South, East, and West units. Larry was an astute psychiatrist and medical director of the children's service. Unlike some younger psychiatrists, Larry was as interested in hearing what his patients had to say as he was in prescribing the newest medication on the market. Good thing, too. The kids in residence needed someone to listen with a caring ear to their often-tragic stories.

In the office with Larry was Linda Weiss, RN, known behind her back as Nurse Ratched. As often happens in facilities with creative staff members, nicknames were pinned on people, typically outside of their knowledge. Someone must have observed Linda wearing a perpetual scowl.

Nicknames often reflected turf battles between mental health agencies. For example, some staff members with master's degrees feel superior to those with less education. In the end, it was all about competence and attitude, but in the tedium of a work week, perceptions can jag at people. I probably had a nickname pinned on me, too, but I doubted that I would ever know what it is. If I had to guess, "Chief Psychobabble" would be reasonable.

I also found the variety of naming conventions to be interesting. Dr. Davison was the most formal thing people called me, but I also got

"Dr. D," "Dr. B," "Dr. Bryce," and sometimes just "doc." Sometimes the same individual used different titles. It was a bit of fun for me.

Most of my ongoing staff contacts were master's level psychotherapists whom I supervised. We met each week to discuss cases, and I felt I was building some good relationships with the three therapists assigned to me. One of them, Wendy, was also in the room.

Fresh out of graduate school, Wendy was the youngest of the therapists on staff—mid-twenties, with wonderful long, red hair that framed the pale skin of her face. The boys on her unit often sought to spend time with her. She was pretty, attentive, and remembered personal details about kids from even brief interactions. Kids could tell she was genuine and always clustered around her when she walked onto the unit. That's one of the ways you can recognize the reputation of a staff member. Fortunately, Wendy was as intelligent and intuitive as she was attractive, and her common sense helped her out of many potentially difficult situations. At this moment, she appeared to be under the glare of Nurse Ratched, who perhaps felt neither as youthful nor attractive in comparison. Not that she couldn't be considered such, mind you, but it's hard to win admirers without smiling. She seemed to do well with Larry, though, probably because he had her pegged.

The rule of the pack: Don't mess with the big dog.

I smiled at Wendy and sat down beside her. It seemed the individual we were about to discuss was going to reside in her unit. Her current patients were already an interesting bunch, but you could never tell what the next admission might do to the mix....

Nurse R. began. "We're admitting a sixteen-year-old white female to the North unit. Name's Maegan Mitchell. She's adjudicated dependent and has a very significant mental health history. She's going to be transferred to us from Northern Pennsylvania Hospital, where she's been treated for the past six months."

We weren't off to a good start. Six months in a hospital was a long time for an adolescent and usually suggested a degree of pathology with the strength of history behind it.

"She was admitted involuntarily following a suicide attempt. Her tool of choice was a straight razor. According to the medical report, the cuts were not deep, but scar tissue suggested that she had done extensive cutting previously. She had significant mood lability during the course of her hospital care. At times, she would follow the program and be a model citizen. Other times, she resisted and refused to disclose personal information. She would not speak for long periods of time. Records indicate a history of sexual abuse by caretakers, including partners of her mother and even a foster parent. The most recent abuse reportedly occurred within the past year."

I felt a knot in my stomach. This girl's life had taken a serious wrong turn somewhere and had grown more tragic over time. I guessed she was risking her chances for full recovery unless she formed a sufficient connection with a therapist and built a strong enough relationship to undo some of the damage.

"Wendy will be a good therapist for her," I noted. "She's nurturing — and this patient's interactions with men haven't been particularly healthy. However, we must also keep in mind she may be very angry with her mother, which also sets up some potential negative transference towards Wendy in therapy."

Larry nodded. "There's no question this girl has some things to work through."

He leafed through the medical record.

"From available information, it appears she's had no recent contact with her mother, although it's unclear as to why this might be the case. We don't know how the mother left things with her."

"What was her discharge diagnosis?" Wendy asked.

Nurse R. scanned her papers. "Post-Traumatic Stress Disorder and Dysthymia."

Wicked combination there, too. These diagnoses suggested not only was this girl having trouble stemming from the abuse, but she also had a history of depressed mood lasting at least one year. "Any psych testing?" I wondered aloud.

"Apparently it was attempted, but the patient refused."

"Might help for us to do some once some rapport is established," I suggested. "This young lady has some secrets she doesn't want to share."

"Are you thinking about some projective testing, Dr. Davison? A Rorschach, perhaps?" Larry asked.

Projective tests are designed to give little clue or structure as to how the patient should respond. Often, this allows the person to react in a manner that their reveals inner dynamics, helping us understand him or her from a psychological perspective. Such a test tends not to be as threatening as one asking direct questions, and won't raise someone's defenses as a result. On the other hand, some patients tell me the ink blots look like, well, ink blots. In psychobabble terms, we call that *resistance*.

"Maybe. There are several possibilities. Let's see how she does on the unit."

"Well," Larry said, scanning his list, "my initial inclination is to take her off meds, see how she does on her own. Find out what we're dealing with at baseline."

Heads nodded in agreement. Sometimes, over the course of treatment episodes with different practitioners, a patient's medication regimen could become bloated.

"This young woman arrives later today. Let's give her the evening to settle in. Wendy, drop by and introduce yourself tomorrow, would you?"

"Will do."

Larry closed the meeting by saying, "We'll staff this case in one week after the key personnel have had a chance to assess this young lady. Thanks for your efforts, folks."

As the meeting broke up, Wendy and I walked out of the office together.

"Wendy," I said, "after you check out this girl, let's talk. We'll tag-team this one."

"Roger, chief!" Wendy smiled, and when our paths diverged at the next intersection, I headed to my office.

CHAPTER SEVEN

I DUG MY APPOINTMENT BOOK out of my briefcase, thumbed to today's date, and glanced over the day. I had some "open-door" time set up for the next full hour, after which I would be doing some supervision. I developed this open-door time so staff members could drop in to talk about a wide range of topics without an appointment. Sometimes, line staff might be reluctant to talk in small group sessions or to make a formal appointment with me. An unstructured time presented a good opportunity for people to check in and not feel like they should stay for some predetermined length of time. So far, it was successful. While the time slot wasn't used 100 percent of the time, its use was frequent enough the powers that be thought we should continue with the program.

If no one showed up, I would complete paperwork or plan future projects. Innovative agencies are always open to new ideas about training staff, supervision, or the development of clinical programming. I often had at least a few ideas floating around in my head.

Sometimes, staff brought in issues related to forensic psychology, such as the identification of malingering — determining if someone is faking symptoms of a disorder, usually in hopes of avoiding jail time (or juvenile detention facilities) for "softer" mental health treatment.

I glanced over at the dead flowers. Temporary amnesia had allowed me to escape from reality. I pretty much crashed upon re-entry.

What the hell was I supposed to make of these? Morbid fears seized me. This was about death. A sign I was marked to die? Or something more esoteric? Surely the dead flowers were not a commentary about my gardening prowess. If that were true, someone was reading my mind, and I had bigger problems than I thought. My early morning conversation with Vicki came to mind.

No. She wouldn't. I dropped the flowers in the trash.

"Hey, got a minute?"

I turned toward the doorway, and there was Nancy.

I glanced at my watch, and said, "Sure, c'mon in, have a seat."

Nancy chose to sit in the chair by my desk. In part, therapists assess folks by where they choose to sit: close to the therapist, near the door, in the farthest corner of the room, and so on. Nancy's choice suggested she was either in a frame of mind for some interpersonal connection or she was too tired to walk any further into the room. I suspected the former.

"Thought you were bringing someone with you," I said.

"I was planning to," she replied, "but the boy has visitors right now, so he's not available."

"Visitors, as in family?"

"Not in this case. Visitors as in cops. They're questioning him about some possible perp behavior. Something we were unaware of before his admission."

Perp behavior. In the real world, that could mean several different things. But in residential treatment, "perpetration" was sexual in nature. While the police were interrogating this youngster, it wasn't clear whether that might involve the boy in the role of the victim or that of the aggressor. I figured we would get to that in a moment. Plus, we didn't have a sex offender unit and typically didn't accept those types of patients. "Who are we talking about?" I asked.

"Jimmy Schwartz," she replied. "He's been on my unit for about a month—long enough for any honeymoon period to be over, but he remains a mystery."

Kids, even those who are viewed by themselves or others as BBAs, or "bona fide badasses," may be overwhelmed upon admission and give an initial impression of compliance. However, this lasts about a week or two at the most, and then the kids begin to display some of the "badass" behavior that led to their admission in the first place. In one respect, such honeymoon periods outlast many marriages. In residential work, however, it only reflects the calm before the storm.

"What do you see with Jimmy?"

"Well, we knew that he was coming in with a history of aggressive behavior. He punched a teacher, threatened his peers, and spent much of his last week of school prior to admission in restraints. Since he's been on the unit, we've seen no aggression; in fact, Jimmy appears to be underactive and amotivated. We were expecting some fireworks by now, but that hasn't been the case."

"How are his appetite and sleep patterns?"

"His appetite goes up and down. Sometimes he picks at his food. and at other times he asks for seconds. He is following the bedtime routine, which means he's in bed with his lights out by ten, but during bed checks at eleven and midnight he's often found to be awake."

"How about interactions with staff and peers?"

"He tends to keep to himself. If he's involved in a group activity, he does the minimum expected requirement. With staff, he's been pretty quiet as well. Doesn't share much about what is on his mind."

"Has he been assigned to a therapist?"

"Not yet. He's getting to the point where the team talks about that kind of an assignment. I wanted to get your input first."

"I'm concerned about this boy's anxiety levels. He sounds depressed, but I wonder if he's wearing out from worry about something or other. Sounds like someone who might benefit from a brief psychological assessment to find out what's going on. How about if we get it set up?"

"That's great. Who would do the testing?"

"I often use Wendy for testing kids not on her roster, which would be the case here. I'll arrange for her to see him. One more thing, though. Do we know exactly what the police are questioning him about?"

"No, you know the cops. They tend to keep their cards close to the vest. Administration thought that it would be okay for them to conduct a brief interview with Jimmy with a night manager present.

In fact, it should be winding down now. I need to get back over there and see if there are any questions for me, since I'm his lead counselor. I can try and find out a little bit about what they're talking about."

"Right. Well, I'll talk with Wendy about the testing, and please keep me posted about Jimmy."

After Nancy left, I pondered the Jimmy situation. Observable behavior, as Freud aptly noted, is so often only the tip of the iceberg. Who knows what lurked deep beneath the surface? With that profound question remaining unanswered, I glanced at the dead flowers in the trash and headed out for lunch.

CHAPTER EIGHT

THE RESIDENTIAL SYSTEM IS A self-contained community. There are classrooms for educational activities, a gym for recreational pursuits, and a cafeteria for meals. Sometimes, I headed over to the cafeteria for lunch, which was cheap, tasty, and always ended with a dessert of some kind. Chocolate chip cookies were my downfall. Not just *any* old chocolate chip cookie, oh no, but the large, fresh-from-the-oven, melting-chocolate-morsels type of cookie begging to be eaten right away, accompanied by the other common partner of the ritual: a large glass of milk. *Wow.*

Today, however, I decided to escape the confines of the building. Perhaps grab a sandwich somewhere, or go home and scavenge something. I could also skip lunch and sit on a park bench somewhere and vegetate. What to choose?

I walked out of the building and into the bright, sunny day. Mild, not too humid, with the light touch of a breeze. A few clouds in the sky, but otherwise a darn nice day. I waited for some fast-moving traffic to pass on the street and headed across to the parking lot where I had parked the Prius. I could see the car from a distance and felt a rush of pins and needles as I noticed something odd about the door. I broke into a run and made it to my car in seconds.

A pair of pink women's panties was tied to the door handle.

Even as I approached, I could smell floral perfume, now all-too-familiar to my nostrils. I turned and glanced around the parking lot, looking for someone in hiding, perhaps someone sitting in a parked car. I saw no one.

I stepped back and folded my arms across my chest, pondering my next move. Should I call the police? Oh, yes, so I could inform the attending officer there were perfumed pink panties attached to my car. I doubted it would be considered a serious report. An uncommon experience, yes, but hardly menacing, at least to a casual observer. All I had a series of minor events, none of them threatening.

But I *felt* threatened.

Someone was zeroing in on me. I was in someone's crosshairs. The moment I had that thought, the hair on my arms raised. I stepped closer to examine the offending panties. As best I could tell, they were new. I carefully detached them from the door handle, held them up for better viewing, turned them over and noticed the writing on the back.

One word: *Closer*.

"Anything wrong?"

I turned with a start. Tom strolled toward me. I crumpled the panties into a ball in my hand and turned in a half-circle, knuckles forward. Tom stopped a few feet from me and looked around the parking lot, his expression blank. I had no idea what, if anything, he had witnessed, or what he might decide to do about it.

"I found some garbage around my car," I said. "I was cleaning up."

Tom nodded. "Oh, glad that's all it was. I wasn't that far behind you, but the way you bolted toward your car—you took off like someone was chasing you. I even looked around to see if anyone else was around."

"Oh. Just you and me, then?"

"Yeah, for now. It's funny. Even though this is a busy area, you often find yourself alone." He paused, shook his head, turned to walk away, then stopped. "Sometimes kids walk through here and leave all sorts of trash," he added, "even though there are a couple of trash bins nearby. Go figure. Well, I need to run an errand before my break is over. Talk to you later."

"Right, have a good one."

As Tom walked away toward his car, I stuffed the panties in my pocket. Was that a line of bullshit he just laid on me, or was I overreacting? I kicked at a pebble near my foot, which struck the rear tire of my car and rocketed back at me, nicking my ankle.

"Ouch, damn it!" I limped toward my car and peered through the windows. Nobody was hiding in the back seat, and nothing seemed out of place. I wasn't concerned about lunch anymore. I needed to get away for a while. I backed out of the parking space, slipped the car into Drive, and moved out to Long Street. I figured I would hit Highway 380 and head out of town toward the Ravenwood recreation area. I tried to space out a bit once I cleared the traffic in town. Within about ten minutes, I made the turn into the entrance of the dam area where I could park and go for a walk.

I had some thinking to do.

CHAPTER NINE

I PARKED IN A SECLUDED area near the dam—easy to accomplish, given that there were only a few cars scattered about the lot today. As I walked away from my car, I heard the reassuring chirp of the horn as the doors locked. I put the keys in my pocket and walked toward the public access area above the dam. On any given day, the Ravenwood lake area is gorgeous. It is a popular area for visitors, fishermen, and picnickers. While I'd never been much of a fisherman, I'd always found water to be relaxing. Plunk me on a chair under a shade tree near water, and I could sit there for hours, taking it all in.

I wished I was there for the view, but I had other things on my mind.

Above the dam, following the concrete path, I noted I had five hundred feet of unrestricted access ahead of me, with no one in sight. I glanced behind me; the coast was also clear. I pulled the panties out of my pocket for closer inspection. They did indeed appear to be new, and were unblemished except for the one handwritten word. Oh, and they were size 6. Perfect. All I had to do was go around and find out who would fit into them, and there would be my mystery woman. It would be an updated, immodest rendition of Cinderella, only with undergarments rather than glass slippers. Swell.

Besides, I wasn't sure whoever was toying with me was even a woman. It could be a man. Nothing about the email, the nondescript voice on the phone, or anything else indicated I was dealing with a female. Anyone could purchase perfume or panties. Or kill some flowers.

The intention of the stalker was also not clear to me. Was there malice involved, or was this behavior considered...*enticing?* After all, neither my townhouse nor my car had been damaged, and if someone wanted to hurt me enough, he or she could easily have done so by now. In spite of this indecision, my instincts told me nothing about this behavior was in the least bit seductive.

I thought back to the parking lot. While I didn't think Tom had seen the panties, his comments about someone chasing me and finding myself alone were troubling. I thought about the chronology of our conversation. Had he added anything to what I had said to him, or altered it in some way? Or was he doing what clinical trainees are taught to do — repeat what someone says, but in a paraphrased manner?

My gut told me something was amiss, but I couldn't wrap my mind around it. Vick had reminded me about the episode in which I had expected the cops to show up at my house, all in overmagnified reaction to a small crisis. Could I trust either my gut *or* my head? What would be helpful, I realized, was to talk to someone — to get some perspective on the things going on. But who? I considered talking to Larry. I could tell him about the panties and the other odd occurrences.

Plus, I had to consider the possibility that "ribschild" was a patient. Perhaps a dangerous one. Seeking consultation would be a prudent course of action, except for the risk that if these activities did *not* involve a patient, I would be sharing my most personal laundry or baggage with my boss. Being a private person, that would take some doing. And in my current world, I didn't have any patients. I was a consultant, an overseer, a reviewer. Why would someone who didn't know me directly be so consumed with getting at me?

I shook my head to clear it. Lots of questions. No answers. But I knew that I could be trapped by inertia. It had happened to me before. Depression could immobilize me. Wasn't that Vicki's beef with me? One of them, anyway?

I also knew that time can be a buffer. I checked my cell phone. One bar. Might not be enough to place a call. Let fate decide. I punched in Vicki's number.

"Hello?"

I heard sounds in the background. Someone singing? But no music accompanying the song.

"Hey, it's Bryce. Did I catch you at a bad time? I thought I heard someone else."

Now there was no sound. "Vicki, are you there?"

"Yeah, no, it was the television. I had to find the remote and turn it down. It's okay. So, why are you calling? I'm in the middle of something."

"I'm just checking in. We haven't talked in a few days."

"Yes, and I'm okay with that. And I probably shouldn't say it, since it only leads to more conversation, but you sound odd again. Like something's the matter."

"I decided to take a drive during my lunch break. Shake off the mental cobwebs a little. Strange things keep happening to me. It's driving me a little crazy."

"In my experience, the only crazy things that happen with you are the ones that you create. The world isn't perfect, you know?"

"Yes. I do know that. But what you said diminishes what I'm experiencing. If I could tell you about the things going on, it might help."

"Oh, Bryce, I don't think I would make a good sounding board for you. I don't have the skills for it.... Plus, I've got things to do."

I realized if tried to counterpunch, Vicki would only become more irate and become more distant. I tired diplomacy. "I don't seem to catch you at the best times, do I?"

"You know me. If I don't keep moving, I don't know what to do with myself. When I'm not at work, I work on things at home. I decided to waterproof the back deck. That's what I was doing when you called. I should get back to it."

"Would it be better if I called you later?"

"I'm not much in a talking mood today. Another time."

"Just so you know, this is exactly what I keep saying. Remember when during our last conversation about how we can't change anything if we don't talk? Well, nothing has changed. I know you need your space, but our exchanges are pretty much limited to caring for Max."

"I have a life, remember? I've been busy. I don't mean to make it seem like I don't ever think of you. I do. But it's always 'push, push, push.' You don't give me room to breathe."

"What if we could schedule some time together? Why don't we see a therapist together? We could talk in front of a disinterested third party."

"I don't need to see a shrink. I lived with one. I've seen their limitations."

That comment drew blood.

"That's unfair. You tell me you haven't made a decision, but you don't want to talk to me. I thought seeing a therapist would be a compromise."

"I compromised enough in our marriage. But, hey. You seem to be struggling with things. Maybe it would be good if you saw someone on your own."

She didn't bother saying goodbye. The pain moved to the forefront. We'd been married for fifteen years. Right now it seemed like our life together sucked, that wasn't always the case. I pulled out my wallet and opened it to a half-dozen pictures that I carried. The first was Vicki's professional head shot. Beautiful smile. Long, soft, brown hair. I loved her hair. When I came up behind her, I would hold her and bury my face in her hair. Lavender. Vanilla. Soothing.

There was picture of the two of us, kneeling and holding tennis trophies. We had played mixed doubles together, and we worked so well on the court. No need to speak. Tears welled in my eyes, and flipped to the next photo. Similar to the tennis pose, but in this one, Max had sauntered between us — a neighbor child had been holding her leash, watching while we played tennis and let her go when she became insistent. The photographer from the paper snapped this shot, too, as Vicki and I laughed and petted Max upon her arrival. It was a great candid photo of our family.

There was one more photo. A posed shot of the two of us, all dressed up after we had performed a duet of a hymn during a church service. Another thing we did well, enough so that we'd been asked to perform during a number of weddings.

I put the wallet away and swiped at the tears with a shirt sleeve. I gazed at the sky and recalled a point in our marriage, about five years in, when I went through my first rough patch. Although I rebounded after some time, the relationship was damaged. I experienced what research has borne out — the likelihood of developing future episodes of major depression is much greater following an initial occurrence.

Although two subsequent depressive episodes further took their toll, the initial experience cast the die.

I had been working in a community mental health center and had several seriously disturbed individuals on my caseload. One day, out of the blue, the sheriff's office had called.

"Dr. Davison? Please hold for Sheriff Stone."

I'd had no clue what this was about.

"Dr. Davison, this is Sheriff Sam Stone from Cypress County. Are you familiar with Cynthia Johnson?"

Ms. Johnson had been one of my patients at the time: late thirties, history of depression, seen by me for psychotherapy and our psychiatrist for medication management.

"I'm sorry, Sheriff Stone. I'm not at liberty to discuss who may or may not be coming in for treatment."

"Yes, sir. I realize that is generally the case. However, we have some special circumstances here. Your patient, Cynthia Johnson, killed herself last night."

"What? Oh, my God, no! What happened?"

"Not a pretty story, I'm afraid. I interviewed the husband. He's the one who told me you were treating his wife. He's pretty devastated, as you can imagine."

"I can't begin to imagine. I'm shocked. Please, tell me more about what you found out."

"Mr. Johnson and his wife were out to pick up some groceries. They had a big argument about something. Not sure what. But it got ugly. Ms. Johnson told her husband that she would be better off dead than in a relationship with him. He admits he told her that if that was the case, she should go ahead and kill herself. He said she was in the glove box before he could even react. She pulled out his handgun, which was loaded, and shot herself. She died immediately. We know the full story, and the facts are corroborated by the forensic evidence. I'm only calling you as a professional courtesy. I know you'd want to be informed."

I don't remember what I said next. I'm not sure I even hung up the phone. I'd never lost a patient before. There were countless times when I was on-call and I had to intervene with people in despair, some with access to lethal means. Each call was rough. Listening for the caller's speaking style, choice of words, even inflection, for clues to guide me in how to respond. So much energy directed to mental tasks, sapped by the fear that I might not find the connection someone needed. I remembered one call that lasted several hours—

an individual whose impulses vacillated between suicidal and homicidal intentions. The call ended with police intervention that I had orchestrated using a second phone. None of those situations ended in suicide.

This one did, but there had been no call.

When my colleagues became aware of what had happened, each was supportive. Still, administrative protocol required review of the medical record by an independent psychiatrist, along with interviewing me. I waited for my face-to-face meeting in my own waiting room, knees shaking, sweating, feeling like I had down something wrong. I knew that wasn't the case, but the guilt gnawed at me.

The critical incident review concluded I could not have predicted or prevented the outcome. I was cleared.

I met with Mr. Johnson several times. His grief was profound. He felt enormous guilt for acting in such a stupid manner that he lost his wife and his children lost their mother. Each of our sessions was filled with anguish and rage. After each session, I found myself drained. But over the course of our short time together, Mr. Jones never once blamed me for failing his wife in treatment. She liked me, he said. Felt I was going to help her. Felt like I heard her reaching out for assistance. Mr. Jones knew that he had pulled the metaphorical trigger. He needed a longer course of treatment with his own therapist. I arranged for him to continue with another therapist in our system and made sure his kids were evaluated by one of our child psychiatrists. I was concerned about how this family could get through this. I should have focused on how *I* could.

Vicki showed great empathy. Each night, she encouraged me to eat, to talk about what was going on inside, and to go for walks with her. Instead, I lost weight and interest in activities, and I felt the sting of searing pain in my psyche. Each day at work, I went through the motions, said the right words to coworkers, and no one was the wiser. At home, I sat and watched reruns while Vicki sat with me and held my hand. While my eyes seemed to look at the TV screen, I was thinking of my patient. She had come to me because her hope was dimming, and she knew something had to change. With support, she had started to imagine a better life. And now she would never reach it. My heart ached for her. If only I had known what to do.

I failed to realize how much the pain of this loss was heightened by an experience from my childhood. Back when I was twelve, on a bleak, wintry day.

* * *

It was a snow day, and a rare day off from school. School never got canceled in my town because most of the students walked, and there was little need to be concerned about road conditions. However, this snowstorm dumped a foot overnight — too much for even the teachers to get through in any reasonable time.

I spent most of the day indoors, either looking out at the snow or immersed in a book. From time to time, I watched small groups of kids pulling their sleds along as they trudged either to or away from the best sledding hill in town. No one stopped at my house. No one called me and asked me to join them. Condensation from my breath fogged the window, and I drew a solitary stick figure with no facial features. I didn't have to label it. I drew a sky but no sun. I sent wishes into this wet sky — wishes for something different. Wishes to belong.

I saw my mother's reflection in the window. I knew she looked in on me from time to time. She baked cookies and offered me one. I ate it as I watched the day grow longer, and as the sun was about to begin its descent, I grabbed my sled and walked the half a block to Church Hill. The sledding area was flanked by the Lutheran church at the top and by the Presbyterian church at the bottom.

I gazed down the long, snowy hill. Glanced around to see if anyone was nearby, perhaps someone shoveling snow. The streets and sidewalks were devoid of activity, which, along with the blanket of white, created a surreal hush to the scene. As the sky darkened, I busied myself making a small mound of snowballs and pitching them at a pair of ice-shrouded bushes. I threw more snowballs until my fingers began to numb. Cotton gloves never keep out the chill after they become even a little wet.

I climbed on my sled, ready to hurtle down one of the grooved sled paths forged by countless runners of sleds covering the same trails. The tracks were smooth and glistened with ice that shone in the dusk. Between the parallel tracks were smooth mounds of snow flattened by sled frames flying over them. Being suspended a few inches above the snow felt pleasant, yet somehow disconcerting. I was at the top of the hill, but I could very well have been watching this event through a window in my house.

What do people think about at these times?

I mean, right at that second. I considered neither the past nor the future. My soul was as numb as my fingers. And perhaps the detached, disembodied, floating-above-the-ground feeling was my cue. I felt neither sad nor relieved as I slid a few inches back and forth, my gloved hands pushing against the snow-covered ground. What I did know, however, was a sense of emptiness more compelling than anything else in my young life.

Okay. Three main ingredients. Sled...path...oak tree at the bottom of the hill.

The wind picked up. Small pieces of ice stung my cheeks. A few snowflakes crystallized against the bare skin between my glove and my sleeve, and a trickle of water traced a path across the palm of my hand. I blew out a long breath, and the fog from my breath appeared, suspended in the heavy winter air. I slid the runners back and forth a few more times, immersed in the crunching of the packed snow. Somewhere deep inside my belly, I became aware of gyrating, pulsing pressure that pushed outward against my skin, shoving my guts against my throat. I wanted to scream, to pound my chest, to rock my sled back and forth. If I had stayed one second more, my emotional explosion would have left me stripped bare, lying at the crest of this snowy hill for the whole world to see. I pushed off, eyes wide, mouth open, letting loose an acid-tasting shriek as my sled tipped and began to catapult downward.

The cold air pummeled my mouth, tongue, and throat, taking my breath away. I tried to look back, but the wind and pressure immobilized my torso. The icy tracks bored into the snow pulled me along. I saw the tracks between the line of trees and the church. To their left: soft, unblemished snow. If I closed my eyes, my sled would carry me all the way to the curb at the next street. Instead, I squeezed my right hand around the rudder, pushed down on the left rudder, and rolled toward my left side, filling the space between my right side and the sled with a whoosh of frigid air. The blades of my sled fought against the tracks, vibrating the sled and shaking my body. I leaned further. The left runner shook out of the rut, and the sled re-oriented. The snow crunched under the wooden slats as I created a new course – with a tree right in front of me.

I smashed into the tree. My body compressed against the sled an instant before I launched several feet into the air, slammed into the frozen ground, and skidded another few feet into a pile of snow before coming to an abrupt halt. The nothingness was gone, replaced by exquisite pain. I couldn't catch my breath. I tried and failed to stand. In that instant, I knew, without even thinking about it, that no pain ever – emotional or physical – came close to the physical hurt reverberating through my body. With great effort, I turned my head to the side and considered my Flexible Flyer, impaled in the snow, misshapen, one runner detached. I thought I heard voices right before everything went dark.

CHAPTER TEN

BIRD CHIRPS REORIENTED ME, AND I found myself gazing at the dam where I still stood, alone. I bunched the underwear into a ball and placed them in my pocket once again. My heart felt huge and heavy. Tears began to fall, and I couldn't stem them. Sometimes, it seemed like it would be easier to live if all memory could be erased. Erasing a memory bank was the stuff of science fiction, and with memory erasure, I would forget how to eat, walk, talk, and so on. So, maybe just get rid of the *negative* memories. If someone could invent the right kind of drug.

I glanced at my watch: 12:40. Time to pull myself together and get back to work. Inside the car, I reached into the glove box and found a CD with faded writing on it. My old "anti-depression" CD. I turned on the ignition, popped in the disc, and the beat of "Nothing's Gonna Stop Us Now" began to play.

I wasn't sure what first led me to make the recording, or what constituted the appropriate ingredients a song must contain to earn a spot on the mix. In fact, some of the songs seemed more evocative of sadness than you would think would be appropriate in an anti-depression tape.

Who knows how the mind works? *An ironic question for a psychologist to ask.*

By the time I pulled into the lot across from the zipper building, the final strains of Bruce Hornsby's "Mandolin Rain" were ending. I turned the car off, appraised my appearance in the mirror, and headed to the office. I needed to attend to other things for a while.

I managed to get back to my desk without bumping into anyone. I was glad. I didn't want to anyone to see me — I still looked like I'd been crying. I consulted my schedule. Time to meet with one of my supervisees.

I looked at the message screen on my phone and noted two messages had arrived while I was out. I hesitated, then hit the speakerphone button and punched in the code to retrieve my messages. A robotic voice verified there were two unheard messages.

The first message was from my supervisee, canceling our meeting because her son was sick. I might need to find something else to get my thoughts refocused.

Message two: "Dr. Davison...I wonder why it is your wife wants to divorce you. Not taking care of things at home? *Tsk, tsk.* Closer than you think..." whispered the voice of my tormentor.

Bile burned my throat, and I fought off a wave of nausea. My hand trembled as I wiped my mouth with a tissue. Some twisted son of a bitch was stalking me and had intimate knowledge of my life — from my work details to my home address, email, and marital situation. I balled my right hand into a fist and pounded my desk. Damn! I hit it again. Paper clips jumped, and a pen rolled off the desk. Who was doing this? *Why* were they doing this?

I felt like a bug under a microscope. I wheeled around in my chair, half-expecting to see someone peering in at me from the hallway. It could be anybody. It could be somebody I even trust.

No one there. I turned back to my desk.

"Are you okay?"

I jumped in my chair. Marge stood in my doorway, one hand to her chin, eyes wide.

"What?"

"I thought you had fallen or something. I heard a couple of booms from my office."

"Oh, no, I'm sorry, Marge. I was just frustrated about something and took it out on my desk. Sorry about that. I didn't realize it was going to reverberate through the building."

Marge's posture relaxed. "Well, I'm glad you're not hurt or something." She smiled. "Sometimes I feel like punching some things, too."

I watched her turn and walk away. Even as I thought that it was nice that she checked on me, part of me still considered even her a potential suspect. My psychic glue was beginning to loosen.

CHAPTER ELEVEN

FORTUNATELY, I WAS OCCUPIED WITH management meetings and new patient reviews for the remainder of the afternoon. By the time I got back to my office, people were beginning to leave for the day. I spent another half hour organizing project files and pitching some dated materials.

I headed across the street; the parking lot was desolate when I got there. I had hyper-scan engaged, and the absence of observable threats did nothing to reduce my tension.

Ten minutes later, I pulled up in front of my townhouse. The balcony from which I had peered during the Night of the Perfumed Pillow was the first thing I noticed. No faces were visible at the balcony window, so I continued up the sidewalk.

As I turned the key in the lock, I heard the familiar clinking sounds on the other side of the door. Max was home! I stepped through the doorway and she ambled up to me, tail wagging like a flag in a stiff breeze. She stood on her hind legs and appeared to want to jump into my arms as she whimpered, low and soft. I bent over and stroked her long ears as she licked my face.

"That's a good girl, Max. Good to see you, too!"

I let Vicki keep a key to my townhouse to return Max from visitations, which meant Max would be waiting for me in the laundry room, although today it appeared she had been given free roam. I'd have to say something to Vicki about that. One more thing to irritate her, I imagined. Of course, in our recent conversations, even discussing the weather tended to irritate Vicki. Was my reaction sadness, or bitterness? Right now, it mattered little, as I didn't know when the next opportunity to talk with Vicki would present itself. I was also unsure about bringing up a subject that might push her away.

I grabbed Max's leash and snapped it on her collar. She was always eager to go for a walk and found it even more pleasurable to ride in the car, sticking her snout out the window as the car moved and drawing in what must to be exquisite scents to a dog.

As we hustled out the door, we almost bowled over a tall, scrawny, middle-aged man, wearing tight jeans and a red T-shirt with a pack of cigarettes rolled up in one sleeve.

"Sorry, Scooch. Max was in a hurry to get out the door."

Scooch was the chief — and I believe *only* — maintenance man for the townhome community.

Scooch blinked and toyed with his mullet. I appreciated his seeming unconcern for recent fashion trends.

"No problemo. You rushing off to the hospital to perform surgery or something?"

The day I moved in, I found Scooch hooking up my new appliances. In the process, he asked me countless questions about where I came from and what I did for a living. Since then, despite all information I presented to the contrary, he continued under the assumption I was a physician. Forget the fact surgeons don't dash to the operating room with their pets in tow.

"Nope. No surgery today. Besides, I'm not that kind of doctor."

Scooch walked away, muttering something under his breath about rich doctors and fancy cars. I watched him go, waiting to see what happened to the hair on the back of my neck. Scooch may be okay, but I had the feeling he didn't like me for some reason.

"C'mon, Max, let's get going."

There was a pet-walking area behind the building up on a grassy knoll, and we headed there. The walking area bordered a wooded stretch of land where a few trails beckoned, although as yet Max and I had not chosen to go further than she needed. Today, however, Max seemed intent on further exploration. I curled her leash around my wrist, and she leaned away from me, insistent. New ground. Was I ready for this?

I loosened the leash. A change of scenery could help clear my head.

The path was only wide enough for us to walk in single file, so Max took the lead, and, nose to the ground, she headed off. She was in a mood to sniff and there was ample material along the path, with plant life on each side

Max's attention to detail reminded me to live in the moment, something difficult of late. I shook my head to clear the cobwebs and checked out the greenery. There was a sense of freshness about the area, as if folks from the townhouse complex neither frequented nor disturbed it. The trail was clear of brush and long enough that both pets and owners could walk for a good ten minutes in one direction. Although I was glad Max selected the road less traveled, I also felt out of place.

Or was I too obsessed with my routine? When had I become so inflexible? Was this one of the things about me that Vicki found annoying?

I swiped at an overhanging branch, scattering a swath of leaves around us. One landed on Max's head, which she shook until it dislodged. She shot an annoyed glance my way before she turned and continued her quest for scents. Cripes. I even irritated the dog!

Max found an acceptable spot and relieved herself. Some people referred to dog droppings as "gifts." I referred to these leavings as "Max muffins." Max inspected her muffins thoroughly following their creation, as was her normal approach, before I stepped in to scoop them into a plastic bag.

With the hard work done, we moved deeper into the woods. The moment I stopped watching her, I was back in stalker-land, going over everything that had happened so far. I wanted to be objective in my analysis, but anxiety interfered. I worried about the next bad thing that might happen. The intensity mushroomed when I thought about the latest taunt about Vicki. Was she vulnerable? I didn't think it was likely that my stalker knew where she lived. I was still uncomfortable, though. I didn't want to drag anyone else into my drama.

Poor choice of words. There was real threat here. Being tracked, watched, being pushed to be on edge.

It dawned on me that Max had ceased her forward progress. She gazed behind us, one front paw bent, ears alert. Although we had never hunted, Max's hound-heritage stimulated bird-dog behavior. I had seen this when birds, rabbits, or squirrels were near.

But something was different. She was growling. A deep rumble from her chest. The hair on the back of my neck twitched. I turned slowly, scanning every foot of the periphery for prey of some kind. Nothing—until my gaze reached the curve in the path as far back as I could see. Something moved. Someone ducked back behind some foliage. I dropped Max's leash and took off down the path. My legs felt like cement as I tried to increase my pace. My heart pounded. I pumped my arms like a sprinter, and I hit the gap in time to see the person clear the opening to the trial. I took off again and lumbered to the trail clearing, hands on knees, gasping for breath. I heard a car spin loose gravel as it raced from the parking lot on the opposite side of my building.

"Damn," I muttered, spitting the word out.

Deep basset barking alerted me to Max coming up the trail. She must have taken off soon after I began running, doing the best she could with while dragging a leash. She approached me, inquisitive, sniffing the air near where I stood.

That's when I noticed it, too. *A strong floral scent.*

CHAPTER TWELVE

I GATHERED MAX UP AND we made our way back to the townhouse. I was still spooked by the incident in the woods and needed some time to unwind. I tied Max's lead to the patio and sat down on a lawn chair. The development was quiet; most people seemed to prefer staying indoors in their air-conditioned units. I was grateful for the relative peacefulness—a sharp contrast to the wild thoughts running through my mind.

I could not imagine who might be watching me. I had not been in town long enough for many people to know such specific details about my life, yet this individual seemed to know everything about me—or at least had access to very private information. Of course, stories about people developing enemies over little things are not uncommon. Someone gets angry because you take too long to pump your gas, and he decides to pull out his gun and take care of business on the spot.

But this situation was different: the identity of my stalker was unknown, as was his or her motivation. This individual was unlikely to have been provoked by some random encounter. I figured whoever was hot about me had a very personal reason.

I stepped inside the townhouse, grabbed a notepad, and sat down with a fountain pen in hand. Going on the assumption this was a personal vendetta, I decided to list some names reflecting such a motive.

First name on the list: Vicki. She had access, knew my personal history, and she could enter my townhouse without my knowledge. Law enforcement professionals always suggest that some perpetrators are overlooked because they seem too obvious. What was Vicki's motivation? I figured divorce would be both satisfying and safe for her. Why go to the trouble of engaging in such a stunt? What could she gain? I had no answer to that one.

I thought about my earlier encounter with Scooch. He had access to every residence in the community. Was my appraisal of him biased because his manner of dress was, well, sleazy? I decided I couldn't discount him, although the perfume connection was lost on me. Next, I considered people I'd met since moving to New Alex. No one came to mind as a potential stalker, as I did not believe I had developed any enemies here. However, as I had considered earlier, that did not mean someone did not consider *me* to be an enemy.

That one would require more thought.

I rolled the pen between my fingers. I had to assume my stalker was mentally afflicted in some fashion. Perhaps even psychotic. Most clinicians would begin by examining a current client list to see if a potential suspect might be lurking there. Only one problem there: *I had no clientele*. I don't evaluate or treat kids in my consulting work, and when I consulted on cases for the adult outpatient unit, I provided direct input to the therapists working there. I hadn't so much as set foot in the same room with a patient. And even then, none of the patients on whom I had consulted would fall outside normal limits with respect to potential for violence.

However, mental health professionals are notorious for failing to predict violent behavior. An individual might meet certain criteria—for example, a male with low socioeconomic status who's scared, angry, or delusional—but situational variables are what trigger the violent response. Who can reasonably predict what situations a person will encounter? So there could be someone I had missed in my mental review—but, once again, I could think of no situation where I might have offended somebody. For example, when doing a custody evaluation, it's inevitable for one side to feel dissatisfied and perhaps very angry with the evaluator, with some potential for "acting out" of some kind. I had, however, completed no such evaluations since moving to town. Nor did I want to.

Someone from my past? That posed some logistical problems. If someone followed me from my last residence to this one, I would have thought I would run into him or her at some point in such a small town. I had a pretty good memory for people, and I was sure I hadn't come across anyone who didn't belong in this geographic area. In this category, I included former patients as well as acquaintances. I eliminated friends. Who would stalk their friends? Plus, the obvious probability of recognition would mitigate against that.

So, that left people who were already here. Coworkers. *Larry.* Larry was my friend, but if I could consider my *wife* as a suspect, I shouldn't leave *anyone* off the list. Larry knew my personal situation. He knew my work hours. He knew where I lived. But he was a no-nonsense physician, and I thought I worked well with him.

Marge. She knew my work hours, but I doubt she knew about Vick and me. But that kind of info gets passed around workplaces like it was reality TV. Marge determines what calls are put through to me. Could she fake a phone call? If so, she had more skills than I knew of.

Nurse Ratched. She would probably be willing to take some risks to get ahead, but she and I weren't on the same career path.

Next would be my supervisees. I thought we had good rapport. I hadn't had any incidents with any of them, nor had there been any disciplinary write-ups. I had the most contact with Nancy. She was positive and upbeat and, to my knowledge, unaware of my marital problems. Again, the grapevine could provide that, but I could see no payoff for her in stalking me.

That left the unit staff. My most recent interactions were with Tom and Nancy. They were the first people I ran into following the perfume incident. Those interactions had felt awkward to me, but that could have been a reflection of my edginess at the time and nothing else. Tom had left abruptly, though. Nancy had touched my arm. The first could have been a timing issue, and some people routinely touch others during conversation.

There were outpatient staff I had met, but they were all bit players at this point. I scratched through that line on my list. Where did that leave me? With a large question mark at the bottom of my page. I knew this was an exercise I had to do, though. And I could add to my list over time.

My rumbling stomach reminded me I had skipped lunch. The tasty cookies I had consumed seemed to have been burned up by my anxiety-fueled furnace. Who could think like this on an empty stomach? I checked the coals in the hibachi, which seemed up to the task. I stepped inside, found some matches, and stepped back on the patio. As I knelt, Max wandered over and put her head near my face, brown eyes looking deep into my own, communicating the unconditional love only pets can provide. I smiled and scratched behind her ears. She sat down, and we enjoyed a few moments of master-dog quality time. When I dropped my hand from her head, Max sighed and sprawled on the patio, eyes ever-watchful of my movements. In addition to the mutual admiration, I suspected Max did not want to miss out on any tender morsels of food that might drop from the hibachi. Maxine is a true chow-hound.

I whipped up a nice cheddar cheeseburger and a side salad with Ranch dressing. I poured a glass of iced tea, flavored with some potentially carcinogenic sweetener. I was living dangerously. I sat down at the small patio table and savored the first bite. Pretty tasty for a hibachi burger.

In my short time in the townhouse, I had not had as much time to appreciate the patio area as I had planned, due in part to the fact that it had been rainier than normal. Today, however, was a good day for being a patio-potato. I took in the lush, green grass surrounding the fence and gazed at the small-but-stout trees in full bloom — oaks, maples, and spruce. They must have been planted when the development was built and had done quite well. It was a pretty area — an important factor in clinching my decision to move here, along with the sense of quiet.

I polished off the salad and gave the last small bite of burger to Max, who was waiting in vain for some crumbs to fall to the concrete slab. She took the meat gingerly and moved to a corner of the patio to enjoy her treat. Little things are important.

Max and I spent the next hour just being. Max was much better at this than me, but I worked hard to follow her lead. I smiled at the irony of working to relax. *Working hard.* I tried to remember the last time I'd had some fun. Strained my brain. Since my separation and move to the townhouse, I had just been trying to stay afloat. Fun seemed to be lower on the priorities list. I knew this wasn't unusual.

People in crisis are worried about getting through them, not how they'll tackle their leisure time.

Mental note: *Do something fun.*

I reached across the table and took pad in hand once more. A quick glance at Max revealed *she* wasn't about to do any work, so following her lead was a bit short-lived. I decided to think about something other than my fear. I had some things I wanted to jot down on paper.

This time, I oriented the list toward ideas for building my private practice. I had spent little energy envisioning this area so far, and it required my attention if I was serious about it, which I was. I'd been out of graduate school fifteen years, working in a variety of positions—both clinical and administrative. I worked with anxiety disorders, medical conditions, depression, and other symptom constellations that could be treated using a mind-body approach. I found it fascinating to observe the response to interventions such as hypnosis and imagery, as well as the efficiency of these techniques.

I'd always enjoyed clinical work, although there were times I daydreamed about doing something else. Owning and running a bookstore was a frequent fantasy. I chuckled when I pictured some bookstore owner out there fantasizing about engaging in a psychotherapy practice. It was part of the greener-grass scenario and provided some distraction when stuff got difficult.

And while escape right now was attractive, it was also a distraction. Distractions wouldn't help me resolve my situation.

Since motivation was a sticking point in my list-building, I flipped to a blank page in my note pad and labeled it "Motivations for Stalking." I started with "romance". But not romance in the typical sense. *One-sided* romance. A thwarted lover. Or someone that wanted love but didn't feel worthy of getting it from a specific person. The victim or target might never know that someone out there desired them.

I sat back and rubbed my chin. The part about the target being unaware troubled me. That would bring Nancy, Wendy, and even Marge back into play. It would include the outpatient staff. It would include passersby on the street. Taking it broader, it wouldn't be limited to heterosexual interest, either, leaving…pretty much the whole world. Except! Except for the fact that the person had knowledge of my separation from Vicki. That took me back to the women noted earlier, plus Larry and Tom. Most likely of the unlikely? Nancy or Wendy had a crush on me.

Rage/revenge. Maybe I had wronged someone, and he was going to get me for it. Rage could stem from a minor insult, but revenge was more specific. I hurt someone, and he was going to hurt me. I had no names to cross-reference here.

Delusion. Somebody was out to get me for a reason that wouldn't be obvious to me. This one was tricky. I would leave it on the list, though.

Random.

As I wrote this word, waves of chills cascaded over my body. This one scared me more than anything else. If someone was targeting me with no reason, I wouldn't be able to narrow the list of possibles down. I'd have to figure out how he would know about Vicki and me.

I put the pad down once more. Maxine slumbered on the patio, and I decided to enjoy the evening. Before I knew it, it was getting dark. I stroked Max's ears to wake her up. We both stretched and went inside.

CHAPTER THIRTEEN

WHEN I WAS YOUNGER, PAJAMAS were too much trouble. Now, in my late thirties, I found pajamas and slippers quite comfortable; plus, they represented a ritual marking a separation between the rest of the day and the time during which one retires for the evening. I slipped into my pajamas, slid into my slippers and a robe, and walked down the hall to my office. I wanted to catch up on any email that had arrived during the day. Who knew, perhaps I would get some good news for once.

I booted up the computer and accessed my email program. Seven messages awaited me. I scanned the names. I was relieved to recognize all the senders. I relaxed a bit in my chair.

One message was from Vicki. I opened it first.

> *Bryce: I have been thinking a lot about our situation. I know you would like me to join you in counseling, but at this point, I don't think there is anything anyone could do to help our marriage. It may be time we consider getting on with the rest of our lives. Solo. Let's talk soon. We need to discuss when you will be bringing Max over again. V.*

I rapped the monitor button with a knuckle and sat back. I couldn't catch my breath. I stumbled toward the window, leaned on the windowsill, chest heaving. *Shit.* I stood up, blew out whatever air was stuck in my lungs, and forced myself to draw in a slow breath. After a few similar breaths I turned and slid to the floor, my back against the wall. I tapped my head against the wall a couple of times, hard enough to notice.

She was doing it. She meant it. She meant to end our marriage. I was of no value to her.

And she acted like she was doing me a favor. "Damn you, Vicki!" I yelled before closing my eyes and wrapping my arms around my torso.

I heard the clink of Max's aluminum rabies tag against her collar as she entered the room. When I opened my eyes, she was sitting beside me, her face a foot away from mine. She looked sad. Granted, basset hounds always have a somber look about them, but now she hung her head, too. Max had always been attuned to me. She would make an excellent therapy dog.

I remembered the day we bought Max. Vicki and I had been looking in the newspaper for weeks, checking out the classified for puppies or shelter dogs that needed rescue. We found a family whose mama basset had recently had a litter of pups. The ad said that half the litter remained available. I called and got directions to the home. In the family's sunroom were the mother and father and four pups — three of them nuzzled against their mother, and the fourth one trying to make her way closer but finding the bodies of her siblings to be a barrier. While we watched, she stopped squirming and looked up at us. For a moment, it looked like she smiled, before trying to climb over the brother closest to her. He tried to nudge her away, but she gave it right back to him and chewed on his ear for good measure. Max, whose name at the time was "Little Jeannie," was the runt of the litter. The eye contact and smile sealed the deal. I scooped her up and Vicki drove us home.

Max was so small, she fit in both of my hands. Her body was hot against mine as I held her. Vicki and I riffed on dog names on the drive. "Tiny" and "Minnie" were options until I brought up the fight to get in with the pack. We agreed she had a heart bigger than her body. That got us to the more ironic "Max" as a common name and "Maxine" for formal occasions. Max grew, of course, to the point that she needed a boost to get her backside into most vehicles. I guess it happens to all of us as we get older.

I took Max's face in my hands and leaned even closer.

"Oh, Max. What a mess I'm in," I said. "We're a long way from where we were that day that you found us. Now, I know you're a loyal dog and you don't take sides. I understand that. I'm going to keep on trying to work things out. We'll get through this. And I won't let anything happen to you."

Max looked at me and walked off to my desk, where she sprawled on the floor.

"Is this your way of saying get back to business?"

Max's tail swished against the floor.

I sat at my desk and turned the monitor back on. Rotated my shoulders, sighed, and pulled my chair closer. I reread Vicki's message again and moved on. I breezed through the remaining messages, then went back to reread the email from the previous night. Ribschild. *Closer than you think.* It was a brain teaser. Obviously, the person was closer than I would like. But there was no one present, other than Max and me. In response to this dead end, I tapped the Reply button and typed the following:

Who are you and what do you want?

"Well, there goes nothing," I muttered to myself.

Send.

I looked through a pile of bills, sorted them by due dates, and made a mental note to pay them off in the next day or two. As I put the bills back on the desk, a tone from the computer indicated new mail. I clicked on the new message.

Returned mail: User unknown.

A bogus email address. Not hard to set up and then delete. Just enough to remind me that my adversary was clever. That ruled against psychosis.

But not against dangerous.

I was too tired to think one more thought. I got up and stretched. Max yawned and followed me to the bedroom. Unlike my usual routine, tonight I entered the bedroom, closed the door behind me, and locked it. Pausing, I found myself sniffing the air. No floral scent as far as I could ascertain. I made sure the balcony door was locked, drew the shades on the windows, and went to bed. Within minutes, I knew sleep was soon to follow.

To sleep, perchance to dream.

Or to slip deeper into the nightmare.

CHAPTER FOURTEEN

THE REST OF THE WEEK was uneventful. Max and I hit the road Saturday morning, stopping only once in the ninety-minute drive to the Pittsburgh area. We agreed that sausage, egg, and cheese biscuit purchased at the McDonald's drive-through was a good way to wake up the taste buds.

On the side roads, Max stuck her head out the window and let her ears flap in the breeze. She moved her snout slightly, back and forth, drinking in as many scents as she could. It may have been the wind, but her jowls fluttered, showing her teeth. With her jaws separated a bit, she appeared to have big smile. She nodded as if to ask for more.

"We may have to get you some goggles for these summer drives," I commented to her.

There was very little traffic when I hit The Town Where I Grew Up. For a small town, there were plenty of churches. There were an equal number of bars. But only one school remained. When my mother had grown up here, there was an elementary school and a high school. Before I was born, the school merged with a larger district. Now the kids went to junior high and high school miles away, just as I had. Each time I traveled from New Alex, the last segment of the drive took me up Church Hill, where I always kept my gaze facing left.

I knew the spot beside the Presbyterian Church was there. I chose not to acknowledge it.

My mother's house, The House That I Grew Up In, sat at the end of a tree-lined street. As I pulled over to the curb, I could see her rocking on the front porch. Her head was visible above the porch wall, her gray hair neatly brushed, her glasses focused on the street, head bobbing slightly, a smile on her face. I knew she was rocking in her favorite chair.

Max shot out of the car like a carnival stuntwoman from a cannon. She loved trips to Grandma's. By the time I was up on the porch, Max was already chewing on a few treats.

"Hi, Mom." I kissed her cheek. "You sure spoil my dog."

"Oh, she's my baby and she knows it. Besides, she has a face that makes me smile."

Max did not appear to be offended by the remark.

"Hey, I have a snack for you, too. Your favorite kind of cookies."

I handed her the vanilla wafers and sat down on the glider.

"Are these sugar-free?" she asked.

"You bet. I know you're on top of your blood sugar."

"I'm used to diabetes at this point. It won't get the better of me."

She was right. When she was first diagnosed, it took some practice to prick her finger and draw it into a test strip. Later, when oral medication wasn't enough to keep her glucose levels down, she had to learn to inject insulin into her abdomen. She gritted through it, though, and now the task was more routine.

"Oh, these are good. Would you mind pouring me a little glass of milk?"

We sat in silence while she ate, watching a pair of hummingbirds hovering about one of several feeders around the porch.

"How are things at work?"

"Things are fine. It's a good place to work. Good people there."

Mom nodded. She knew the value of good people.

"How's the arthritis been?"

"Not too bad today. I'm not getting around too quickly on my walker, but I'm in no hurry, so that's fine."

"True. No geriatric races for you. Have you had any visitors lately?

"Monday through Friday, the hot meals man from the senior center stops by around noon. Usually, on Sunday afternoon, Pastor Cook brings a tape of the church service over for me. I like to hear the choir sing and listen to the sermon."

At one time my mother and I had sung in the choir together. I knew she missed singing.

I must have been quiet for a time. When I looked over, my mother was watching me. When we made eye contact, she smiled and winked. "Bryce, I'm older and wiser than you, and I'll always be your mother. I know when something is on your mind. What aren't we talking about?"

I hesitated. Took a breath.

"Have you looked at the brochures for those assisted living apartments that I dropped off?

She sniffed. "Those are for old people. This is my *home*."

"That's right. This is your home and you should enjoy it. But I worry about you. It's not like I live next door. I'm concerned that something could happen to you, and you wouldn't be able to get help quickly enough."

"I carry the phone in my walker basket."

"I know you do. And that's good. But…would you at least *look* at the brochures?"

"I'll think about it. Have you talked to Vicki lately?"

My mother loved Vicki like a daughter. Whenever they were together, tears would often flow from their laughter. "Here and there. Just a day or two ago, as a matter of fact. Not much has changed. She's doing well."

"Knowing Vicki, she may not be doing as well as you think. She's a proud woman. She's from that strong, Scandinavian stock that so many Midwesterners share. We used to talk about it. Plus, she works around a lot of men, so she needs to be tough. I know you two are having a rough patch, but I know you can get through it."

"I appreciate your support."

It was true, I did. But I spared my mother from the details. She had enough to worry about.

"Your dad really liked Vicki. He thought that she had a great sense of humor. Although sometimes it was at your expense."

"What are you talking about?"

"She told me something one time that even I didn't know about you when you were younger. You never told me that you thought the light fixture in your room looked like a big spider when it was dark and you were in bed. She said you thought it was getting closer and closer to you."

I had forgotten about that. Maybe Vicki was right—I always was a little intense.

"True story. And I agree with what Dad thought. Except it's changed a little. Now she has a sense of humor — except where I'm concerned."

"Oh, go on. It's just the way the world is today. In my day, you married for life. "Until death do you part." Now, you can get married and divorced in the time it takes to microwave a TV dinner."

"Man, that brings up some memories. Those frozen chunks of unidentifiable food with aluminum foil over them. Dad struggled to tell the food items apart. Remember the one time he though the meatloaf was a brownie?"

My mother laughed. "Poor man was crestfallen when he found he had put salt on his brownie."

"But you're right about what you were saying. You and Dad had over fifty years together in this house. Thick and thin. Today, that amount of time won't often be equaled."

"Don't give up, Bryce. You forget how resilient you are. And I'm not saying that because I'm your mother."

CHAPTER FIFTEEN

MAX AND I MADE DINNER. Well, I cooked. Max supervised.

Grilled cheese sandwiches and tomato soup. Comfort food.

"This hit the spot. Thank you."

"You taught me well," I replied. "This was always one of my favorite dishes as a kid."

"We didn't have it very often. Your dad liked meat and potatoes for supper after a day at the mill. There are only so many ways to fix meat and potatoes. But he enjoyed every meal, except for those TV dinners we were talking about."

"I remember when I was in college, and I brought my roommate and a couple of other guys from my residence hall wing down for the weekend. I asked you to make the meat pie that I loved. We were here to get away for the weekend and visit the local fall festival, but the only thing those guys talked about for weeks after was that pie."

"I do remember that. It was good to see you with some buddies."

"I lost track of those guys not long after graduation. By the time we were seniors, we had grown apart for one reason or another."

"Oh, that reminds me. Some mail came for you the other day. Now, where did I put that?"

I hadn't lived in the house for over two decades, but at times I still got mail, most often regarding high school reunions or related requests for financial support.

"Oh, good. More reunion news. Yippee." I pitched the first piece of mail in the trash.

I glanced at the second envelope. My vision blurred for a moment when I read the address. *Dr. Bryce Davison.* No one from my high school days knew about my career.

I put the envelope on the table. That caught my mother's eye. "It's not a bill, is it?"

"No, I don't think so. I just need to hit the bathroom before Max and I get ready to go."

Inside the bathroom, I paced as much as I could in the small space. Dr. Bryce Davison. Not even my college buddies knew I had my PhD. I doubt few people in town did, except of maybe friends of the family that my mother would have told. But none of those people would be sending me mail out of the blue. I should have brought the damn thing in with me. My mother saw me put it down. She just doesn't know why. I'd have to go out there and open it, no matter how much I wanted to avoid it.

I flushed the toilet and washed my hands. Took a long, slow breath, and opened the door. My mother was sitting at the table where the envelope was waiting.

"I got my letter opener from the desk for you," she said. "Paper cuts can make you bleed like the dickens."

I took the opener and slit it open.

Plain paper. Computer-generated type: *There's nowhere you can go that I can't get to you. Or those you love. ribschild.*

Oh, shit. My lips felt parched and my mouth felt like aged paper. I covered my mouth and coughed to buy a moment. I had to recover.

"Oh, this is interesting," I said. "Um, when did this come?"

"Let's see. You so rarely get mail here. I believe they both came the other day. Last week one day. What, is it a bill after all??"

"No, but not only was I invited to...to the next high school reunion, this one informed me that I was elected to be on the planning committee. Can you imagine? That people remember me enough to include me in something so important?"

I folded the note and envelope and stuck them in my pants pocket.

Mom shook her head. "When you graduated from that school, I was pretty certain the only way you were ever going to go back was if you were the principal. Like what happened with one of your cousins. But you majored in psychology, not education. Well, their loss. But good for you for doing what you do and helping so many people. I'm proud of you."

CHAPTER SIXTEEN

I SAT IN THE CAR after saying goodbye. I couldn't start it. I felt like I was going to hurl my guts out.

I fished an opened bottle of water from the back seat. The warmth of the water almost made me gag. I tried just to sip it.

"Don't lose it, Bryce. Get a hold of yourself. You need to sort this out. Just one moment at a time."

I started the car, then pulled the message out of my pocket. I knew what it said. But I needed to take the physical action. Was something expected of me? No. It doesn't tell me to do anything. "Ribschild" wanted me to know he knows me. He knew my whole world. Nothing in my life was out of his reach. He could get to me wherever I went. He could get to my mother if he wanted.

My god, would he *do* that?

It didn't matter. The mere hint that he could was all that he needed, and my nervous state reflected that. My heart threatened to choke me. In that instant, I looked up and realized where I was. Without meaning to, I had driven the car to the top of Church Hill. I gazed at the road at the bottom of the hill. Felt myself sliding down the glass. I closed my eyes and held my breath.

* * *

I opened my eyes. My father had his hands on my shoulders, shaking me.
"Bryce, can you hear me?"

"Yes...yes."

"Can you sit up?"

He took me by the right arm and elbow and helped me up. I flopped back down again.

"It...hurts!"

"We have to get you over to the truck."

No ambulances worked our town. The nearest hospital was twenty miles of rural road away.

"I know this is going to hurt, but you have to stand up." He shifted his position. "Here, take my arm and pull. I'll help you stand."

I doubled over. Billy Wilde had punched me in the stomach once during gym class. It felt like that, only worse. Like losing your breath and feeling that the next one will never come.

Once he had me up, my father wrapped my left arm around his shoulders and slid his right arm around my waist. For a few seconds, I floated outside my body, watching myself hobble while also observing that darkness was descending.

We made a quick stop at the house where my mother had been waiting. She rushed to the truck. A burst of icy air flooded the cab. She helped move me to the center of the seat so she could climb in.

"Don't let him fall asleep," I heard my father say. *"Bryce, look at me. Just keep your eyes open for me. We'll get to the hospital as soon as we can."*

"The snow."

"It won't stop us. The truck has four-wheel drive."

The heavy truck seemed to make little noise, all sounds muffled by the snow blanketing the road. I closed my eyes. I wanted to float again.

"Bryce, you have to keep your eyes open for me. Just a little longer."

"He's going into shock."

My mother unzipped her coat and managed to wrap it partially around me.

I watched the wiper blades flick snowflakes from the windshield. Out in front of the truck where the headlights appeared to intersect with the falling snow, the white cascade seemed to swirl. I gazed transfixed at the glittering vortex.

I heard my mother whisper, *"We need to go a little faster."*

CHAPTER SEVENTEEN

I COULDN'T SHIELD MYSELF FROM the thoughts that bombarded me as we drove home. I wanted nothing more than to escape. I envied Max, who was sound asleep. I didn't feel like listening to music or talk radio, but I felt too alone with my thoughts in the quiet.

I punched Vicki's number.

"Hey, it's me. Max and I are on the way back from Mom's house."

"How is she?"

"Mom is doing fine. Just the usual bumps and bruises that comes with age. She mentioned you in our conversation and sent her regards."

"She's a sweet woman. I have to get down there sometime soon and visit her. Maybe I'll take Max along for a ride."

I thought about my wall of glass.

"I had a little trouble there. When I left. Couldn't seem to drive past, you know, the hill. The tree. Shook me up."

"That's understandable, isn't it? I don't get it. You know from professional experience that these kinds of triggers could affect someone for many years, right?"

"Yeah, you think I would be used to that by now. I know that it's normal, but sometimes, like today, the feelings grip me like icy tentacles."

"Icy tentacles? C'mon. Isn't that a little dramatic?"

"I just want you to understand."

"It's not important that I understand. I'm dealing with my own feelings as we go through all this, you know. It's not right for you to expect me to be a sounding board every time you feel upset."

"Isn't that what married couples do? Support each other?"

"We're separated. We're in a different category."

"I thought that the goal was to work things out. Our recent conversations don't sound like that. And then the email message that you sent me. *Moving on with our lives.* Who decided that was the best thing for each of us? I love you, don't you know that?"

"I do. And there was a time when that would have been all that I needed to hear. I'm sorry. I can't keep going to that well of despair with you. It's too draining. I need this time away to sort out who I am…"

When did we become such strangers? The thought jarred me and I searched for landmarks along the road to get my bearings. Everything was off-kilter. Or was it just me? I gripped the wheel and arched my back. Did I still know how to have a normal conversation?

"It would be nice just to sit down with you," I said. "Even if it's for a cup of coffee. We need to deal with things together?"

"Yeah, we can try that. But nothing heavy. There's been enough of that. Even so, call me first, though, in case I am wrapped up in work."

"Sure…I'll call you."

I had driven another ten miles before I realized that I was still holding the cell phone in my hand. I tossed it on the passenger seat. My muscles ached as my body slid further down the wall of glass.

By the time we turned off the interstate, I was exhausted from anxiety. Staring into the black, moonless sky was like looking in a mirror.

CHAPTER EIGHTEEN

THE NEXT MORNING, MAX AND I made our rounds. She took her time savoring the scents. She didn't mind at all that I wasn't paying attention to her. We moved further along the grassy knoll, closer to home. Max took advantage of the full rein to explore the farthest boundaries of her reach. I decided that it was time for me to find some ways to de-stress, and a face-to-face with Vicki would be a good place to start. If I went to her in person, and if we could have a heart-to-heart talk, then we would get somewhere.

Max finished her duties, and we headed back to the townhouse. I dug through the box in the cupboard and found her treats, fished out two for her, and tossed them on the mat near the door. She pounced on them with fervor, tossed one in the air, and ate them both. It was rather merciless, but such is the way of the mighty basset hunter. I couldn't help but smile a little. Max was the biggest pacifist I knew, and I was sure that the dog biscuits weren't treated particularly cruelly.

"Max?" I asked after she had eaten, my voice rising as I said her name.

She was at my feet in an instant, big tail swishing against the carpet. She knew that such voice inflection often preceded a request regarding a favorite pastime of hers.

I spared her any additional anxiety from waiting. "Do you...want to go for a ride?"

We hustled to the car, I helped her in, and we were on our way. Max was in her element, but I noticed some tension in my neck. Every trip to see Vicki brought me to what had been our dream home — a colonial with a wide yard, big deck, and a porch swing beneath the deck, accessible through the walk-out basement. It was still hard for me to see the place, even if I was just driving by. I tried to avoid it as much as possible. I pulled into the driveway, scanned the yard, admired some of the perennials that were gracing a landscaped area, and headed up the sidewalk.

I took a big breath and rang the doorbell. No answer. Tried one more time and glanced at Max in the car while I waited. She was watching me, her nose almost pressed against the glass. She liked to have a good view of whatever she was watching, even if nothing important was going on.

I heard the deadbolt turn, and I faced the door, ready to apologize to Vicki and preempt a likely argument.

"Hi, I was..." I began as the door opened.

It wasn't Vicki in the doorway. It was a man, wearing a bathrobe and boxers, the robe gaping open down to the elastic waistband. A second later I noticed that it was an old bathrobe of mine. My heart beat faster.

"Can I help you with something?" Mr. Bathrobe-Wearer asked.

"Who the hell are you?" I asked.

"What do you mean? Let's try who the hell are you?"

I stepped into the foyer, bumping the man back. "You're wearing my robe, asshole. Does that give you any clues?"

"Wha—?" he sputtered.

"Can't figure it out? I'm Vicki's husband, and you're in the wrong place at the wrong time."

"Oh, *shit*, man, I didn't know. She didn't say she was married." He raised his hands in front of him.

"Yeah, Vicki can be at a loss for words when you need her to speak up. I bet she'll be more talkative once I leave."

"You should leave now, then. Please."

I pushed his hands down.

"Well, since you said please."

He sighed and relaxed his posture.

"But I'm not leaving without my robe."

With a quick yank, I had the robe off the man's shoulders. I twirled him around and pulled it off the rest of the way, causing him to spin out of the foyer in the process. He turned back to me, his face beet red, fists clenched, sputtering something that I couldn't quite make out. He took a step toward me and then retreated again, almost self-consciously.

"Just tell my wife that I came to get the rest of my stuff." I slung the bathrobe over my shoulder and headed down the sidewalk as whoever-he-was glared at my back. I heard words exchanged, then Vicki's voice. "Oh Jesus, Bryce, don't go. Wait a minute."

I glanced back to see Vicki stick her head and shoulders out the doorway. I turned and kept on going. I opened the Prius, threw the robe inside, started the car, and pulled out of the driveway. Max hung her head and ducked down in the back seat, out of my view. I spun the car onto the highway, gunned the engine, and roared away from what used to be my home.

Less than a minute later, after I had slowed down within legal limits, I felt my eyes burn a split-second before they released a flood of tears. The sobs that I had held back for so long shook my body. Blinking to clear my eyes, the road looked hazy. I wiped at my tears with the back of one hand while squeezing the steering wheel with the other. I slapped at the wheel with my free hand. "Damn!"

The car rocked, and I leaned forward to focus on the road. I shouldn't be driving. It triggered a memory, hurtling through the snow on my sled. A feeling of calm washed over me. But I heard Max rustle in the back seat, and I pushed the feeling away. I saw an opening on the berm and pulled over. With the car in park, other images emerged.

* * *

I must have dozed off. Where was I? Noises. Bright lights. My guts feel like they're being ripped out of me. Not enough breath to cry out. Someone help me!

"Why are we sitting? What are we waiting for?" I heard my mother say. We're still in the emergency room, but in a different place. God, this hurts!

Someone pulls on my arm and wraps a black thing around it. It jerks my body. It hurts.

"It should only be a few minutes. Where are those abdominal films?"

Someone new comes in and slaps pictures on a screen. I put my head down. It hurts to lift it to watch the activity.

"This kid's bleeding all over the place. Can't see what's going on in there. He needs to get to surgery, STAT!"

* * *

Vicki. My heart filled my chest and then constricted, like tearing off layers of skin and muscle. I laid my head against my arm on the steering wheel until the last tear fell. Max whimpered in the back seat.

CHAPTER NINETEEN

I'M NOT SURE HOW I made it back to the townhouse, and I don't recall the route that I drove to get there. I navigated by autopilot. Somehow, I found myself in the parking lot of the complex with Max in the seat beside me, looking at me, waiting for a response.

I drew in a deep breath, stroked Max's neck, gathered up the bathrobe, and climbed out of the car. It felt like climbing out of a pit. Max jumped down from the car right behind me. I closed the car door, locked it, and leaned against it for a moment.

"What a crappy week," I said out loud, thinking of the pink panties, the trip to the dam, and the perfect ending to the day — discovering exactly why my wife didn't want to try and work anything out with me.

"What's the matter with me, Max?" I asked, half-expecting an answer. "I have a job, a place to live, and a full head of hair. I don't belch in public, and I open doors for little old ladies."

Max sat there, panting. I wasn't going to get any words of wisdom from her on this topic.

I trudged up the sidewalk toward the townhouse, glancing once again at the second-floor balcony. I never used to give it much notice, but now I wouldn't take things for granted ever again.

I unlocked the door, stashed the keys on a small side table where I kept the mail, and caught a glimpse of my reflection in the hallway mirror. The casino refugee had returned, and I caught myself glancing around, still not quite accepting that the face belonged to me.

I slipped off my shoes and walked into the kitchen. Max was busy slurping at her bowl of water. I opened the refrigerator door to see what was available. Some milk, some apple juice, and a two-liter bottle of ginger ale. I needed to get to the store. I poured some ginger ale and downed half of it while standing against the sink. I couldn't get the image of Vicki out of my mind, that one glimpse. With such a brief glance, I had still memorized her appearance: panties and an old t-shirt of mine. Her bedroom attire. She'd was stepping through the doorway while her new lover pulled on her arm. *Shit.* I didn't need to see any of that. I closed my eyes and tried to clear the images.

Although no tears remained, questions filled my mind. What was it about me that she could move on so easily? Until today, I had some hope in spite of the messages Vicki was sending. Now I felt lost. Empty. No, more than that. It felt like a gaping hole in my heart, a vortex of pain that enveloped me. I was unwanted and unwelcome, at the edge of a precipice, where the weight of my despair threatened to push me over.

Those were the feelings that had driven me to the top of that snowy hill years before. The winter of my first year in junior high, in the midst of a failure to adjust to a different school, a forty-minute bus ride, and being one of the youngest students in the building.

Images swirled. I held onto the counter behind me, feeling nauseous. Sweaty. My heart began to race. I recognized a panic attack starting and pulled a kitchen chair from under the counter. I closed my eyes and tried to take slow breaths while abject terror ran roughshod over me. The feeling, I knew, was only a push from a primitive part of my brain to fight or flee, to somehow save myself from whatever was threatening me. However, it's hard to flee from oneself, and I reminded myself that I had to ride this out.

Within a few minutes, the sensations had reached their peak. I could almost feel the chemicals flushing through my bloodstream. I felt weak. Ashamed. In fact, I was feeling a combination of all the dysphoric emotions known to my entire species.

What was that quote? Shakespeare? No, someone else. Kipling. Something about treating both success and failure as impostors. I told myself to think of the suicidal thoughts as impostors. *Ghosts.* Vestiges of bad days gone by, triggered by the associated feelings that the experiences of today shared with those early adolescent days.

"Leftovers," I muttered to myself. I was dealing with emotional baggage. *Leftovers.* I tried to put things in perspective.

I glanced around the room. The kitchen sported lots of oak, which I favored. Light-colored cream walls helped brighten the entire space. I could see the living room from where I sat, and it struck me that the walls were empty. Not a single picture or print or wall hanging to suggest that someone lived here. Up until a short time ago, I had viewed my townhouse as a transition to something more rewarding: a better time, complete with a reunion with Vicki. Now this dream was dying. I felt as empty as the walls were bare.

I also realized that I had yet to eat something. I wasn't hungry, which was unusual for me. Some people stress-eat. I stress-starved. But I had to eat something. I took a second look into the fridge and this time opened the freezer and vegetable bins.

I thought back to my recent visit with my mother. What I needed was comfort food of some kind. I wasn't sure what would be most comforting, but a tuna sandwich was easy enough. I toasted some bread, sliced a tomato, whipped some mayo into the tuna, and made a sandwich. I pulled a plate from the cupboard, tossed on some whole grain crackers — which I hoped weren't stale — and walked up the stairs to the second floor. As I moved through my bedroom, I glanced at the pillows on the bed, reminding myself I could have a full day of things to worry about if I so chose.

I went outside on the balcony, which, at this time of the day, was in the shade. A gentle breeze beckoned me to calm myself, and I sat down on a lawn chair. I heard the screen door open as Max nosed it out of her way and joined me. This spot was her favorite place in the entire house. She loved sticking her nose between the rails of the balcony and sifting the aromas.

As I munched on my sandwich, I gazed out across the expanse of field that I could see in the distance. My townhouse was on the highest ground in the complex and afforded me the opportunity to look above the other units. I knew there was a farmhouse somewhere over the far horizon, but all I could see was the dark brown earth that had been tilled, surrounded by deep green grass. It was a pastoral scene and I found myself just gazing at it. I set my plate down on the small table beside me and rested my head against the wall.

Tired. Very tired.

CHAPTER TWENTY

THE FEELING OF MOISTURE AGAINST the bare skin of my forearms roused me from my catnap. I sat up and saw the sky was now dark; thunder rumbled somewhere in the distance, and light rain began to fall. The wind had picked up just enough to send some raindrops to the balcony. I gathered up the now-empty plate. Max had invoked the unspoken basset rule that any food near mouth level was fair game. She licked her mouth as I looked at her, as if to accentuate her enjoyment of the remainder of my sandwich.

"C'mon, Maxine," I said, smiling at her and patting the top of her head. "Let's prove we know enough to get out of the rain."

Back in the bedroom, I checked outside to determine if the wind was going to propel the rain into the room, but it seemed okay to me. I latched the screen but felt no need to close the main door. I walked down the hall to my office and pulled out the desk chair. I sank into the soft leather with a sigh and examined the accumulating piles of unopened mail and other documents to read. Today would be a good day to tend to those. Later.

I turned on the computer and logged in. For a moment, I recalled the slow days of dial-up access and thanked the computer gods for broadband. In a flash, I had called up my email.

Three messages downloaded. Not much activity. The one that caught my eye was from Vicki. I opened it.

Bryce: I am so sorry that you saw what you did today. You should have called first, and it would never have happened. But we can't change that now. Tony was furious with you for how you treated him, and I can't say that I blame him. You should know that he is going to be moving in with me. It's time for me to go through with this divorce. V.

So. His name was Tony, and he was angry with *me*. Poor man! Tightness seized my throat, and my brow furrowed. I was angry, too, and it felt good. I leaned back in my chair and wondered how I had come across to Tony. He seemed to want to be in charge of the situation, but that changed pretty quickly. I hadn't been in a fight since elementary school, even though I was a target of bullies in junior high. Bullies who targeted me because I was kind toward other cast-off kids with no friends. I learned to fade into the background and make myself look small.

This coping style later proved useful when I entered the consulting room with a small child, I looked big in the doorway but once I was on the floor and playing with toys, kids didn't bat an eye. With Tony, I made myself look bigger.

"Tony had better watch his ass," I said to the computer. "Or I'll kick it from here to Cleveland."

But there was Vicki. It seemed obvious she thought this was all my fault. The fact that she had been dishonest with me hadn't even entered her mind. That's the way things had always been. I carried the guilt for both of us. Vicki didn't have the time for that. She was always too busy forging ahead. Had she always done that?

I picked up a framed photo of Vicki and me and examined it. One of my favorite pictures of us. Arm in arm after having climbed Squaw Peak in the mountains near Phoenix. We were smiling, probably giddy after walking steep paths in the heat. Fortunately, the next woman who climbed to the top agreed to take our picture.

But the walk—at one point I had rolled my ankle, which swelled right away. I had to hobble on it, but Vicki rejected the idea of turning back. She told me not to let the ankle get the better of me. To "man up," as it were. Whether challenged or stupid, I kept going. She was well ahead of me and waiting for me at the top. The view took my breath away, though, and I was over the incident.

I put on my clinician's hat. Vicki was a jock. She was a leader. She liked to win, and she won a lot. Tennis, golf, volleyball. Even playing Scrabble revved her competitive engine. I also did many things well and had a shelf of trophies to show for it. But I was more laid back, more deferent. This was the result of nurture rather than nature. I was shaped by experiences to be as comfortable assisting in the winning point as scoring it.

Was it an oil and vinegar relationship, then? Lately, yes. I put the photo back on the shelf. Straightened it. And then picked it up and placed it upside down on a row of books.

One other email message caught my eye, a message from Lawrence Jones:

> *Bryce: Joan and I are having a barbecue of sorts this Saturday afternoon. We would like it if you joined us. It will be a small gathering, but it should be fun. Yours truly will be doing the grilling. People will begin to gather around 3 pm. No need to bring anything. Just drop a reply if your schedule will allow you to come. Thanks, Larry.*

I hit the "reply" icon:

> *Larry: Although my social calendar is demanding, I have cleared my schedule to attend your barbecue. Someone will need to supervise the grilling, and I am volunteering for the job. See you around three. Bryce.*

I sat back in my chair and considered the occasion. I could use the opportunity to meet some people, and so far, such opportunities had been almost nil. It was about time I got out and enjoyed myself in the land of the living.

A final message was set up to appear as a response to a message from me—but I knew that such was not the case. My heart skipped a beat. The timing. Something wasn't right with this email message. It might harbor a virus. I kept my antivirus software updated, but it only takes one bad email slipping by to jam up the works. I right clicked my mouse and scrolled down to "delete." Let go of the mouse. Drummed my fingers on the desk. Rubbed my chin. Then I leaned forward, hit the ESC key, and clicked open the message.

> *Dr. Davison: While your wife may be done with you, I certainly am not. But what are your options? Without your marriage, perhaps you should consider leaving town. Yes, leave, before something happens to you. Of course, wherever you go, I will find you. Perhaps you should consider a more permanent departure.*

It was signed "ribschild."

A shudder traversed my body. This was the most ominous, most direct and threatening message I had received yet. I thought back to the earlier incidents: the panties and the phone call at work. It all felt like a bad dream, one that had come out of nowhere, like the panic attack I had experienced earlier. It was clear that I was going to get little sleep tonight.

I considered my options. I felt like bolting, but I had nowhere to go. I chided myself for even thinking like that. "C'mon, Bryce, pull yourself together. You've been through worse than this."

I was right. At least with respect to what had transpired thus far with "ribschild," I had been through much worse. Losing my father was worse. What was happening with Vicki was worse. It was a dagger to the chest. Myriad experiences could fill the list. All I had to do was keep my wits about me.

Which was about as easy as keeping an ice cube from melting on a hot sidewalk.

CHAPTER TWENTY-ONE

I DECIDED TO DO SOME research. I searched for ways to track email for a while but lost interest after a half-dozen web pages. I moved on to psychological literature and stumbled on some interesting information about stalkers. I wondered if that was the most accurate term for whatever I was facing.

My research suggested that most stalkers were men and that a significant proportion was mentally ill, but only a minority was predisposed toward violence. However, there were some subtypes that could further distinguish stalkers. A rejected stalker feels wounded from rejection and seeks vindication. A resentful stalker is self-righteous and makes threats, typically without acting on them. A stalker seeking intimacy believes he is loved or will be loved by the victim. This type is delusional. A predator type is all about violence, control, and sex , and may not know the victim — and the victim may be unaware of being stalked. There's also the incompetent type who is sexually awkward and doesn't mean harm. The rejected and predatory types were the most likely to assault their victims. Some stalkers are charming and may show no signs of problem behavior until something sets them off.

I wondered if my luck was such that I had the worst of the worst targeting me. I also felt in my gut that the perfume and the panties were less likely to have been used by a male. That line of thought moved me to look at the literature on female stalkers.

Female stalkers appeared to be most interested in getting close to their victims — usually other women — and while there could be some same-sex romantic overtones, a female stalker is usually more interested in a best friendship. While perfume and panties *could* be considered romantic, the messages were becoming more menacing, more predatory in nature. The behavior I was dealing with had elements of both male and female stalkers.

One possibility was that whoever was orchestrating this behavior was manipulating the variables to keep me off-balance. Stalking might not even be the best term for what was happening to me. The bottom line was that I had to take the stance that my predator was dangerous, and I needed to watch my back.

I shut down the computer, dimmed the lights, sat back in my chair, and found the remote for the CD player. I hit the button for drawer one and listened to the opening strains of "Hotel California," one of my favorite songs. On this run-through, though, I paused to consider the lyrics regarding the seductive female character, so enticing from the doorway, but who trapped her victims in the manner of a black widow spider. Interesting....

The song ended. I was exhausted. I shut off the music, switched off the remaining lights and walked back to my bedroom. I didn't even feel like I had the energy to get into pajamas. I slipped out of my clothes, slid under the covers, stared at the ceiling, and tried to will the hair on the back of my neck to relax.

That message. My thoughts in the kitchen earlier this evening. The invitation for a permanent checkout. A demand too powerful to ignore? I closed my eyes to quiet my mind, but in doing so, I opened the window to waiting horrors.

* * *

I was moving but I didn't know where I was. I looked around. I was on a gurney, pushed along by attendants in white coats. Everything was white. White walls. White lights. Someone was paged over a loudspeaker. Pungent ammonia smells in the hallways. Where was I going? What was happening to me? I heard automated doors open. I lifted my head a few inches from the pillow and saw my parents' worried faces as my bed moved past, into the next room, where new faces appeared as people gathered around me. Someone lowered one of my bed rails; a metallic, clinking sound filled my ears. I was moving again, slid from my bed to a cold table. Someone put a mask over my face. My heart raced, and I didn't know what to do. Someone told me I would be okay. I didn't know what to do. Count backwards from one hundred. Why was I counting? Things got foggy, and I struggled to hold on to the moment, unsure of where I would go or if I would awaken. Things got foggy.

No, wait! WAIT!

CHAPTER TWENTY-TWO

I OPENED MY EYES AND glanced at the clock. *Whoa.* Ten hours. I hadn't done that in a long time. I was so tired I must have fallen right into deep sleep. But now it felt like my defenses were down, like I was vulnerable. I felt disoriented. I looked around the room, checking for evidence of ill-doing. Nothing. Everything was where it had been the night before. No out-of-the-ordinary scents—save for those emanating from Max, who had joined me during the night, curled up near the head of the bed, deep in sleep and breathing right in my face.

"Time for breath mints, pooch," I said as I slid out from under the covers. Max stirred only for a moment and inched a bit closer to my pillow. I caught myself thinking about how good a dog's life could be…sleep, eat, play, sleep some more. What a life.

I was groggy enough that it took me a minute to figure out what day it was. Monday. I was due into the office at ten o'clock. Plenty of time to take a long soak in the shower, eat a light breakfast, and breeze into work.

In the bathroom, I shaved, followed by twenty minutes in the shower. I let the hot water run over my muscles, lingering on the tight areas in my lower back, a primary stress point. As a psychologist I not only sit a lot, I also sit with people who are in distress. I act as a holding vessel for their emotional pain as we work to resolve issues. As a result, my body often holds the tension that I've built up in focusing on others' pain. My muscles were just beginning to loosen when I shut off the water. Max, now awake and looking lazy, watched as I went about getting dressed.

When I got to work, I found my usual spot near the tall shade trees. Most of the employees start earlier than I do as a contractor, and such was the case today. Few parking spaces remained, but not a person in sight. That was fine with me. I wasn't in the mood to run into anyone who might want to harm me.

I decided I had ruled Marge out as a potential assailant, so I stopped for a moment to speak with her.

"Good morning, Dr. D, how's it going this morning? Someone baked some goodies for the staff today; they're back in the kitchen."

"Marge," I said, "one of your jobs must be to try and fatten me up. Either that or you think I need to be a tad sweeter."

Marge grinned. "Dr. D, you're already one of the sweetest men I know. You certainly don't need any help there. I just know you sometimes enjoy a muffin when you make your tea. I keep a close eye on you, Dr. D."

I stiffened. "What? What do you mean by that?".

"Why, well, nothing," Marge sputtered. "I-I just wanted to tell you there was food available."

What the hell was the matter with me? I mustered a smile.

"Thanks, Marge. I do appreciate you help keep me on track. I'd be lost without you. I'll grab a muffin. Any messages come in for me?"

Marge handed me two slips of pink paper without looking at me.

"Just a couple of phone messages—nothing urgent—and several intakes you need to review."

Part of my job involved reviewing intakes, or initial assessments, completed by staff members who meet with people seeking mental health services. The initial assessments include a psychosocial overview and a description of signs and symptoms, leading up to provisional psychiatric diagnoses and recommended services.

"Thanks. I'll be in my office for about forty minutes before I meet with Wendy for supervision."

I headed back to my office, kicking myself the whole way. What was I doing, snapping at Marge? I went from ruling her out to treating her as if *she* was my stalker. What the hell was I doing?

With a long sigh, I stopped to select some tea and something from the baked goods department. Brownies. Well, there was nothing I could do to resist a brownie this morning. Thinking paranoid thoughts requires energy. I took one, grabbed a napkin, and walked the remaining ten feet to my office.

The message light was not flashing, meaning Marge had grabbed the calls coming in so no one needed to leave a voicemail message. I examined the phone messages. One from a student inquiring about a class, and the other from a former colleague wondering if I could present at a conference on children's services.

I busied myself with paperwork until ten forty-five, when I heard a soft rap on my door. Wendy had arrived for supervision, and I welcomed her into the office. She walked to the chair beside my desk, ever graceful, and settled in. She wore cream-colored slacks and a soft blue short-sleeved sweater that highlighted her eyes. She used little makeup and didn't require much to accentuate her soft complexion.

"How are things on the unit, Wen? Any problem cases?"

"Things are fine. May I tell you again how much I love my job?"

Wendy was only six months out of her master's program but was one of those people who seemed to be a perfect fit for work as a psychotherapist. She was calm and caring, and could defuse the most volatile situation with little difficulty. She had, I discovered, a manner of speaking to people in a tone of voice that put them at ease. She always seemed to say just the right thing, leaving those in her care feeling understood.

But there were some things only experience could teach.

"That's great, glad to hear it. Just keep in mind, with the kind of kids we get in here, there may be rough days ahead. I've seen situations on units that required police intervention. I need you to keep your wits about you once you unlock those doors."

"Thanks, Dr. D. I really value your help and support. And I'll make sure I don't let my guard down." Wendy smile was genuine. It was if her whole body smiled.

We discussed some of her more longstanding cases and moved on to more recent cases.

"Oh, before I forget—there is a boy on your unit but not on your therapy caseload I think could use some psychological testing. His name is Jimmy Schwartz, and Nancy is his behavior tech. From what

I've gathered from talking with her, there may be some anxiety driving his behavior, and I think we should take a look."

"Sure, no problem." She opened her planner. "I can get to him next week. What exactly did you have in mind?"

"Let's do the Smith Youth Anxiety Scale, and let's throw in the Adolescent Psychopathology Scale while we're at it. I know the APS is a lot longer, but Jimmy's not going anywhere soon, and it may give us other information about symptom patterns the staff aren't necessarily catching on the unit. You know how these kids are — they show you lots of stuff behaviorally, but it's often a cover or defense for the emotional stuff that seeks expression or release elsewhere."

"Right. I'm on it. I should be able to administer and score those instruments before we meet next week so that I can go over them with you. I also wanted to let you know that I've met with Maegan Mitchell a couple of times. She's the girl we staffed a week ago, the one from the long-term psychiatric hospital."

I thought back to the discussion, remembering the history of PTSD and the chronic depression.

"Great. Tell me your initial impressions."

"Well, she's going to be a tough one, I think, for a couple of reasons. First, the girl looks like a young Nicole Kidman, but with very dark hair. She's high-energy. And she's no wallflower. She's been engaging and attracting attention, which she enjoys and which reinforces her behavior. However, she's pretty cool toward her female peers and they're already beginning to refer to her as 'Ice Princess.' I've tried chatting with her, superficial stuff, but she barely acknowledged me."

"It's going to take some time with her," I said. "Her history — relationship with her family members, family dynamics, etc. — has shaped how she relates to others. It would be helpful to have more history. A lot of that information will come from the treatment records that haven't arrived yet. In the meantime, if she's icy, just continue to chip away at it. Nothing heavy — just regular, supportive interaction."

"Right," Wendy said. "Every day I am here, I'm going to seek her out, even if it's just for a minute or two. But I think her presence is going to make a major change on the unit."

"True. The sexual dynamics. We need to make sure the unit staff is on the lookout."

Wendy's eyes appeared to widen. She didn't respond.

"Wendy?"

"Oh, sorry, Dr. D. What you said. The 'lookout' part. It just reminded me of something nagging at me, but...."

I waited her out.

"Well, I almost hesitate to say anything. It's not like I have any hard data to go on."

"Go on. This sounds important."

"It's just, well...I've noticed more than the boys on the unit looking at her. I've caught male staff members leering as well."

"Leering?"

Wendy blushed. "Like I said, it's just something I've noticed. I saw one staff member who just seemed to be...staring at Maegan's ass as she walked down the hall."

"Wow. Was it that obvious?"

"It just happened I was looking in his direction at the time. I doubt anyone else would have even seen it. And then, when he caught me looking at him, he just smiled at me and went back to his paperwork."

"Sounds pretty significant — and unprofessional — to me. Who was the staff member you caught staring?"

"It was the unit leader. Tom."

I must have looked flabbergasted.

"Do you know him well?"

"Actually, not well at all. My interactions with him have only been professional, but he seems to be well-liked by the other staff and the kids. However, we need to take your observation seriously. Let me think about how to deal with this."

"OK, sure. Whatever you think is best..."

I checked my watch. "We need to wrap up. I need to do my rounds on the units. Gotta keep tabs on what's going on with staff and kids. How about I walk up with you to your unit first?"

Wendy and I took a brisk stroll up the back stairwell to the locked door of her unit, the west wing of the facility. It was nothing like the Presidential Suite of the White House, however.

"Hey, are you going to Dr. Jones's get-together tomorrow?" Wendy asked.

"You bet I am. Someone has to help eat the food. Wouldn't want Larry to feel like his grilling expertise wasn't appreciated." I paused a moment. "But with all the cookies and treats people bring in here, I may need to avoid the dessert table."

"Well, I think a fair number of staff members will be there. As for the dessert table, I'll keep an eye on you, if you like."

I was unlocking the unit door when she said it, and I almost dropped the keys. My mouth was dry. I watched as Wendy crossed into the unit. Nothing in her manner suggested the realization she had delivered a trigger phrase for terror. With some fumbling, I locked the door behind us.

When I'm on the units, kids seem to come out of the woodwork. They associate me with some kind of status and try to see if I have enough clout to grant them some favor or privilege that unit staff can't.

Today was a bit different. While there was a hum of activity, none of it centered on Wendy or me. And I saw the reason.

At the end of the hall, a small crowd had gathered around an individual whom I couldn't yet see. Wendy and I hustled to the opposite corner, and some of the kids moved aside for us. Two staff members restrained a teenaged girl, who, based on her appearance, could only be Maegan Mitchell. Tears streamed down her face, accompanied by an almost plaintive wail. Tom stood behind her and held her arms while another staff member used her upper body to cover Maegan's legs—a typical two-person passive restraint position.

Staff from other units had begun to arrive and were ushering the gawking residents away. Wendy knelt beside Maegan and spoke to her in a soft voice. I waited for Tom to make eye contact with me.

"What happened?"

"We were about to do some small group work when Maegan began to really freak out. She began screaming and then started to tear at her eyes with her fingernails. We had to chase her down the hall and restrain her to keep her from gouging her eyes out."

Maegan appeared to be oblivious to the activity going on around her. Wendy continued to speak to her and moved her face into Maegan's line of vision. She wanted Maegan to look at her, to help ground her and bring her back into the present. At this point, though, Maegan was not focusing on anything. Although her crying had subsided, her breathing was becoming erratic, and her eyes were glassy, her facial muscles slack.

I sensed the explosion a second before it erupted.

"Slut-bitch, get the hell away from me! No-ooo-o!"

She hissed and spat at Wendy, who cringed in response at the surprise assault. All eyes turned to watch Wendy's response to the rebuff. Wendy turned toward me, eyes wide. Maegan's breaths came in bursts. She struggled against the restraint, and then her muscles seemed to go limp.

I watched her for a minute. Wendy remained frozen. Staff members looked at one another. This "restraint and recovery" was unraveling. I needed to help Maegan and support Wendy without causing her to lose credibility.

"Wendy, it's okay," I said. "She's dissociating. Sit back and catch your breath, but stay close. I'll need you shortly."

Wendy blinked and slid back, eyebrows raised. Spurned or relieved?

Regardless, I didn't have time to deal with Wendy's issues right now. I squatted beside Maegan and spoke in a soft-but-firm tone. "Maegan, my name is Dr. Davison. You're being restrained because you tried to hurt yourself. I need you to focus on me. We want to work you through this restraint as soon as we can. Talk with me, and we'll get you through this quickly."

Maegan snapped her head up. "Another...fucking...shrink?"

"That's right. Your friendly neighborhood psychologist. Do you mind if I talk with you?"

"Would it matter...if I did?"

"Sure it would. I would respect your wishes. It just seemed like you were having a tough time."

Maegan's muscles relaxed a little, and she scrutinized me.

"You're...kind of big for...a shrink...ain't you?"

I smiled.

"That's got to be the wittiest observation I've heard today. Can I repeat it if I promise to give you credit?"

I thought a flicker of surprise crossed Maegan's face. She took a deep breath and blew it out.

"That's all I need. A fucking Chris Rock shrink. I can tell you why you're not out on tour. You suck!"

"Hey, that's only your opinion. Don't worry, though, I don't plan on quitting my day job. Right now the main thing is that you're feeling better."

"I feel like shit."

"Understandable. It's not fun to be restrained."

Maegan glared at the staff member braced against her legs. She tried to look at Tom, but his head was right behind hers.

"Any chance we can get these assholes off me?"

"Sure can, if you promise to talk with Wendy afterward."

"I'll try, but I ain't making no promises."

"The fact you're willing to try is good enough for me."

I stood and stepped a couple of feet away, nodding to Wendy as I did so. Her brows knit for a moment before she took my place beside Maegan.

"Stay close by," I said to Tom and his partner, "but let's see how she does on her own."

"Okay, Maegan, we're going to let go now," Tom said as he let go of her arms. His partner unwrapped herself from Maegan's legs, and both staff members moved to a crouching position several feet away.

Maegan leaned against the wall, muscles slack. I saw the glaze in her eyes continue to clear. She looked at Wendy, wiped at her eyes, and then turned to confront me.

"Who the fuck called you, anyway?" she demanded.

"No one called me. I just happened to drop by."

"Yeah. I heard about you. You're the head shrink." She snorted at her unintentional pun.

I smiled.

"Maegan, don't stop now, you're on a roll! Perhaps you should go on tour with me. We'll start with county fairs and work our way up."

Maegan groaned. The remaining crowd began to disperse.

"You are so lame. Next time you plan on coming up to my unit, call the staff so I'll have time to hide."

"Not my usual way of working, but it's a deal."

I turned to Wendy.

"She's all yours. Don't let her pull any funny stuff."

I began to walk away.

"Hey, doc!"

"Yes, Maegan?"

"No matter what people say about you, you're the best head shrink I've met today."

"I appreciate the vote of confidence, Maegan, and I promise you I'll try to live up to it."

Maegan's eyes twinkled for a second.

"But for now, I know you're in capable hands with Wendy, so, until next time...."

I left Wendy with Maegan and headed toward the staff area. As I approached the doorway, I overheard something that caused me to pause.

"What a dramatic display that was. She's got everyone sucked in. We should give her negative consequences for throwing a fit like that."

"What do you mean?" someone else asked.

I stepped into the room. Tom was talking to another male staff member who had been on the periphery of Maegan's restraint.

"Are you guys talking about Maegan?" I asked.

"Well, yeah," Tom muttered.

"What are your concerns? Maybe I can help you sort them out."

He cleared his throat. "Well, it was just she was fine one minute and going off the deep end the next. I think she was manipulating us."

"Really? To get what?"

"I don't know what you mean."

"Well," I said, "if she was manipulating us, it would be to gain something for herself, some kind of advantage."

"Well, maybe she wants us to feel sorry for her so we'll cut her some slack on the unit."

"I see. Do you have much experience with flashbacks and other PTSD symptoms?"

He averted his eyes. "Of course I do. I'm the unit director, and I have a lot of line experience."

I looked at the other guy. He looked like he wanted to be anywhere else but there. I turned back to Tom.

"I'll share my experience with you. Residential staff act as parent figures. They're right in the mix of everything that happens. Sometimes, during the course of dealing with the tension that dealing with adolescents brings, it's easy to direct feelings toward the kids that sets up barriers to understanding them."

"Are you saying I—"

"I'm *saying* that you have to step back and realize that these kids are hurting and need the best that we can give them. In Maegan's case, that means cutting her a break. Her trauma history is terrible. It wouldn't be unusual for that to lead to dissociation, flashbacks, or even self-injurious behavior. I don't think she was manipulating anyone. What was going on prior to the restraint?"

"Well, it was rough. It happened so fast, and Maegan was just so...out of it. Just freaking out. Scared me out of my wits."

"I saw that part. I mean before that."

Tom scowled. I maintained eye contact.

"Well, we were just calling the group together for a unit meeting. Out of the corner of my eye, I saw Maegan coming to the circle. Jimmy Schwartz was following her. Next thing I know, Maegan starts tearing at her eyes."

"Where were they prior to that?"

"I'm not sure. I think another staff member was rounding the kids up."

"Sounds like something happened that you didn't see. After things calm down on the unit, and Maegan is resting under supervision, it would be a good idea to interview the staff and pull the rest of the kids together and see what they know. I bet you'll find an answer there somewhere."

"OK, will do. And, hey, I'm sorry about what I said earlier. I was just blowing off steam. You know, from the restraint."

"Yeah, that could account for it. But as I heard the conversation, I was concerned that it was insensitive. You're the unit leader, so what your staff members see and hear from you guides them as to how they should respond."

"Right. My bad. I'll do better."

"It's probably a good time for me to set up trainings for each unit focusing on trauma. How to understand it, and how to have these units be safe places for the kids."

"Training would be good. If you need my help with that., just let me know."

"I'll keep you posted."

I started to leave the room but turned back to him. "How has Maegan been integrating on the unit?"

Tom seemed caught off guard. "Well, uh, she's been fine. No problems to speak of."

"This was my first time meeting her. She's an attractive young lady, isn't she? Is she stirring up the guys on the unit?"

"She turns heads, doc. Not much we can do about it. It's human nature."

"I'm sure she draws attention. Just let me know if you think she's getting too much of it." I paused for a moment. "From peers or staff."

I felt holes being bored into my back as I walked away.

CHAPTER TWENTY-THREE

I MADE IT THROUGH THE rest of the week, managing supervision, general rounds on the units, and attending a couple of management meetings. Back in my office, prior to the end of day, I reviewed initial evaluations. I found myself thinking about Wendy's promise to keep an eye on me. It seemed just too coincidental — and too creepy.

Could Wendy be my stalker? What would her motive be? I didn't know much about her background, but that was true for most people who worked in the residential treatment facility. I wanted to dismiss the notion without further analysis, which only reinforced the need to continue to consider the possibility. I blew out a deep breath and turned the lights out.

I headed out with the crowd as the agency closed for the week. I followed several line staff out the door, said hello to a few others in passing, and walked to my car in the parking lot. If anybody had been watching me, they might have seen me focused on my car and the area around it. I was looking for something out of the ordinary, but found nothing.

Or perhaps my stalker could do subtle as well.

Friday evenings at one time had meant fun and relaxation, but during my separation, weekends had been less than thrilling. I recalled my earlier vow to have more fun, but I was baffled. I decided I would rent a couple of movies and pick up some food at a nearby restaurant.

I made a quick stop at Redbox and scored a couple of flicks: *Foul Play* with Chevy Chase and Goldie Hawn — an oldie — and *Sneakers* with an all-star cast including Robert Redford and Sydney Poitier. Nothing to tug on the emotions too much, plus some laughter to elevate my mood. A second stop yielded a turkey-and-cheese sub, and then I was ready for the evening.

I turned the key in the front door and waited for Max to greet me. I was met with silence. Puzzled, I stepped inside, closing the door behind me.

"Max?" I called, perhaps thinking she was in deep slumber. No response.

I peeked into the laundry room. No Max. I was starting to get concerned.

I walked into the kitchen, dropped my keys on the table, and laid my movies and sub down. A piece of colored paper caught my eye.

It was a note from Vicki:

Bryce: I know I was supposed to pick up Max tomorrow, but I was able to get her an appointment with a groomer for early morning. I hope that's okay. I'll call you Sunday about picking her up. V.

Letting out a deep sigh, I stretched and groaned. Looked like I was batching it tonight. Max would enjoy the pampering though. I could use some pampering myself.

I stepped back outside just long enough to get my mail. A couple of advertisements and a cable bill. The fliers got pitched; the bill went into a letter rack I had hung up for such a purpose. It would soon make its way to the piles on my desk.

After changing into some shorts and a T-shirt, I pulled a cold soda from the fridge, popped it open, and debated about which movie to enjoy first. I decided to begin with the comedy. Serotonin infusion before I hit the adventure. I hadn't seen *Foul Play* in quite some time. For a moment, I wondered about the choice. Was it a movie I had seen with Vicki? Was I grasping at nostalgia? If I was, was it a bad thing?

I decided it didn't matter. I put the DVD in the player, grabbed my sub and some chips, and plunked on the couch. It was funnier than I had recalled and had a good mix of drama and adventure. Plus, the sub was great, enhanced by the fresh-baked roll—a special flair of the restaurant. I felt myself beginning to relax. And then the phone rang.

"Damn," I mumbled as I stared at the ringing phone.

I glanced at the wall clock: 8:30. Still in the civilized time period. After ten p.m., I would have treated the call with more suspicion. Still, it was unlikely to be a telemarketer, as that breed only calls during the dinner hour for maximum disruption. Or, as the chills ran down my spine, might this be a psychological intrusion of another kind?

I picked up the phone.

"Hello?"

There was a pause.

"Dr. Davison?" asked a breathless, female voice. One I did not recognize. I found myself holding the phone in a death grip.

"Speaking."

"I'm really sorry to bother you at home. This is Nancy Rodgers, from work."

It took me a second to realize who Nancy Rodgers was. I wasn't used to hearing her last name.

"Nancy, sure. What can I do for you?"

Another pause. I heard her sniffling.

"I just had a huge fight with my boyfriend. He, uh, hit me, and threw me out the door, and, uh, told me not to come back." She began to cry. "I'm sorry, I called work and got your phone number from the staff roster. I didn't know who else to call. I need your help."

"Nancy, where are you calling from?"

"Umm, a pay phone at the mini-market downtown."

"You should call the police, Nancy. They can deal with your boyfriend and help you find a shelter."

"No!" she wailed. "I don't want to involve the police, I don't want to press charges. That's too much mess. I don't want to be in the paper."

"How about a girlfriend?"

"My two best friends are out of town until tomorrow. They're staying in Pittsburgh tonight after a concert."

Crap. "Umm.... All right. I can come down and get you, and we can sort this out. Okay?"

"Oh, please, would you? That would help me out so much."

I told her that I would be there in ten to fifteen minutes. It took twenty. I pulled in close to the entrance, shut off the engine, and glanced around. There were a couple of customers at the gas pumps, and it looked like a few more were inside the store, but I didn't see Nancy. I took a deep breath. The moment I climbed out of the car, however, I heard her voice. She had been sitting on a small stone wall beside the building, out of my line of vision.

"Oh, Dr. D, thanks for doing this. It means a lot to me." Breathless. Anxious. She cast a furtive glance around.

I saw why she had been sitting in the shadows. First, her left eye was swollen and puffy, and it looked like she was going to have quite a shiner. Second, she was underdressed. She was wearing light slippers, short-shorts, and an oversized T-shirt that I suspected was her pajamas. Her arms were folded across her chest, but it was clear that she was also wearing no bra.

"That's fine, Nancy," I said, hearing my awkward cadence. "Why don't we get in the car and we can talk about this."

My first thought was just to talk, but I saw that Nancy was beginning to cry. I decided that we should go somewhere other than the mini-mart.

I drove to the diamond at the center of town. It housed a gazebo, benches, and plenty of places to park without a lot of attention. I pulled into a vacant spot, rolled down my window, fished a Kleenex out of the center console, and offered it to Nancy. The tears came in earnest.

"I'm s-s-so-sorry," she said as the tears rolled down her face. "I f-f-feel s-so helpless."

"You've been through a lot, Nancy. Don't worry about the tears. If the water gets too deep, we'll just open the doors."

Holding a tissue to her face, Nancy looked at me and managed a smile. I turned from her and looked out the window until the only sound I heard was the traffic from the street. Nancy's voice pulled my attention back inside the car.

"God, I don't know what to say. One minute my boyfriend and I are having pizza and beer, and the next thing he's using me for a punching bag."

"Sounds pretty rough. Do you have any clue what triggered it? Did he have much to drink?"

"I should have known something was going to happen. He had started in on the beer well before the pizza came. He must have had a pretty bad day at work, but he didn't want to talk about it. He never wants to talk about anything!

"By the time we started to eat, he was well into the second six-pack. All I said to him was, 'Honey, why don't you slow it down a bit?' and that's when he blew up. He told me that it was his place and if he wanted to have a beer or two, that was his privilege. And no 'bitch' was going to tell him what to do. I told him that if he was going to talk to me like that, I was going to go out until he calmed down. That's when he grabbed me up off the couch, hit me with the back of his hand, and pushed me out the door. He threw the deadbolt behind me. I was cold and scared. I pounded on the door, begging him to let me back in. I saw through the window that he went back to the beer. I don't really know any of my neighbors. Besides, none of them have been especially friendly. Flick's a loudmouth and alienates everybody. I walked about a mile into town and stopped at the pay phone at the mini-mart. I pleaded with the clerk to give me some change to use the phone. She saw what I looked like and gave me the money right away."

"Nancy, you need to call the police. No one deserves to be treated like this. You should press charges."

She shook her head. "I know. You're right. I'm not sure I can do that to him right now. He can be okay. He just doesn't handle stress real well. Plus, he only hit me once before. And I don't want to go to the cops. You know how this town is. I'll end up on the front page, or, at the very least, a big chunk of the police blotter section."

I thought about that. News like this did tend to find its way into print. Besides, it was the second time I had brought it up, and I didn't want to push it on her.

"Is there somewhere I can take you?"

She turned away.

"Friends? Relatives?"

"I've only been here a few months. Carrie and Lisa are about the only ones I know, and they're gone. My dad lives a long way from here."

I thought about putting her up in a hotel but felt like a heel. She had just been through the wringer and had reached out to me for help. But, still....

"There are a couple of hotels out near the interstate. Can I take you out there? I can cover the cost for you since you don't have any money or credit cards with you."

Nancy unleashed a torrent of sobs. "I don't want to be alone," she gasped. She looked like she was going to bolt.

"No, wait. Of course you don't want to be alone. I get that. You...can crash with me for the night. I have a futon couch in my office, and as a bed, it's not too bad."

The words were no sooner out of my mouth than I wondered...was this a setup? Could Nancy be my stalker?

Next—what the hell was the matter with me? This woman needed my help.

She looked at me with wet brown eyes and whispered, "Thank you."

Her tears eased my doubts.

CHAPTER TWENTY-FOUR

I GAVE HER THE NICKEL tour. Nancy was polite but was beginning to look drained. I offered her a drink, and she asked for some ice water. She sipped it as I excused myself and went upstairs.

I pulled the futon couch out and found some sheets, a comforter, and a pillow for her to use. I managed to scrounge an old pair of sweatpants that had shrunk over the years but were still good enough to paint your house in if you were so inclined. I also rounded up a bath towel, a fresh T-shirt, and an old bathrobe that had been my father's. Picking up the robe, I remembered Tony in my old robe, which I had since thrown in the laundry room. Didn't plan on touching that one until it was deloused and laundered.

I returned to the living room, where Nancy was sitting on the couch, staring at the wall. I wondered if she was in shock.

"Here, Nancy, I brought you some things to wear. Look, I'll be down here. You can go upstairs and change. If it would help you feel better, I can get you a fresh towel, and you could take a shower, if you feel like it. Whatever helps. When you come back down, we can look at that eye."

"Thanks, Dr. D," she said. "That might help."

A few moments later, I heard the bathroom door close and water running in the shower.

I took her half-empty water glass to the sink, passing the mirror on my way. I looked pretty rough. When Larry sees me tomorrow, he may prescribe shock therapy.

I sat down on the couch and flipped through a myriad of television channels. Looked like my second movie would have to wait for another day. Amazing how life happens and plans change.

I had just picked up the sports section of the paper when Nancy returned. Her hair was combed back, and she had the robe on over the T-shirt and sweatpants, which were bunched up around her ankles. Her eye was becoming more swollen.

"Geez, Nancy, you look very comfortable in those hand-me-downs."

Nancy lifted one leg and smiled as she glanced at the excess material.

"I want to say again how much I appreciate you doing all this," she said as she sat on the edge of the recliner "I don't know what I would have done if you hadn't been here." "Not a problem. Let's have a look at that eye."

I knelt beside her chair and turned her face toward the light. I touched the periphery of the bruised area and she winced.

"Yep, I can see why that hurts," I said. "Let me get some ice."

In the kitchen, I put some ice cubes in a plastic bag, wrapped a dish towel around it, and knelt beside Nancy again.

"Here. Take this and hold it against your eye."

She did so, leaning back into the chair.

"The cold feels good but kind of hurts, too."

"I know what you mean. In a few minutes, hopefully, you'll only notice the feeling-good part."

I returned to the couch. We both gazed at empty walls.

"I hope you don't mind," she said, "but I used your comb in the bathroom. It didn't even dawn on me until after I got out of the shower that I don't have one single thing other than my clothes. No brush, no makeup, no toothbrush—nothing. Zip."

"Well, for the comb, of course I'll have to charge you. We'll work on getting your purse and other stuff tomorrow. Right now, I think it's time for you to turn in. I'll get you some Tylenol PM. The antihistamine in it will help you sleep."

"You're the doctor," Nancy said. This time, she mustered a big smile.

She followed me up the stairs and we entered my office.

"This is my office away from the office, but tonight it's yours. There's a stereo if you like music that's probably older than you, but if you get terribly bored, you can always play solitaire on the computer."

"This is nice."

She walked over to my CD collection and browsed a few titles.

"Hey, I actually know these groups! They remind me of songs that my dad would listen to..."

"Yep, that's what I meant. Classic rock."

Nancy smiled. "Music is ageless. There are people younger than me that listen to oldies from the sixties."

I groaned. "We should stop at that and move on. I'll see you in the morning. I'll set the Tylenol PM out on the bathroom sink for you. Try to keep that ice bag on for another ten minutes or so."

"Great. Goodnight. See you in the morning."

I closed the door, found the pills in the medicine cabinet, and set the bottle on the sink. I washed my face, brushed my teeth, and headed down the hall to my bedroom where I flipped on the light on the table beside my bed and closed the bedroom door. Once more, I felt too tired for pajamas, so I just stripped off my clothes and crawled into bed.

As I looked up at the ceiling, I contemplated my circumstances. Here in my home, not twenty feet down the hall, was an attractive young woman, the first overnight visitor in my house. She'd called me for help. I tried to shuttle her to a hotel, but here she was. While I was being kind, I was aware of my feelings since she arrived. It felt good to engage with someone outside of work who didn't snap at every word I said, or try to get out of the conversation entirely. If Nancy was a damsel in distress, did that make me a hero?

I didn't feel like one. I felt like a dirty old man. She thought I was her father's age. Well, no matter. I wasn't going to act on my feelings. And I reminded myself that it was okay to be human. Hero or not, I didn't need to be perfect.

CHAPTER TWENTY-FIVE

FOR THE SECOND TIME IN less than a week, I was awakened by a smell. This one I recognized. The aroma of eggs and bacon frying. And, I believed, toast.

I crawled out of bed, wiped the crust from my eyes, and threw on a pair of jeans and a T-shirt. In the kitchen, Nancy had set the table, quick-thawed some frozen orange juice, and was hard at work on breakfast. She turned when I entered the room and smiled. The purplish-blue bruise around her eye looked nasty, but the swelling had lessened. Otherwise, she pretty much looked as she had when I had said goodnight, with the exception that her hair was dry.

"Wow, this is great. What time did you start all this?"

"I thought I at least owed you breakfast. I've been up for about an hour. Even with the pills, it was a hard night of sleeping. I got up early, even took your advice and played a few games of Solitaire, and finally decided to just come down here. I peeked in your fridge and found just the right ingredients for breakfast."

"Hey, I'm sure glad you did," I said. "I wasn't looking forward to having to fight with you over that last bowl of Cocoa Puffs in the pantry."

Nancy laughed. "You, sir, are a funny man. Now go sit down and let me take care of you."

I did as I was told. It was nice to see a woman in my kitchen. It reminded me of more pleasant days.

Within moments, breakfast was ready, and Nancy had joined me at the table. She lifted her glass of orange juice.

"To new beginnings."

"Indeed. New beginnings," I concurred.

We made small talk for a while and enjoyed our breakfasts.

"Dr. D, if you don't mind me asking, where is your wife? For some reason I had assumed you were married. I mean, I noticed you wear a wedding band...."

I looked at my ring. "Well, I guess I am, technically speaking. However, we've been separated for over six months, and it looks like things are moving along toward the end."

"I'm sorry. That stinks. You look pretty worn out. Are you doing okay?"

I couldn't remember the last time someone had asked me such a question.

"Well, yeah. I'm not sleeping well. It's been pretty rocky these last couple of months. I'm sure all this is for the best...somehow." I said the words, but they felt half-hearted.

I leaned back in my chair and looked at Nancy. "What about you? What's your next step?"

She glanced at the clock on the wall. Just about ten a.m. "Well, I need to see about getting some of my things. Especially my car keys and my purse. Would you mind driving me over there?"

It sounded like the right thing to do.

"Okay," I said. "But let me take a quick shower."

Nancy stood and started to gather up the dishes. "I'm going to call my friends and see if they made it home yet. Okay if I use your phone?"

I nodded and then excused myself. When I returned to the kitchen, it was spotless, and Nancy was looking out the window.

"I like your place," she said. "It looks like you need something on the walls, though."

I laughed. "You're right. I thought that just the other day. The place looks like it's been occupied just long enough to move on to something else. I need to make it more homely."

Nancy snorted. "You mean *homey*, right?"

"Yeah, right." I winked. "Homier."

"I'm sure that will all come in time," she said. "Hey, my friends decided to drive back early today, and they said there's no problem with me staying with them for a while. They said that either you could drop me off there, or they could meet me at my place."

I thought about the previous night. "How about I take you to their place after you gather up a few things?"

"You're the best, doc. I'll never be able to repay you for your kindness."

"Tell you what. Sometime down the road, you can buy me a cup of coffee in the cafeteria and fill me in on how you're doing between now and then. Sound Okay? You can also keep my clothes until then if you like."

She looked down at herself. "Ya know, maybe I should just keep them...I've become quite attached to them!"

We both laughed. It felt good to laugh.

We stepped outside. I made sure the front door was locked, and we headed out of the development. She gave me directions as I drove, and it wasn't long until I pulled into the parking lot of her apartment building.

"I'm on the ground floor" she told me. "It shouldn't take me a minute to get my things. It might be best if you wait here for me. It'll be easier for me to talk my way through this that way. I'm guessing that he's gonna pretend to be remorseful about last night and will try and make things right with me."

"Well, I'll stand by the car and wait for you. If you need me, just call me."

I watched as she swished away in my old clothes and disappeared through the main entrance of the apartment building. I tried to imagine what might be going on.

It didn't take me long to begin to get an idea.

As I leaned against the hood of the car, I heard the door slam. I turned my head to see an angry-looking man striding toward me. He was dark-haired, average height, and wearing a typical gym-rat sleeveless tank top. I noted the STUD tattoo on his right bicep. He wasn't running, but had picked up his pace.

Butterflies collided in my stomach. I wanted to bolt, but didn't move a muscle.

"Hey," he said. "You and me need to talk."

See? He only wanted to talk. I'd be a good listener.

I turned to face him but held my ground, still leaning against the car. I wasn't sure what he intended to talk about, but I wanted to show him that I wasn't going to just jump in my car and leave, in spite of my internal response.

He stopped a few feet away from me. He was breathing hard, appeared to be a bit flushed, and was flexing his pectoral muscles — perhaps unconsciously, like a primate who wanted to show dominance.

"What can I do for you, Mr....?" I offered.

He took another step toward me until he was about two feet away, and jabbed the air between us with his finger. "You need to keep your nose out of other people's business. What are you doing, driving her around like this? Did you sleep with her or something? You better start talking, boy."

He had my attention now. And leaving was no longer part of the equation. Instead, I stood and folded my arms across my chest. Not a good clinical move, but I wasn't feeling very therapeutic right then. I made full eye contact with him but spoke in a soft voice.

"First off, I'm not your boy, sonny. Second, I'm not looking to interfere in anybody's business. But I'm concerned about what you did to your girlfriend's face. You also need to get out of my face. It wouldn't bother me to call the cops and let Nancy show them how a real man like you treats a woman."

His whole body twitched. I thought he was going to explode on me when the door of the building closed again. We both turned to look.

Nancy had changed into a T-shirt and jeans and was carrying her purse and pulling a large suitcase behind her. Mr. Stud moved to intercept her as she made a beeline for my car.

"Baby, wait a minute," he said. "Come on back in, and let's talk this out."

She brushed past him, opened the back door, maneuvered her suitcase on the seat, and closed the door.

"So," she said. "You want to talk?"

"Yeah. Yesterday just sucked at work. It was a bad day. I drank too much. Then you got mouthy and pushy, and you made me hit you."

There it was. The classic line of a batterer. It wasn't his fault. She had provoked him. She deserved what she got. I anticipated her sharp retort.

Her reply stunned me.

"Oh, sweetie, I knew you'd had a bad day. I just wasn't able to help you feel better like a good woman would have done. Will you ever forgive me?"

I saw him relax. He shot me a gloating sort of look before he addressed her.

"Of course. Everybody deserves a second chance."

She reached her hand toward his face as if she was going to caress his cheek. However, she pulled her hand back and slapped him. He stumbled backwards....

"You son of a bitch. You won't ever lay a hand on me again. I'll get my car tonight, and I'll be back tomorrow with my friends after my Sunday shift to get the rest of my stuff. *Don't be home.*"

With that, she left the speechless Mr. Stud sputtering in the parking lot and climbed into my car. I got in, still wary, and started the engine. He didn't move and said nothing more. I was pretty sure that his masculine pride was wounded, and anything he might have done would have made things worse. A few moments later, his form disappeared from my rear-view mirror.

Out on the highway, I looked at Nancy. "My God, you certainly stood up to him. Where did that come from?"

She looked straight ahead. Then buried her face in her hands. "God, what did I just do? Now I have no place to live. I'll be alone. Maybe we should go back."

"From what I just saw, I think you'd be wise to respect your instincts. The way you nailed Flick, that wasn't a woman who was worried about being alone."

Nancy looked at me and remained silent for a minute. "You ever think about being a therapist?"

"Nah, I'm looking to open a bookstore."

Nancy rubbed her hand. "This sure hurts."

"It'll take your mind off your face."

She touched her bruised cheek. "Not a day to write home about, that's for sure. But what about you? Are you going to be okay?"

"Me? I'm fine."

"I mean, I've put you through some shit, haven't I? And I don't think Flick is going to be your friend after this."

"Since we weren't friends to begin with, I haven't lost anything then. Right?"

CHAPTER TWENTY-SIX

I DROPPED NANCY OFF AT Walmart where her friends were waiting. They assured me they would take care of helping Nancy pick up her car and her belongings later. Nancy, for her part, gave me a demure kiss on the cheek as a further gesture of thanks. I left her somewhere around noon.

Was it only Saturday? The way the weekend had started, I'd covered a lot of emotional ground already. It also struck me that I had an important social engagement on my calendar. I'd almost forgotten about Larry's barbecue! I pushed the Prius above the speed limit and sailed the rest of the way home, interrupted only by a few stoplights.

I changed my clothes, spruced up a bit, and checked the clock. I still had about forty-five minutes until I had to leave. Being a creature of habit—a more innocuous attribution than calling myself a highly compulsive, overanxious individual—I decided to check my email.

While the computer went through its system checks, I opened the two windows in my room to let in some fresh air. There was a hint of mugginess, suggesting that the rest of the afternoon was going to be both hotter and more humid.

I sat down and clicked my email. Half a dozen messages. I scanned for the most interesting ones. Once again, a message from Vicki had arrived.

B: just wanted to let you know that Bill Winters is going to handle the divorce. It will be very straightforward. I'm not asking anything of you, and I'm sure that you and I can amicably share duties pertaining to Max. Oh, I was in the grocery store this morning and bumped into Dr. Jones. He made reference to seeing you at a picnic this afternoon. I'll probably drop by your place while you're out and put Max in the laundry room. V.

Right. So, full speed ahead with the divorce—and trying to avoid any contact with me whatsoever in the process. Lovely. Made me wonder if we would ever do anything "amicably" again.

As I considered Vicki's frosty message, a computer beep alerted me to a new email. A preview pane popped up and the email subject line broke my rumination: *So Close.*

My heart pounded in my chest. I walked away from the computer. I couldn't deal with this. The walls felt close. I poured a glass of water, took a small drink, dumped the rest.

I slid back in front of the computer. Stared at the email message header. I clicked on it.

Dr. Davison. Tsk tsk. Your wife doesn't want you. Even though you don't seem to be getting the message, you let a strange woman stay in your house. What did you do while she was in your house? Would it bother you if your wife knew you were sleeping around? Pathetic. It should be obvious by now — even to you — that I'm watching your every move. Who knows what surprises are coming your way? I will tell you this: you are in for one hell of a ride. ribschild. ps. Do you hear footsteps? It's not too late for a final exit.

I felt the butterflies doing advanced acrobatics in my stomach. I shut off the computer without going through the usual shutdown procedure—something I never do.

I swiveled in my chair, took a few deep breaths, glanced at the clock. About twenty minutes until I needed to leave. The picnic, however, was the farthest thing from my mind. I was living in a fishbowl. My life was completely exposed to someone who could strike at will. The images of lambs headed to slaughter flashed through my mind. I rushed to the windows and looked out, as if I would find someone out there, hovering in a hot air balloon or hanging from a bungee cord to get a good view of me. I closed the windows and locked them.

Like clockwork, I felt rumblings from deep within, and I knew that I had to get to the bathroom. I rushed down the hallway and got there just in the nick of time as my bowels exploded.

"Christ, Bryce," I muttered to myself. "What a clear demonstration of the instantaneous nature of mind-body communication. You must be a psychologist."

I washed my shaking hands, glanced in the mirror. The casino refugee, while still present, looked just a shade more presentable. I locked up the apartment and hit the road, deciding that I may as well head to the shindig. If something happened, at least there would be witnesses.

It was also important for me to find a way out of the fishbowl.

CHAPTER TWENTY-SEVEN

THE JONES RESIDENCE WAS A wonderful three-story home with several impressive pillars supporting a massive front porch roof. In addition to the huge house, there was a carriage house and three-car garage in the rear next to a spacious yard that was surrounded by split-rail fencing. I pulled into the driveway and noticed that there were already a few cars parked behind the house. I felt a moment of relief that I was not the first guest to arrive. As I turned the corner, I caught a glimpse of Larry going inside through the screen door. If I wasn't mistaken, he was wearing some "Kiss the Cook" type of apron. If that was the case, my intention was to pass.

I climbed the steps to the deck, where Joan was arranging plates and silverware. She saw me coming and greeted me with a hug. I kissed her cheek.

"So good to see you, Bryce," Joan said. "It's been too long since you paid us a visit."

"It's kind of what pushed me to come today. I realized that with all the things happening in my life, I hadn't done much socializing."

"Well, now that you're here, you'll get a chance to meet some people. Maybe that will lead to other opportunities," Joan said.

"Maybe I can help with that later," Larry said, returning to the deck. "I'll introduce you to some people, once things are rolling."

"Take your time, Larry. I'll wander over to the chairs on the lawn and see what's going on."

As I was left the deck, Wendy was approaching. The change in her appearance was striking.

"Wendy, you cut your hair!"

"Hi, Dr. D, nice of you to notice. It used to be a regular routine for me. Grow my hair out and then cut it when the weather gets hotter. It's been long now for a while. I figured it would maybe help me make some other changes, too."

"Anything we need to discuss at work?"

"No, no, nothing like that. Like I told you, I love my job. No, it was just getting to the point that I was working and then going home to watch television. I used to be more active. Music, exercise classes, stuff like that. So I'm going to get back into some things. And I cut my hair."

"I get it. Sometimes taking a break by hitting the couch becomes a habit rather than a temporary fix."

"That's it. It's good to run into you here. I don't mean to step out of line, but you've seemed a little out of sorts recently."

That caught me by surprise. "Dr. D?"

"Wow, I'm sorry, Wendy. No, not out of line at all. I've been a shrink long enough that I thought I had developed a good poker face, including keeping my home life separate from my work life…. But from working with you, I know you're very observant. What you said is right. I've been pretty tired lately, and out of sorts in that way. And that's why I'm here."

"Good. I'm sure I'll bump into you again later. Enjoy yourself."

I watched Wendy walk away. My casino-refugee persona was my private experience. But I wasn't hiding it very well. Wendy was the second person to mention it lately, so it may be obvious to others—including people who wouldn't feel comfortable sharing such an observation. I needed to take better care of myself.

By three-fifteen, most of the partygoers had arrived. A few physicians from town had joined the group of chairs where I was sitting, including a gastroenterologist, a pediatrician, and an oncologist. When they heard I was a psychologist, the discussion turned to psychological intervention to support medical treatment. I was in my element, and whatever social anxiety might have been present quickly dissolved.

Toward the end of the discussion, a newcomer joined our group. He listened to the conversation, sitting forward in his chair. When other conversations formed, he turned to me and offered his hand.

"Jerry Raphael."

"Ah, Dr. Raphael, so nice to meet you. Bryce Davison. I'm a consulting psychologist with the local human services agency. I see your name on the sign every day when I enter the building. Folks in the outpatient department speak of you with reverence."

Dr. Raphael laughed. "Reverence, eh? I'll have to remember that. But it's true that I provide medication management to a number of the clinic outpatients through my practice. But your name also means something to me. There aren't a lot of psychiatrists in this town, so I know Larry pretty well. He has told me about you, specifically about your diagnostic and therapy skills."

"He's too generous."

"I'm thinking not. He's a straightforward physician. He likes you and what you bring to the table. Which, incidentally, is one reason I'm here today — to meet you. Larry said he had invited you. Do you have a private office yet?"

"No, but hopefully soon."

"Perhaps we can work something out. I understand you have a background in anxiety disorder treatment."

"It's one of my clinical interests. Do you see many patients with anxiety disorders?"

"I do, yes. For the past year, I've been developing a panic disorder program. It's getting much busier. Good referrals from cardiologists and family practice docs. I'm afraid, though, that I have limited time to offer psychotherapy. I also have office space available, so we should talk soon. How about a lunch meeting?"

"That would be great. I'd be very interested in hearing more about your practice."

He handed me a card. "My email address is on the back."

I dug for my wallet. "Thanks. Here's my consulting card." I jotted my cell phone number on the bottom.

"I'm a compulsive email checker, Dr. Davison, so that may be the easiest way to get in touch with me."

He glanced at a pocket calendar. He noticed me watching him, and smiled.

"I may like electronic mail," he said, "but I prefer paper products for many things, including my appointments."

"I'm a fountain pen guy," I said. "That makes me a paper guy, too." Dr. Raphael nodded and looked back at his calendar.

"Say, a week and a half? Wednesday at twelve thirty? We could meet in my office and order lunch."

Good luck for me. Providing assessment and treatment for an anxiety disorder clinic would be a great way to build my practice. And he had office space!

At that moment, Larry approached the group with his arms raised, seeking to quiet the conversations.

"Folks, your attention for just a moment. As the grill master for this gathering, I want to thank you for coming. You have your choice of several specialty items: although we have the usual hot dogs and hamburgers, we also have summer sausage and a new item for this year — *rack of ribs* slathered with a secret Texas sauce."

The attendees cheered. I sat quietly with my hands clenched on the arms of my chair. I didn't have enough spit to whistle.

What the hell? Ribs? Was this a message from Larry to me? Or another in a growing line of coincidences? My paranoia meter went up several notches, each one adding a furrow to my brow.

I watched Larry go about his business, waiting to see if he would make eye contact. He looked relaxed and happy. He scanned the crowd as if to assess their positive responses. When he saw me looking in his direction, he gave a little wave.

I had no choice. I had to scratch Larry from my list of trusted parties.

CHAPTER TWENTY-EIGHT

THE REST OF THE AFTERNOON was pleasant enough. The food was good, and, as Joan had predicted, I had met some new people. So despite how it had started, the day had turned out much better than I had anticipated, although I realized that I had more reasons to worry than I had before the day had begun.

Mr. Stud. Larry. I needed a spreadsheet to keep track of all the threats.

Possible threats, I reminded myself.

I stayed after dinner to help with cleanup. Less than an hour later, the deck and surrounding area were spotless. I stopped to thank my hosts before I left.

"Thanks for the cleanup efforts," Joan said, touching my arm. "It helped make quick work of it."

Larry shook my hand. "Did you have a good time?"

"I did. Usually the gatherings I attend don't have so many medical professionals. At those parties, when I tell people I'm a psychologist, people start telling me their dreams or ask if I can read minds. It got to the point where I started to carry balloons with me just in case someone asked me to create balloon animals, too."

Joan laughed. "That's hilarious. I take it Dr. Raphael and others responded more appropriately?"

"Yes. He was great. The all were. I'm glad I came."

When I reached the end of the driveway I put the car in neutral. For the first time in a very long time, I felt like I should be *doing* something — like the night was still young, and there was no reason to be heading home so soon.

The question was: what? I mulled over some possibilities. I could drive up to Presque Isle, walk along the beach, and gaze out at the sun setting over Lake Erie. I could catch a movie, although I wasn't sure what was playing. I could do some shopping, look for some of the latest gadgets that I enjoy.

I didn't want to spend more time in the car, which a trip to Erie would entail. I remembered that I still had a movie to watch. I put the Prius in drive and turned toward home.

As I approached the turn for the development, a white pickup truck barreled through the intersection, fishtailing in front of me as the tires sought concrete to grip. I had hit the brakes when I first saw movement, but I pressed down harder as if I could stop the truck, too. I watched its tail end shimmy and turned my head to follow the path of the truck. When its stability was ensured, I saw the maniac driver speed by while giving me the finger. I sat and watched for a moment, wondering which telephone pole the driver might wrap his vehicle around. And then I drove home.

CHAPTER TWENTY-NINE

SUNBEAMS ACROSS MY FACE COAXED me awake Sunday morning. The warmth felt pleasant, and I chose not to move for another few minutes. There was no reason to rush and nothing on the calendar. I had the whole day in front of me. A short time ago, this would have engendered dread, but I felt an optimism today. I had done something positive yesterday, and it had a rippling effect. It's what I had been chiding myself to do.

When I finally moved to get out of bed, I rapped Max's head with an ankle as she slept at the foot of the mattress. She raised her head and looked at me.

"Sorry, Max. I didn't realize where you were."

Max looked at me for a few seconds longer and then put her head down and closed her eyes. She was sleeping in—and rightly so. When I had arrived home the night before, we'd had a joyous reunion. She joined me on the couch for the movie and a bite of my leftover sub. We had stayed up late.

Over a bowl of cereal, I looked at my list of suspects. I jotted down Mr. Stud and Larry. Mr. Stud was a latecomer to the events, but he was definitely in play now. He might even become a secondary stalker.

That made me laugh out loud. I put my pen down and let my belly laugh run its course until it was time to wipe the tears from my eyes. *A secondary stalker!* As if my life wasn't complicated enough. As much as I disliked the phrase "it is what it is" because I considered it to be dismissive, the truth was, I needed to keep my eye on this list, even if it got to the point of including third-string stalkers and beyond.

Mr. Stud would fit the mold of a "wronged individual." Although I was an innocent bystander in his drama with Nancy, I was now associated with it. I wasn't sure I was an easier target than Nancy, but he might direct his energy toward me to justify his anger.

Larry. I jotted down "cooker of *ribs*" next to his name. A man who, by his own admission, was offering the dish for the first time. Motivation? I couldn't even come up with a creative response to that. But I wouldn't be confiding in him anytime soon.

I finished my cereal and rinsed out the dish, mulling all the while about ribschild. On impulse, I jogged up the steps and into my office. I studied the physical structure of the CPU. I picked up the keyboard and examined it, and then followed the cord behind the unit and unplugged it. Something was attached to it—something I hadn't put there. I disconnected it from the keyboard cord, plugged the cord back in the CPU, and then sat down to boot up the computer, staring at the cylindrical item sitting in front of me on the desk. It had its own cord and plug to which my keyboard cord had connected. The cord on the other end of the cylinder had connected to my computer. I didn't know what it was, but I had a good idea what it must do.

I did some Google searches using a physical description of the item, and then modifying my search terms to include new language I learned. What I had on my desk was a keylogger. It had been recording everything I had been typing for God knows how long. Perhaps even mere days after I had set up my computer.

With guidance from YouTube, I inserted the device into a USB port and accessed it. At that point, I discovered that this particular keylogger was encrypted. Without a password, I couldn't determine the information contained on it. So maybe I couldn't tell how long it had been installed, I now knew how my life had been exposed.

Or did I? Was everything that I communicated via email what ribschild had referenced in messages to me? I would need to check that out. The keylogger also told me that someone had to have been in my house. I mentally reviewed that list: Vicki, Scooch...and

Nancy. She not only was in my house, I had invited her to access my computer! I berated my naiveté, then took a breath. The ribschild stuff was happening before Nancy had stayed here.

I pulled an invoice from a desk drawer and dialed the number listed on it. What time is it? Should be okay.

"Logan's Luxury Townhomes, how may I help you?"

"Hi, this is Bryce Davison. I'm in unit 310D."

"Yes, Mr. Davison. This is Charlotte. I think I was the one that leased the townhouse to you. What can I do for you?"

"I have a bit of a sticky situation. I just found out that someone attached a device on my computer to capture keystrokes. Is it possible to know how often someone enters my townhouse on official business, or let's just make it for any reason?"

"Well, first let me say that I'm troubled to hear about this. We are very serious about our residents' privacy, although as you know from filling out your lease agreement, you agreed to provide access for maintenance, inspection, complaints, and so on. I'm pulling your app up now."

"Complaints? What does that refer to?"

"That would be like someone telling us that rotten odors might be emanating from someone's space — something along those lines. Okay, I have your app on my screen. Now I do see that you requested an additional key so that your wife, Vicki, would have access. Have you checked with her?"

I had several times, none of which went well.

"Yes, I'm aware of allowing Vicki access. I don't think she is monitoring my computer activity."

"What would you like me to do, Mr. Davison?"

"Let's start with who has accessed my place. Scooch was here when I moved in. Is there a log of his activity?"

"Of course we keep track of that. Neither Scooch nor anyone else can enter units willy-nilly."

"Good. No willy-nilly. So how about approved access?"

"That will take me a minute. Hold on, please."

I heard a file drawer opened and closed, followed by paper shuffling.

"Yes, we have Scooch in your unit on entry day to hook up your new appliances. It looks like he was in one other time, about a month ago."

"What was that about?"

"It was routine AC maintenance, including checking your thermostat. We sent out notices about that a week or ten days prior."

I remembered receiving the mailing.

"Anyone else? Outside contractors?"

"No, no record of other access. I'm sorry."

"Thanks for checking for me. I'm glad I called you. Thanks for your time."

"Any time, Mr. Davison. If you need anything else, just call or stop by. And if you need to report anything further on this issue, please contact me as well."

I took the keylogger and put it in a drawer with the invoice I had taken out. Drummed my fingers on the table. And then changed my login and email passwords, and, for good measure, my online banking password.

"Advantage Davison," I said to the computer screen before I shut it down.

CHAPTER THIRTY

AS THE AFTERNOON STRETCHED ON, I grew tired of looking at the computer screen. Max had joined me and was sprawled out in the doorway.

"Time for some fresh air, Max. Feel like hitting the trail?"

Max's tail thumped the floor.

"I'll take that as a yes. Let's go downstairs."

Max waited until I stepped over her and started down the stairs before standing up. The snapping of her leash clasp quickened her pace. As she hit the bottom step, I managed to hook her leash on her collar in one fluid motion.

Outside, we stood on the sidewalk. We could take a loop around the development or head back on the trail. The last trail trip hadn't ended well. The more we avoided the trail, though, the more anxiety would be associated with it.

"Sorry, Max. I know *you're* not avoiding anything. That's all on me. Let's go back to where we last explored."

I remembered the point where my reverie had been interrupted. We hit that spot and kept going. Around the next corner, we hit something unexpected—a large, cleared circle of land, maybe a couple hundred feet in diameter. There were a couple of benches on the periphery and a flower garden in the middle, protected by stacked wooden beams. It was quite pretty.

"Wow, Max," I said. "If we had known about this, we could have come sooner."

I unsnapped Max's leash, and she trotted across the clearing until something caught her attention. Then she crept along, nose to the ground. I walked the edge of the circle until I came to the first bench. There was a plaque dedicating the bench to the residents of the townhome community.

I sat down and watched Max do her thing. I puzzled over the access to this area. The lack of a mowed path all the way back made it less likely that people would find it. It should be better advertised, too — perhaps a sign along the trail. I'd have to make that suggestion to the leasing office.

"Woof!"

Max was standing near the garden but staring toward the end of the path. I couldn't see through the shrubs, but something moved behind them.

"Who's there?" I asked as I approached Max. I slipped her leash back on.

Someone stepped into the clearing. It was Scooch, and he was holding a knife.

CHAPTER THIRTY-ONE

"WHAT ARE YOU DOING HERE?" Scooch asked, arms at his sides.

I looked at his knife. It had an unusual blade. But it *was* large.

"Max and I were just out for a walk. Were you following us?"

Scooch rubbed his mullet with his free hand. "Following you? Why would I follow you?"

I stepped closer to him. Max stayed behind me.

"You didn't just walk out and show yourself. Seemed like you were hanging back and watching."

Scooch averted his eyes.

"Scooch?"

He looked back. "Nah, that was nothing. I heard noises so I was trying to figure out where they were coming from. Must've been you two."

That didn't seem like an honest response, but I wasn't going to challenge a guy holding a knife.

"We just found this place. I was trying to figure out why it wasn't better presented, like with a mowed path and signs."

"That's why I'm here. To do some of the weedin'. As for the other, this area ain't quite done yet. That's why it ain't been mowed all the way back."

Max moved up and peered at Scooch around my legs.

"That makes sense. Max and I just found it early."

Scooch pointed at Max with his knife.

"Is that a wiener dog?"

"Nope. Max is a basset hound. She's long, but she's bigger and stronger than a dachshund. Bassets were bred for hunting small game. They're great trackers — almost as good as bloodhounds."

Scooch wasn't really listening. He was looking at me and twirling the knife handle in his fingertips.

"Mind if I see that? That's an interesting knife." I held my hand out.

Scooch took the knife by the blade and offered me the handle.

The blade was curved and the edges were dull. Only the tip was sharp.

"That's a digging blade," he said. "It gets down to the roots of the weeds and pokes through them."

"Impressive." I handed the knife back and willed my shoulder muscles to loosen. "Max and I had better move on and leave you to your work. Thanks for chatting."

Scooch nodded and took a half-step past me. Max backed up a step and growled, the hair near her tail standing up. Scooch hesitated, then kept going, eying Max on his way past.

"Good girl, Max," I said, guiding her to stay with me as we walked toward the trail. When I looked back, Scooch was standing beside the flower garden, leaning to look at the soil.

When we were out of sight, I knelt down and rubbed Max's face. "That guy gives me the creeps. Thanks for having my back."

Max wagged her tail and licked my face. I patted her head and we continued along the trail. She took her time with the scents, and I stretched each time we stopped. It wasn't like Scooch had been carrying a broadsword or machete. It was more a digging than cutting tool. He was probably there to do just what he said. But Scooch even gave my dog the creeps, and for me, that was validating.

We got to the end of the trail and out into the common area of the development without incident.

CHAPTER THIRTY-TWO

I FED MAX AND WENT to wash up and change my shirt. A quick comb through my hair, and I headed downstairs. I gave Max the run of the house and a new bone to chew on. She took it from me politely and carried it to the kitchen doorway, where she flopped down and started to gnaw on it....

Sunday nights were difficult for me. The end of the weekend and the preparation for a new week. Vicki and I had developed a ritual for these nights. It was our time to step away from any electronic equipment. No TV, no email. We started playing board games. Usually Scrabble. Sometimes by candlelight. Like most things we did, there was a competitive nature to the games. And attention to rules. We kept a dictionary close for any debates about illegal words.

Game night was always a success. It was relaxing and provided a gentle close to the weekend. But ever since being alone, I hadn't found a good replacement for Scrabble. I thought about how people in movies would play chess alone. I even tried it once. But I always knew what the next move would be, so it seemed pointless. I probably wasn't approaching it the right way.

The night before, I had thought about going somewhere but hadn't. Tonight I *was* going to do something different than stay home, captive to my fear and my stalker.

I drove to Cracker Barrel and asked for a table by a window. From where I was sitting, I could see over the hillside toward the lights of New Alex. It was a charming view. I selected a breakfast entrée and iced tea and focused on my meal, and then on a second glass of tea after I put my fork down.

"Dr. D?"

I kicked the table leg and saw my glass of tea start to wobble. I caught it before it tipped over.

"Sorry to startle you," Wendy said. "I just stopped to say hi."

"Hi Wendy. I was more lost in thought than I realized. What brings you here?"

"Just here with a couple of girlfriends." She gestured toward two women waiting for her near the fireplace. "We talked about starting a book discussion group. This was kind of our first meeting. I just happened to see you sitting here. I see you had your dinner, but don't let me interrupt your dessert."

"I was just going to sit here with my iced tea. Would you like to join me for coffee or something?"

She looked toward her friends and back at me. "Well…yes, that would be nice. Just give me a second to say goodbye."

I thought Wendy would just talk with them and return. Instead, she brought her friends with her, both blondes and taller than Wendy.

"They said they're always hearing about this Dr. Davison guy," Wendy said, "so they wanted to meet you. This is Jan and Maggie."

I stood up and shook their hands. "Nice to meet you two. Have you known Wendy long?"

"We grew up together," Maggie said. "We even went to the same college. Jan and I went into education. We're both teachers."

She turned to Wendy. "You didn't say he was so *tall.*"

Wendy blushed. "Yeah, funny how that wouldn't come up when I talked about *work.*"

"How do you fit in a Prius?" Maggie asked me.

I looked at Wendy, who blushed again.

"I just remarked one day that you drove a Prius. That's all."

"She's right, Dr. Davison. I was just being silly. But Wendy is the easiest person to razz. Her blush gives her away every time. We love her, but she's hard not to tease."

"Thanks, Jan," Wendy said, "I owe you some embarrassment."

"Nice to meet you, Dr. Davison," Maggie said. "Wendy, give me a call later this week."

Wendy sat down and watched her friends leave the room. A minute later they tapped on the window as they walked by on the sidewalk, waving.

"Troublemakers, those two," Wendy said, smiling.

"They seem like good friends to have. But they do seem to like making you squirm."

"Jan's right. My cheeks have always given me away, as my peers first discovered in elementary school."

"Yep, peers always pick up on those things. How did you learn to deal with it?" I asked.

Wendy smiled. "That's a really good question. I learned right away that the more upset I got with the teasing, the more it exacerbated the blushing. I started laughing with them, laughing at myself. It took away their power. Who could tease someone who's in on the joke? I guess it was one of my first steps toward self-acceptance."

"That's a great story. I can see where the seeds of becoming a psychotherapist were planted."

"It's funny you say that. For a long time I worried that my tendency to flush would give me away or interfere with talking to clients. But the more I focus on the other person in the room, the less I notice it. It was the like the second lesson. First self-acceptance, then being present in the moment with people."

"That's terrific. Have you—"

A sharp rap on the window made us both jump. Maggie leaned close to the glass, tears in her eyes.

"Your car. Come quick!"

I jogged to the parking lot. Wendy was a few steps behind me. Maggie pointed at the Prius. The windshield was smashed; pieces of glass covered the front seats.

"We stopped on the porch and looked at the lights for a while," Maggie said. "When we walked toward the car, I saw the Prius. I figured it had to be Dr. Davison's. I'm really sorry!"

I clenched my fists and punched the sides of my legs. I wanted to explode.

"Thanks for coming back to let us know." I walked closer to the car. A large rock sat on the driver's seat. I reached in and pulled it out. On a flat area of the rock, a piece of paper had been taped, with a message printed in block letters:

Closer still, you son of a bitch.

"Oh, God, what is that?" Wendy asked.

"Well, it's not a love note," I said.

"Someone did this to you on purpose? I mean, singled you out from all these other cars?"

I smacked the roof of the car. Out of the corner of my eye, I saw Wendy back up. Maggie and Jan moved closer to her.

I shook my head and took a breath.

"Would one of you call 911, please?" I asked.

CHAPTER THIRTY-THREE

A PATROL CAR ARRIVED IN a few minutes. I waved the officer over. Wendy and her friends leaned on Maggie's car.

Officer Reiss, as he introduced himself, walked slowly around the car, taking notes. I handed him the rock.

"Heavy," he noted. He turned the rock over, and read the message.

"Seems like someone's angry with you. Any idea who might do something like this?"

"I don't. I agree, someone must be angry with me. I don't know who would do this. It seems like something a delinquent would do. I work with disturbed kids, but they're in a secure facility."

"Have you had any other incidents like this?"

I hesitated. "Well, I've received a couple of anonymous email messages, a couple of crank calls...but nothing like this. Sending an email is one thing. Destroying someone's property takes it to a whole new level."

"If the acts are all connected, I'd say you're right. The situation is escalating. I'll look around the parking lot, question staff inside — there's a kitchen entrance near the lot. I'll be back. In the meantime, you should clean this up. You'll need a tow, too. You can't drive this."

As Office Reiss walked away, Wendy approached.

"What next?" she asked.

"Cleanup, tow truck, and I have to get a ride."

"Jan and Maggie came together. I can give you a ride."

"That would be great."

Maggie approached with a broom and dust pan. "I got these from the restaurant. Should make the cleanup go faster."

Maggie opened the passenger door and started to sweep. Wendy and I picked up larger pieces and dropped them in a plastic bag I had stored in the glove compartment.

Officer Reiss returned. Jan joined the group.

"No one saw anything. As best I can tell, the girls here were the last ones to leave the restaurant over the last half hour. No camera back here either. I suggested they get one."

He tore a page from his notebook. "Here's a report you can submit to your insurance company." He pulled a card out of his shirt pocket. "And here's a couple towing companies you can try. As for the rest, I recommend that you stop by our office soon and talk with one of our detectives. You should follow up on that stuff that you told me about."

I thanked the officer and then Wendy's friends.

"We're glad to help. Sorry again about your Prius. Wendy said she'd give you a lift, so Jen and I are going to head out."

When her friends had gone, Wendy and I walked to the porch and sat down on rocking chairs.

"This would be a peaceful evening out here if it wasn't for vandalism," Wendy said.

"When I was eating dinner, the lights over the town caught my eye. This is a good spot."

I pulled out my cell and called the first number the officer gave me. The dispatcher told me it would be at least a half hour.

"Sorry to make you wait," I said. "We're going to be sitting a little while."

"Not a problem. I'm good for the evening. Laundry's done and folded, dishes are clean, and lunch is packed for tomorrow. Other than sleeping, I'm all set for tomorrow."

"I envy your organization."

Wendy laughed. "Haven't you noticed my appointment book at work?"

"No. Something special about it?"

"It's almost embarrassing. I have things color coded, and there are sticky notes everywhere. I don't want to miss anything."

"Over the years, I've noticed that a lot of mental health professionals are into office supplies. At some point, I became a pen junkie, myself."

"I've actually noticed that. I see different pens on different days. I meant to ask you if you had a system of some kind."

"I like to rotate them. I won't tell you how many I have, though. It would make me look, um, *eccentric.*"

"Let's just say 'unique.' We are a couple of unique mental health professionals."

In a short time, I heard a truck shifting gears as it lumbered up the hill toward the restaurant. A few seconds later, the tow truck emerged. I stepped onto the parking lot and waved it around the corner. Within minutes, the Prius was ready to go.

"Where do you want to take the car?" asked the driver.

"Well, how about the garage on South Street, the one across from Wendy's?"

"Cruiser's. Yep, that's as good a place as any. They do good work there, plus they'll take care of a rental."

Wendy and I followed the truck in her Honda Civic. After the Prius was rolled into a parking slot, I paid the truck driver and crawled inside the car to get out a notebook I kept in the glove box. I scribbled a note with my phone number, folded the car key into the paper, and dropped it into the secure slot in the door.

"Do you feel like a cup of coffee or anything?" I asked.

"Yeah, that would be good."

"We could go to your place," I said, indicating the Wendy's across the street, "or you could take me home, and I'll introduce you to Maxine."

"Is she your wife?"

"Nah. She's more of a roommate. You'll see when we get there."

As I directed Wendy along the route to my place, I pursued Wendy's last question.

"You had asked if Maxine was my wife. Do you know anything about my marriage?"

"No, er, I don't. I mean, I know you wear a wedding band, so I figured you were married. But I don't know anything about your personal life. It doesn't come up."

"You're right. I just didn't know if there was discussion at work, you know, gossip type stuff. Like what kind of car I drive."

Wendy glanced at me, eyes wide. "Oh, no. That was just a passing comment."

"It's okay, I'm kidding. But otherwise, no gossip that you know of?"

She shook her head. "I haven't heard a thing. But other than talking with the other therapists, I don't have those kinds of conversations with people. I'm not much for gossip. I have enough to do at work without it."

"Good to know. I was just curious. Thanks for filling me in."

We pulled into the parking lot.

"I never knew this place existed," Wendy said.

"It is off the beaten path a little, but still close to town. I like it. Are you ready to meet Max?"

"Maxine? Max? Yep, I'm pretty curious at this point."

I turned the key in the lock. I heard Max approaching the door. The moment it was opened, she squeezed through the space and hit Wendy's legs broadside.

"Oh, *hi*, Max!" Wendy said, kneeling down. Max licked her face and then flopped onto her side.

"Some dogs shake hands. Max asks for a belly rub."

Wendy obliged, and Max closed her eyes.

"C'mon Max, let's let Wendy get in the house."

We proceeded into the foyer.

"Coffee? Tea? Ginger ale?"

"Ginger ale would be good."

"Why don't you and Max head into the living room. I'll be in with our drinks."

I sat on the recliner. Wendy sat on the side of the couch near an end table. Max sat on the floor at her feet, leaning against Wendy's legs.

"She is so funny. She's leaning on me."

"Max likes to be close to people. If you move suddenly, she'll fall right over."

"Well, we won't let that happen," she said, speaking to Max as she stroked the dog's ears. "Dr. D, you were saying something about your wife."

"I was?"

"Yeah, kind of. Maybe indirectly."

I had asked about the gossip. She asked a fair question.

"Married for fifteen years. Separated half a year."

"That sucks. I'm sorry to hear that. Any chance to reconcile?"

"I thought so, but it looks like we'll be ending things."

"I'm sorry, Dr. D. Divorce is hard. I went through it with my parents. I was fifteen. But I'm glad you told me. Sometimes I wish I knew you better."

I knew she was right.

"It's part of being a clinical supervisor. Some therapeutic distance. But I've been a private person all my life. I probably chose a style that I was most comfortable with."

"I've learned so much from you. I watch how you deal with people. You have a good eye for what's going on, and you don't hide behind shrink-speak. You're not the analyst sitting behind the patient, smoking a pipe."

I laughed. "I appreciate the feedback."

Wendy looked at her watch. "I don't mean to rush, but I should head home. This was fun. Except for the part with your car."

CHAPTER THIRTY-FOUR

I WOKE UP ON MY recliner feeling pleasantly warm and unusually heavy. I realized Max was asleep on my lap. She has always considered herself a lap dog, no matter her size. I stroked her ears and tried to remember how it was I had happened to fall asleep in my chair.

I remembered Wendy leaving. I had sat down with the intention of watching some television, but instead, I had dozed off. Probably a sign I needed to catch up on my sleep.

Six a.m. Too late to go back to sleep. Too early to get ready for work. I counted it as a blessing. I could take a leisurely shower, get some light breakfast, check the local news, and by then, it would be time to head out.

Around nine, my doorbell rang. I looked out through the peephole. A young man in a Cruiser's hat waited.

"Mr. Davison?"

"Yes. Did you bring my rental?

"Sure did. A new RAV-4." He looked me over. "Should fit you a lot better than your Prius. I just need to get your insurance info."

The transaction was completed in minutes. I gave Max the run of the place and a couple of treats. She plopped down and watched me leave.

My rental car was easy to spot. It had a magnetic Cruiser's sign on the driver-side door. Once inside, I moved the seat and adjusted the mirrors. I was ready to roll.

As I pulled up behind a couple of cars at the first light, I took in the view from the perspective of a SUV. I could see over the roofs of the other cars. I liked it.

I rolled through the intersection, still getting used to the feel of the vehicle. It took me a minute to realize that I had passed a white pickup truck sitting off to the side of the road. My heart jumped into my throat.

I made a U-turn at my earliest opportunity and headed back to the intersection. No sign of a white truck. I moved through the area, and a couple of left turns got me back on South Street. I scrunched my shoulders as I drove, trying to unlock the knots in my back.

I kept my eyes on the rear-view mirror the whole trip. When I hit the parking lot, I sat for a few moments and surveyed the area. Nothing out of place that I could see. I headed across the street toward the main entrance.

The halls were empty. No one sat at the reception desk. I puzzled over this until I saw the handwritten note posted on the glass of the reception area window: *Staff meeting in progress.* That meant all the full-time staff was in attendance. Independent contractors, like me, were excused.

Ever the creature of habit, I unlocked my office door, a cup of tea in hand. Once in the office, I glanced at the phone. I noticed that I was holding my breath. I exhaled once I realized the red light was not blinking. For such a little thing, the relief was large and real. I placed my briefcase beside my desk, found a coaster for my cup of tea, and settled in my chair.

I had about twenty minutes before my first treatment team meeting. I decided to walk through the residential units to get a feel for the atmosphere. You can sense a good deal about the mood of the residents simply by stepping onto a unit. There's either an immediate hit of tension or things are boisterous. There isn't a lot of in-between.

I unlocked the door to the Western unit where a young Nicole Kidman in passive restraint had cursed me. I recalled that she was slated for discussion in one of the team meetings later this morning. I also recalled I had not yet heard a response as to what had happened *before* the restraint. I needed to check on that.

I passed several teens milling about the unit, two of whom acknowledged me ("Dr. Bryce!") and gave me high fives. That was one of the pleasant things about working with adolescents. If they like you and you treat them with respect, they are more consistent and positive—even when they have bad days. Sometimes, the behavior of the unit staff members is considered disciplinary because one of their primary roles is to enforce the rules, which can lead to lost "points," a drop in privileges, a time-out, or even a restraint. As that was not part of my job, I was more apt to be accepted by default. The unit staff members have thankless jobs, made more difficult by the need to mete out discipline.

A blonde teen huffed at me as I passed. I glanced at her.

"Yo! Dr. Shrink! Back on the nut ward?"

It took me a second. "Maegan—hey! I didn't recognize you standing up."

"Yeah, right," she scoffed. "That was just a bad fu…fricking day."

She looked different. Not only was her hair color completely different, it was brushed, and her makeup was neat. She looked comfortable in jeans and a T-shirt. She could be any typical, middle-class teenager you might see in a shopping mall.

"You really *didn't* recognize me, did you?"

"No, not at first. Your new hair color threw me off. Looks nice, though."

"Maybe I should have greeted you differently, with something you would be more used to."

"What do you mean, Maegan?"

"Well, how about this?" She held her arms out and pretended she was cranking a motorcycle throttle. "*Vroom, vroom.*"

"Honda or Suzuki?" I asked.

"Aw, c'mon. Davison. *Harley* Davison!"

"Now that sounds like something *I* would say, not you. And you would groan about it."

"Yeah, I guess. But you wouldn't believe what some moron said last night when we were watching TV."

"What happened?"

"The idiot. This motorcycle commercial came on and he said, "Hey, Harley Davison. I wonder if Dr. Bryce's name is Harley. He could be rich!"

"Oh, I see. What did you say?"

"I told him he needed some more IQ points. He just got finished saying your name was Bryce. So how could your name be Harley?"

"Well, I appreciate you setting him straight. And I liked your bike pantomime. You've got talent."

"You suck, Dr. Harley."

"Some things never change, Maegan. Speaking of, how are things going on the unit?"

Her mood darkened in a flash.

"Um, it's not the worst place I've ever been, but there are some fu…fricking jerks around here."

"Anything I should know about?"

She gazed around the unit, self-consciously. Looking for someone, or just checking to see who was watching? I thought I saw her eyes glass over for a split second. She didn't respond.

"Maegan?"

"Oh, well, um, nothing I can't deal with. I've dealt with shi…stuff like this all my life. No biggie."

"I don't doubt your skills, Maegan. Just remember you don't have to do everything on your own. Lean on Wendy if you need to. Talk to other staff members. Whatever you do, just don't bother *me* with this stuff. You know?"

Maegan snorted but tried to recover. I gave her an out.

"Have you met with Wendy recently?"

"Yeah. She's cool. Different than you and the other shrinks I had."

I smiled. Rather than taking the bait about whatever coolness I might lack as a shrink—when, in fact, I had never worked with her at all—I wanted to reinforce her willingness to deal with Wendy.

"Well, not only is Wendy cool," I said, "she is an excellent therapist. And do you know what?"

She lifted her hands, palms up, toward her shoulders.

"Wendy works well with bright, articulate young women. That means you two should get along fabulously."

Maegan blushed, started to speak, then turned and walked away. Sometimes people, for whatever reason, are reluctant to let their strengths show. A therapist I once worked with used to say something like "Your light can't shine beneath a bushel basket." Or something along that line.

I walked toward the staff desk. Tom and Nancy were huddled over a log book, speaking in low tones.

"What do you mean it's not in there?" Tom said.

"Do you see it? If you do, show me, 'cause I sure don't see it."

"Do you two live here?" I asked.

Tom jerked, knocking the log book off the desk in the process. I picked it up and nonchalantly thumbed to the recent entries.

"Oh, hi, doc. Sorry. I didn't hear you walk up. Nancy and I were just looking at the log from the last shift."

Staff members on each shift added entries to a log book, discussing which patients were doing well, which ones were problematic, and which ones were in and out for appointments. Staff would take kids to the family practice clinic for regular medical care or to dental offices. Sometimes, on the worst of days, there might be a trip to the emergency room. As I scanned the entries, in the periphery of my vision I thought I saw Nancy glare at Tom.

"Maegan has complained to staff that Jimmy has been trying to sit next to her at any opportunity, even though he has been told not to get within ten feet of her," Nancy explained.

"Has anyone witnessed this going on?" I asked.

"That's just the thing. No staff have observed Jimmy trying to get close to her—but it's not like he's under constant surveillance. Any time a staff member turns his back, some of that stuff might go on," Nancy answered.

"Well, it's something we need to consider seriously, given her history. There might be a lot of mixed signals going on. But if Jimmy has been told not to go near her, that's the main behavior we want to put a clamp on." I handed the log to Tom. "We don't want anyone making Maegan feel uncomfortable."

"Uncomfortable? I don't know what it is that you're implying, but I can tell you that nothing—*nothing*—happens on my unit without me knowing about it," Tom reported.

I leaned toward him, one hand on the desk. "Well, that's not entirely true, is it, Tom? We still don't know what set Maegan off and caused her restraint, do we?"

"Well, yeah...I mean, no, we don't, but that's the exception to the rule."

The pause hung heavy on the air.

"Glad to hear it. Well, let me know if I can help with anything."

Nancy chimed in quickly. "We'll make sure to note in the staff log that everyone on each shift should watch for any subtle or not-so-subtle interactions between Jimmy and Maegan."

I headed for the exit. Nancy caught me just as the door was ready to snap shut.

"Dr. Davison, I just wanted to thank you again for what you did for me. I've moved in with a girlfriend, and I've had no more contact with that, um, idiot."

"That's great, Nancy. You deserved much better than what you were getting. And besides, the breakfast you made was the best I have eaten in a long time!"

I thought her smile was sad as she stepped aside and let the door close.

CHAPTER THIRTY-FIVE

THE STAFFING IN LARRY'S OFFICE convened promptly. The usual characters assembled, and Larry reminded us it was time for our follow-up on Maegan.

"What's been going on?" Larry asked.

Wendy, as the lead therapist, began. "Well, a couple of things stand out. First, she's already been restrained once, but not because of any acting out on her part. After discussing the case with Dr. D, it looks like Maegan experienced a dissociative episode. I'd have to say, since that time, she seems to be adjusting okay to the unit, but this is a girl who keeps things inside. She doesn't readily let anyone see her soft side.

"Second, there looks to be some unhealthy dynamic between her and Jimmy S. We have one of those circumstances where we have both a perpetrator and a survivor on the same unit. We all know that's like mixing fire and gasoline."

Larry nodded. "In terms of staffing, that unit is the best equipped to deal with both kids. Staff members have been told to be extra vigilant, and since the boys and girls sleeping units are on separate hallways, we should be fine."

He looked at me. "What do you make of this dissociative episode?"

Professional and to the point. Or was he a better poker player than me?

"Well, having witnessed the tail end of the restraint, I strongly agree with Wendy's description. Maegan was physically present, but mentally she was in a different place entirely. It took significant, persistent intervention to reorient her. Her affect was intense and very much self-protective in nature. She lashed out at Wendy as she apparently had toward the staff members who restrained her. I'm very concerned, though, that the staff didn't seem to have a clear picture of exactly what precipitated the incident with Maegan. I've got the feeling something troubling went down, but instead it seems like the whole restraint scene materialized out of thin air. Maybe more information will arise during Maegan's therapy, but this wasn't some innocuous trigger. This girl thought she was fighting for her life.

"I just bumped into her up on the unit. While she looked more together — complete with a self-styled mini-makeover — she referred to 'jerks' on the unit. I think she had something more to say but couldn't bring herself to say it. And right at that moment, she dissociated in the blink of an eye...."

Maegan's comment reminded me of a previous discussion.

"I may be missing some other information. Last I knew, the state police were interviewing Jimmy. Is there more to the story than that?"

"The boy has been charged with indecent assault, Bryce. Apparently, before his time with us, he exposed himself to a younger child. A hearing is supposed to be scheduled soon," Larry reported.

"Do we know of any other sexual acting out on his part?"

"Not at this time. It also appears Jimmy was sexually abused by a neighbor when he was about eight years old. In fact, his alleged assault was perpetrated against an eight-year-old as well."

"Identification with the aggressor," I said quietly.

"Looks like it."

Head Nurse Ratched mused, "Well, we began discussing Maegan, but here we've developed some potentially helpful insights as far as treating Jimmy."

"Actually, we're due to staff Jimmy next. Wendy has completed some preliminary testing with him, and she'll stick around after we're done discussing Maegan," I said.

The remainder of the discussion regarding Maegan centered around the dissociative episode, training the staff to know what to look for, keeping her safe, and helping her to develop some self-protective skills.

When it came time to discuss the psychological testing she had completed with Jimmy, Wendy perused her notes.

"Basically, what I see so far, and Dr. Davison concurs, is that Jimmy appears to be highly anxious — but rather than deal with it or release it through more positive channels, it builds up until it overwhelms him. Given what we talked about earlier, I think we can now consider one of the ways Jimmy 'explodes' is through sexual acting-out. One of Sharon's tasks in therapy, it appears, will be to assist Jimmy in recognizing and identifying his anxious feelings, and then proceeding to respond with more favorable coping mechanisms."

Sharon was taking notes. "That's great info, Wen. Kids like Jimmy are very slow to open up if they open up at all. And although I would like to work at his pace, with a hearing soon, all kinds of crap could be triggered. If I can teach him some anxiety management skills, we can head off some trouble. If he cooperates."

As the meeting broke up, I hung around, waiting for the last person to leave the room. I may be cautious, but my duty to patients supersedes that.

"Larry, do you have time for me to run a couple of things by you?"

Larry consulted his agenda. "I have a few phone calls to make, but nothing that can't wait." He closed the door and joined me at the conference table.

"What's up?"

"Well, of all the units, the Western unit appears to be a bit...unstable right now. There's all the tension between Maegan and Jimmy, plus, I'm not sure the staff is on top of things. When I was up there earlier, I felt like I had walked into a heated discussion between two staff members."

Larry nodded. "Anything else?"

"Wendy told me that she observed a male staff member staring at Maegan's butt recently. When he saw that Wendy was watching, it was her opinion that he seemed rather indifferent to being caught red-handed."

Larry considered this. "That's all good information, Bryce, but no firm data to go with just yet. However, I'm glad you brought me into the loop."

I was prepared to feel him out regarding the more difficult topic when the phone rang.

"Excuse me just a second, Bryce."

Larry spoke with Marge and then turned to me, one hand cupped over the receiver. "Bryce, I'm sorry. It's one of the state senators. I need to take this. Was there something else?"

"Just a personal situation I wanted to talk to you about."

"Another time, then?"

He turned around to his desk and began his conversation without waiting for me to leave.

"Another time," I mumbled.

CHAPTER THIRTY-SIX

BACK IN MY OFFICE, I considered the conversation with Nancy. I was glad she moved on from Mr. Stud. I didn't know her well at all, but he seemed way too crude for her. What had she gotten from their relationship? Was he a bad boy that she found exciting, or perhaps was trying to rescue? That didn't seem right to me. Maybe I'd ask her some time, if there was ever a good time to do it. She stopped me to tell me she had moved out, so she would probably be open to conversation.

A flash of color in my peripheral vision startled me. Marge burst into the office.

"Dr. Davison, oh my. I've been looking for you. A neighbor of your mother called from your mother's house. There's been some kind of accident."

"What? When?"

"Just ten minutes ago. That's all I know. The caller sounded rushed, and she didn't want to go into details with me. I tried to find you on the units. I just missed you."

I grabbed the phone and punched in my mother's number.

"Is there something I can do?"

No answer on the phone. I turned to Marge. "I'll let you know. But right now I can't reach my mother on the phone. I need to get out of here."

On my way to the car, I debated about what to do with Max. I wasn't sure how long I'd be gone. I didn't know what Vicki's schedule was. It was on my way. I decided to stop and get her. Within minutes, we were rolling.

I tried my mother's number repeatedly. No answer. I called 911 and was transferred to the community dispatch center. In my mother's town, there was one individual dispatcher working simultaneously for several agencies.

I explained my situation.

"I'm sorry, sir. There is a serious car accident on Route 981. All available police, fire, and emergency personnel are already on the scene."

"Is there anyone there who can check in on her?"

"I'm sorry. I'm the only one in the office right now. When someone is freed up, I can let you know."

I hated living my life according to Murphy's Law.

Max and I drove on. I called directory assistance and asked for phone numbers of a couple of people I knew lived in town. Their numbers were unlisted. Images of the scenarios I had recently talked with my mother about looped in my brain. My mother falling or having a hypoglycemic event. I accelerated.

We entered the town by an alternate route to avoid the car accident. Max matched me stride for stride as I bolted to the porch.

I found my mother in the dining room. She was having toast and tea.

"What are you doing here? I didn't even know you were coming!"

"I got a call. Are you okay?"

"I'm fine. I was just having a snack. Haven't seen a soul all day."

I picked up the nearest handset. No signal. I checked every phone and cord in the house. At the junction box outside I found a single lead that was not connected.

With the connection reestablished, the phones worked fine.

I slumped into a chair beside my mother.

"Loose connection."

"That's a relief. Who called you?"

"The receptionist said one of your neighbors called. I couldn't get hold of you, and I couldn't find anyone to check on you. There's some bad accident outside of town and all the police and emergency workers are involved with that." I looked away momentarily. "I thought something bad had happened to you."

My mother touched my hand. "No, no, I'm fine. I'm sorry you had to rush down here like you did, but it's always nice to see you." Max nuzzled her leg. "And my sweet little dog, too."

We chatted a bit before I excused myself to use the bathroom. It was a pretense that allowed me to check most of the windows to ensure all the locks were engaged. While my mother stroked Max's ears, I quickly checked the downstairs windows as well. All the locks were in place.

Before I rejoined my mother, I sat down on the bed in my old bedroom. I looked up at the light fixture and remembered my fear of the boogeyman coming to get me.

Had he finally found me?

The message I had received here last time, compliments of the US Postal Service, was to show that my stalker knew where my mother lived. Today's message was to show me that he could get her at her house. She was vulnerable, and it gave me another thing to worry about. *Or figure out how to fix.* I knew she wouldn't leave. I couldn't stay here. Maybe I should leave Max with her. But that would give her extra tasks to do. As sweet as Max was, she also had regular needs to be meet. I had to come up with something, but whatever that was, it wasn't coming to me at the moment.

I stood up, and dizziness grabbed me. I stumbled toward the dresser. Whoa. Woozy. Maybe I needed something to eat before I left.

"You two doing okay in there?" I asked.

"Yes. Max and I were just talking about you. I told her she needs to keep an eye on you when you don't stop to take care of yourself."

"Are you saying that's what I'm doing now?"

My mother grinned. "Not at all, dear. I was just telling you about the topic of conversation."

That made me smile. "Message received. Speaking of which, do you mind if I make some toast? Yours smelled good when we got here."

"Sure, help yourself to anything. I just use butter and a pinch of cinnamon. Cinnamon is supposed to be good for blood sugar."

"That's what they say. I think I'll try your recipe out."

The toast was really good. I could have eaten more than two pieces. I gave a couple bites of crust to Max, and all three of us seemed content.

"Well, Mom, I need to head home. When we leave, I'll lock the door behind me. Make sure you keep the doors locked, even during the day, okay? If someone needs you, they can ring the doorbell."

"I'll keep the doors locked unless I'm out on the porch. Will that make you feel better?"

"Yes, it will. You probably think it's silly to worry about things like that. You've lived all your life without having to lock your doors. But it's better to be safe than sorry."

"You're worrying me now. You seem jumpy. Is everything okay?"

Perceptive woman. Or I'm more transparent than I ever imagined.

"Sure, Mom. Everything's fine. I'm just trying to look after you. It's either that or leave Max here to take charge."

Max thumped her tail against the floor.

"She's welcome to come and visit whenever she likes. That goes for you, too."

I waited until I was sure my mother had returned to the dining room area, where she probably would turn on the game show network for a while. I sat on the front porch step and let Max roam a bit.

As I was watching Max, it dawned on me that luring me here was a great way of getting me out of town for a while if someone wanted to get into my house. The tension in my back was almost painful. It felt like even the slightest movement would snap my spine.

* * *

My eyes drifted toward Church Hill. I could see the grass at the crest of the hill. Although we were far from winter, this simple glance was all that was necessary to conjure snowy memories. They broke my defenses easily, and this time I didn't even need to close my eyes.

* * *

I woke up in a dimly lit hospital room. I could feel the tube in my nose, see the IV dripping, and hear muffled noises from nearby. The pain in my abdomen was incredible.

A surge of anxiety hit me and I tried to sit up, but weakly fell back against the bed.

"Easy, honey," I heard someone say. "You just rest now. Your mom and dad will be in to see you shortly."

The nurse walked into my view, a young black woman with kind eyes, wearing a starched white uniform. She stroked my hair and tended to the IV drip.

"You're in the intensive care unit, and we're going to take good care of you here."

I closed my eyes and drifted off to sleep.

I reawakened to my mother's voice.

"Bryce, can you hear me?"

"Mom?" I asked.

She was standing beside the bed and when I looked up at her, her eyes were filled with tears.

"Oh, Bryce," she whispered. "We almost lost you."

CHAPTER THIRTY-SEVEN

ANOTHER LONG TRIP HOME. I was beginning to wonder if they would ever feel normal again. Or was this my new normal? I recognized the trough I was beginning to dig, and reminded myself to let go.

Let go.

Unfortunately, that was followed by a rogue, evil thought: I could wait until I hit a rural stretch of road, guide the car off the road, and smash myself into a tree. All could be well and my loved ones would be safe if I just "checked out." The fact I was having such an internal conversation was another sign I was losing my grip. But I had enough of a hold to realize I wasn't about to do anything that would place Max in jeopardy.

Thank God she was in the car with me.

I realized I would make it home before the end of the workday. Did I want to go back to the office? I had some things I needed to finish up. Plus, it would be distracting enough to keep me from dwelling on threats and trees.

I dropped Max at the house and headed back to work. Other than stopping to let Marge know everything was okay, I didn't talk to anyone else. No phone calls interrupted me. I even managed to scratch a couple of items from my to-do list.

Even though I enjoyed my consulting work, I also looked forward to that one moment, just before shutting off my lights and going out the door, when I experience a relaxed, I'm-done-with-my-work-day stress slough-off. I needed that today. I savored the moment and then headed out the door.

I was about to cross the street when a white F-250 pickup roared up to me and stopped, brakes screeching. The driver side door opened, and out jumped a man with a face contorted with rage. As he approached, I realized it was Mr. Stud.

Crap, did I somehow wish this on myself?

He stopped less than three feet from me, body quivering with anger. He jabbed a finger in my direction.

"Who the fuck do you think you are, pal? I know Nancy spent the night with you right before she left me. What makes you think you can fuck around with another man's woman and get away with it?"

I glanced around. No help forthcoming. My main concern was that this lunatic might have a weapon and was stupid enough to use it. My breathing quickened and my pulse throbbed in my temples. How to get out of this?

I raised my hands, palms outward, announcing that not only was I unarmed, I also had no aggressive intent. Mr. Stud stepped closer and smacked one of my hands away. I could sense the testosterone pumping in his veins as clearly as I could smell the beer on his breath.

I took a step back. "Listen, um, I'm sorry—I don't remember your name. And I didn't sleep with Nancy, she just crashed at my place, and that's all."

"That's not how I heard it. I head you did it *all night long.*"

"Well, you heard wrong, then. You should talk to Nancy about it. Clear this up."

"She's the one who *told* me, asshole. She threw it in my face when I came here to talk. And now she ain't talking to me. I'm holding you responsible for that."

"Convenient. Have you considered that getting drunk and beating up your girlfriend might be the real cause of all this?"

He jabbed at me with his finger. "You're a real smartass, ain't you? You don't know shit. And no matter what that bitch says, you ain't a better man than me. I could take you out right now. End of conversation. End of the line for you."

I pulled out my cell phone and punched in 911. "I don't have time to deal with you. Either get out of my way, or I'm calling the cops."

"Oh, I'll get out of your way, asshole, but I'll be back. I'm going to hurt you. You'd better put your head on a swivel, 'cause you won't know where or when, but I'm bringing trouble."

With that, he backed away, climbed into the cab of the Ford, and spun a streak of rubber on the street. I waited until I saw his taillights disappear, and realized that I had been holding my breath. It hurt. I breathed out, felt my muscles tremble, and had trouble catching my next breath.

I sat down on the curb. At least now I knew who owned the white truck. Which led me to another thought: this jerk knows where I live. If not the exact location, he had the townhouse development scoped out. I dropped down on one knee. I felt unsteady.

The image of Pig-Pen from the *Peanuts* cartoons came to mind. A little boy followed and surrounded by a cloud of dirt. I seemed to be a target for all sorts of people a few crackers short of a pack.

Mr. Stud was wrong about one thing, though. My head was already on a swivel.

I stumbled to me feet and walked in careful steps toward my car, searching either for damage or someone who shouldn't be there. Nothing seemed to be disturbed—other than me. I thought about men who felt they owned women. The caveman mentality. That category fit Mr. Stud well. And I fully realized his impulsivity made him very dangerous.

I stopped ruminating and drove right to the police station. The officer who took my statement didn't appear to be particularly concerned about my experience. When Mr. Stud had confronted me, I couldn't come up with a name. But in the police barracks, after I had described the guy, I said I thought his nickname was Flip. The officer didn't miss a beat.

"Nope, not Flip. *Flick.* His name's Flick Dale. Sad thing is, it's not even his nickname. Can you believe his parents named him that? He's a loudmouthed punk who thinks everything should go his way. He can't keep his mouth shut about anything. We've never hauled him in, but we're aware he can make a nuisance of himself."

"Nuisance or not, this guy threatened me. What can I do about it?"

"Well, sir, I could chat with Flick. That could go either way. Either he will lay low for a while, or he'll get more riled up and figure he's been wronged by you. The bottom line, though, is without witnesses, it's just another "he-said, he-said" kind of thing. Flick could flat-out deny the whole thing—which he would. He lies better than he breathes. But there would be nothing we could do about it."

"I'm concerned about his mental state. He already thinks I've wronged him; now he has me in his sights. What am I supposed to do if he assaults me?"

The cop leaned back in his chair. He looked me over.

"Just don't hit him first. If he lays a hand on you, we have grounds for an arrest."

This was an unending nightmare.

"Let me get this straight. I should wait until he hits me before I react? What if it isn't just a punch, but the guy has a knife or a gun or something? He could kill me before I blink."

"I'm sorry, sir. That's the way the system works. We can't arrest people for thinking bad thoughts."

"You guys should have a record of something else that happened to me. I had a rock thrown through the windshield of my car. That sure sounds like something this delinquent would do. What about that?"

The cop considered me. "Yeah, I could see him doing that, sure. But we don't have any evidence to support that."

"I feel like I'm bound in red tape. If I have to wait until this guy kills me to take action, there won't be any action to take."

The officer shrugged his shoulders.

"Okay. When Officer Reiss spoke to me when he investigated the rock incident, he suggested I come in and talk to one of your detectives. I want to do that now. How about arranging for that?"

"No detectives in right now. Both are out working cases. But I'll leave your contact information with them, and one of them should get back to you soon. In the meantime, try not to get too uptight. To my knowledge, Flick has never taken anything beyond words."

"Not very reassuring, Officer. What do you think I should do? Better yet, what would you do if you were me?"

He sighed. "I would watch my back, avoid being alone, and make sure I was in good enough shape to run if I had to. But I think you're overlooking something."

"Really? What am I missing?"

"Have you looked in the mirror lately? What are you, six-three?"

"Yeah, pretty close. Six-four."

"I get that your first instinct is to talk. You're a man of words. But your size can be intimidating. Use it."

Back in the Prius, the heat felt oppressive. It felt like the car could collapse in on me at any second. My chest was tight. So hard to breathe.

I turned on the air conditioner, switched on the radio, and scrambled for something soothing. The channel surfing fed the chaos in my head.

I shut off the radio, gripped the wheel with both hands. I had to do something to push through this. My clinical experience taught me that sometimes, the fastest way to get through tension is to increase it. I squeezed the wheel, gritted my teeth, and tightened as many muscles as I could. I held it until it was unbearable. My body shuddered and I gasped for air — but it worked. I'd expelled the worst of the tension, but I was wiped out.

I started home, but recalled an image of Larry in his apron. Serving ribs and announcing it. I did a U-turn.

CHAPTER THIRTY-EIGHT

I PULLED INTO LARRY'S DRIVEWAY, as far off to the side as I could in case someone needed to get by en route to the garage. I needed to push Larry about the picnic. About the ribs.

About shutting me down the last time I talked with him.

Joan answered the back door.

"Bryce, what a surprise!" She looked past me toward the garage. "Is Larry with you?"

"No, I just had something I wanted to run by him. I thought he might be here by now."

"He called a bit ago and told me he needed to wrap up a few things before he left the office. That's why I thought he might have arrived when you did." She hesitated. "But my goodness, where are my manners! Won't you come in? Can I get you something to drink? Beer? Wine? Soft drink?"

"If you have any ginger ale, that would be great. Otherwise, a glass of water would be fine."

Joan had me wait in the living room. Lots of photographs of Larry and Joan in exotic locations.

She returned with a ginger ale on ice. As I took a sip, she sat on the edge of a nearby coffee table.

We sat in silence for a few moments.

"Um, did you follow up with anyone from the picnic?"

"Not yet. I'm supposed to have lunch with Dr. Raphael soon, though."

"That's great. He's a good guy. We go back a ways with him. He's been to a number of our picnics over the years."

"Yeah, the picnics. What did you think about Larry serving ribs for the first time?"

Joan's brows knit. "I don't follow."

"Don't follow what, dear?"

Joan's body jerked a little as Larry entered the room. She knocked the coffee table a couple of inches out of place.

"Hi, honey. I didn't hear you come in."

Larry kissed her on the cheek and moved the table back into place with his foot.

"I saw Bryce's car in the driveway, so I knew we had company. Have I kept you waiting long?"

I thought he addressed the question to me, but he looked at Joan as he said it.

"Bryce has only been here a minute. Just long enough for me to get him a soft drink."

Larry looked out the window.

"Something you needed, Bryce?"

Joan looked at Larry. Her face muscles were taut.

"I don't mean to interrupt, so I'll step out. I need to get dinner started. Thanks for stopping by, Bryce."

"You may want to hold off on dinner for a little while. A couple town council members are stopping by for drinks. Should be here any minute."

I wanted to talk, but I didn't want Joan in the middle of anything.

"Sorry, Larry," I said. "I shouldn't have dropped by unannounced. I certainly don't want to interrupt."

Larry held out his hand for my glass. I guessed we weren't going to have any time for even a short conversation.

"Let me walk you to the door."

"Thanks for the drink, Joan," I called into the kitchen. No answer.

As Larry opened the back door for me, he leaned toward me. "Did you really come here to see me, Bryce, or were you here to see Joan when I wasn't home?"

I was a step from the door. I turned to look at him.

"What?"

He was half smiling. "Just thought I would check."

A car door closed.

"Councilman Rogers. Impeccable timing as always. This is Dr. Davison, a local psychologist. He was just on his way out."

"Councilman." I shook his hand and hustled away.

What the hell had just happened? Was Larry accusing me of fooling around with Joan? And why was *she* so jumpy? My head hurt. I felt like I had entered some parallel universe and the clones were running the show.

CHAPTER THIRTY-NINE

I WAS MENTALLY EXHAUSTED BY the time I got back to my townhouse. Thank goodness Max was happy to see me. Some days, but for the love of a dog....I took Max for a walk, and then we played ball outside near the patio. A game that I developed, called "bassetball." In reality, it gave me more exercise than Max.

It would usually go like this: I would hold a tennis ball in front of Max, who would dance excitedly. I would throw the ball about fifteen feet away, and she would dash off like a greyhound, usually skidding to a stop near the ball. She might bark at the ball or even leap on it as if she was a lioness pouncing on her prey. However, since the beginning of modern record-keeping in bassetball, she had never, not once, ever picked the ball up in her mouth and returned it to me. So for each throw, I would tromp across the yard, change the direction that I faced, and throw the next ball from where I retrieved it.

I found it ironic and wondered, for the umpteenth time, if *I* wasn't the one being trained. Max watched me and panted lightly, preferring not to engage in the discussion.

Completely beat, I snapped Max's lead on and collapsed on a lawn chair, watching the dog with the golden nose assessing the aromas emanating from the grass.

I jumped up again almost as soon as I sat down...I went inside to get my notebook and a pen. I turned to the suspects page and added some comments.

Mr. Stud drives the pickup truck. He has threatened me.

Larry is suspicious of me.

Someone has threatened my mother.

I closed the notebook. My head was beginning to throb like a balloon was being blown up inside my skull.

"These people are going to have to form a line," I said to myself. "This is getting out of hand."

CHAPTER FORTY

THE NEXT MORNING, AS I sipped some tea, I saw Dr. Raphael's business card on the counter. I decided to send off a quick email:

> Dr. Raphael: Looking forward to meeting you for lunch in a couple of days. Regards, Bryce Davison.

While I was at it, I sent a quick message to Vicki:

> Hey, I have a couple things going on. Can you stop by later and pick up Max for a day or two? No need to confirm. I'll be out of the house for the rest of the day.

There. Done. I expected she would pick up Max sometime after three, just to make sure it was before I got home. Today, though, I didn't care. It was good to have something else on my schedule.

I gave Max her instructions, then headed off to Titan College and parked myself in the psychology staff lounge. By the time the sun displayed its afternoon hues, I had banged out my course syllabus and outlined the first several chapters of the textbook.

It felt good to get out of town for a while. Peace and quiet in the academic world—at least until the students arrived on campus for the fall semester.

I logged on at a workstation in the library and pulled up my home email account. Two messages, one of which was a reminder about a conference on treating children with PTSD. The other message was from Dr. Raphael.

Hi Bryce. Still on for lunch tomorrow. I have your cell number if I need to get in touch with you. Bring your appetite. We'll get something from The Bistro. Best. JR.

Nice. The Bistro was well known for superb deli sandwiches and salads. Perhaps good food and conversation would brighten my spirits.

I thought about picking something up for dinner, but I was ready to get home and wind down.

As I had expected, Vicki had picked Max up. I would miss her, but I knew she needed time with Vicki, too. I had a bowl of cereal and went to bed early.

Wednesday morning, I slept late and made a beeline for the shower upon awakening. When I returned to the bedroom, I noticed the message light on my cell phone was blinking red.

"Bryce, it's Jerry Raphael. Listen, I'm sorry for the late notice, but I have a new patient who's in crisis. I'm going to need to work her in over lunch today. But, hey, I'll reschedule with you at your convenience. Please get in touch with me later today or tomorrow. Thanks, bye."

I knew the turf well. Private practice created lots of scheduling issues and missed lunches. So, what to do now? I could nap, exercise — or mope.

I opted for novelty. I grabbed my driver and a couple of other clubs and headed out of town toward the combination driving range-ice cream drive-in.

My muscles were starting to stiffen by the time I got home, but I was glad to have stepped out. I rarely get visitors so I assumed someone was trying to sell me something. I was going to ignore it, but the buzzer was insistent.

A well-dressed, trim, man, forties, crewcut man stood in my doorway.

"Dr. Bryce Davison?"

"That's me."

He offered his hand.

"Lieutenant Dean. I'm with the regional police. May I come in for a few minutes?"

The lieutenant accepted my offer of bottled water and sipped it as he took in my home.

"How can I help you?" I asked.

"Do you know Dr. Jerry Raphael?"

"I do. I just met him," I said

"He's been murdered."

"What?"

"One of his patients found him. He was sitting at his desk."

"Oh my God, that's awful. What happened?"

"I'm afraid I can't tell you more details right now. I was hoping you could help."

"Help? What can I do?"

"Do you know much about drugs?"

"Street drugs?"

"Medications. Psychiatric medications."

"Well, sure, but you may want to talk to a psychiatrist. I'm a psychologist."

"I'm aware of the difference, Doctor. Do you know if Dr. Raphael prescribed any...*exotic* medications?"

"Exotic?"

"Meds with a high street value. Drugs readily abused."

These days that field was wide open. Even cough medicine was suspect. People would probably grind up toilet paper and smoke it if they thought it might get them high.

"From what I know, Dr. Raphael treated adults in general practice. He wasn't known for treating patients with substance use disorders. So I wouldn't think he would have medications on hand for individuals withdrawing from opiates, for example."

He pulled a list from his jacket pocket.

"This was the inventory of his drug closet. It was pretty well-cleaned out."

I reviewed the list. Typical stock for a psychiatrist — anti-anxiety meds, antidepressants, and some of the newer antipsychotics.

"The minor tranquilizers could be attractive. Those might get some action on the street."

Dean made a note in a small notebook. Paused. "When did you last see Dr. Raphael?"

"I had only met him once, about ten days ago. At a picnic thrown by Dr. Lawrence Jones."

"No contact since then?"

"Well, we exchanged email messages."

"You didn't see him today?"

"No. We were going to have lunch, but he canceled. He called and left a voicemail message on my cell. He had a patient in crisis he had to work in."

"Your name was in his appointment book for twelve thirty."

"That's what I was saying. We had a lunch meeting, but he canceled it."

"Where were you today between eleven thirty and one p.m.?"

I felt the blood drain from my body. My mouth was full of cotton. I licked my lips and sat a little straighter.

"Am I a suspect now, Detective?"

"Just answer the question, please, Doctor."

"After Raphael canceled, I decided to go out and hit some golf balls. I drove out to the ice cream place in Seven Valleys to use their driving range."

"That's a ways to go to hit some golf balls, isn't it? There's a driving range just outside town."

"It's the ice cream, Lieutenant. I had a cone after I was done."

"So you would have a receipt handy, right?"

"It's not that expensive. I paid in cash. But I'm sure the woman at the shop would remember me. We had a short conversation."

"Easy enough to check on. So, Dr. Raphael, did he have a family?"

"Larry — Dr. Jones — had told me he had a little girl."

"Tragic." He stood to leave. "I appreciate your cooperation. If necessary, I'll be back in touch."

I sat, stunned, for a good twenty minutes after Lieutenant Dean left. Dr. Raphael had been murdered, and I had been interviewed as a possible suspect — or, to use the jargon, a "person of interest." Guilt began to creep in. What if no one verified my whereabouts from earlier today? Would I be arrested?

I thought about driving out to the ice cream shop or calling the driving range. Then I realized that no innocent person would try and shore up his alibi.

I slapped the arms of the chair.

Why was I punishing myself like this? *I didn't kill Raphael.* People saw me at the driving range. No sooner had I asked myself the question that answer emerged. Because nothing that had happened to me so far made sense. It was one thing piled on another. So of course the next thing on the pile should be getting arrested for murder. Perfect.

Letting go was impossible. Negative thoughts smacked me around. Even though I went to bed at a decent time, I knew sleep wouldn't happen. I tossed and turned and finally sat up on the side of the bed.

My thoughts drifted to work, to my last time on the units. Tom and Nancy were hissing about something that I interrupted.

Something about the log book.

I changed my clothes and drove to the residential facility.

A dozen cars filled one corner of the parking lot. I joined the pack and killed the engine.

What was I doing? I should be home in bed. Leave the detective work for the pros.

Screw it. I needed answers.

From my office area, I made my way to the back of the western unit. I closed the door softly behind me. With the lights in the hallway dimmed, some desk lamps burned in the staff area. No one sat at the desk, which concerned me.

Who was running the shift?

I moved past bedrooms, saw sleeping bodies in various positions. A few of the kids with stuffed animals. Vulnerability in the safety of sleep.

I nearly crashed into Tom as he stepped out of a bedroom.

"Shit, doc. You scared me. What's going on? Is there something wrong? Why are you here?"

"I had some paperwork I needed to catch up on. Thought I would stretch my legs and walk the units."

"Oh, right. Paperwork. You a late worker, doc?"

"When the spirit moves me. Who else is on for this shift?"

"Just me and Nancy. She's handing out some PRN meds on the girls' side."

"No one was at the desk. Isn't that a breach of protocol?"

"Not really. Things are quiet and we're locked in. I'm only thirty feet from the desk. And we're down one worker tonight. Things still have to get done. If it makes you feel better, I'll sit at the desk."

He started across the hall. I followed, looking for the log book.

"Hey, Tom, Maegan's..." Nancy stopped in her tracks when she saw me.

"Maegan's what?" I asked. As I turned toward her, out of the corner of my eye I saw Tom moving something

"Oh, Dr. D. I didn't know you were here. Is something wrong?"

People were sure concerned tonight.

"I'm just visiting. I was in the neighborhood. But what's up with Maegan? What were you about to say?"

"I was just going to tell Tom Maegan is sleeping. Restless, but sleeping. She often needs some medication to help her down, but it looks like she is doing okay on her own tonight."

"Good to know." I turned back to Tom. He was standing beside the staff desk, shifting his weight from one foot to the other. "You okay, Tom? You seem pretty restless."

Tom looked at Nancy and back to me. "Like I said, you scared me. And then you started lecturing me on protocol. Seems to me protocol says you don't just barge on a unit at night. You have to be cleared."

"I'm a consultant. I have my own protocols. I don't answer to you."

Tom scowled.

"This is my unit. I'm calling this in. This isn't right."

"Tom, don't," Nancy said.

Tom looked at her but picked up the phone.

"Doc, I'm sorry about this," Nancy said.

"Me too," I said, and walked toward the exit nearest the staff desk.

CHAPTER FORTY-ONE

THE BACK HALLWAYS HAD A life of their own at night.

Periodic sounds of unknown origin echoed through the corridors. Exit signs hummed as I passed them. It felt like eyes were watching me. I half expected to see someone lurking around each corner I turned. But the halls remained deserted. Twice I paused with the intention of turning around.

I fixed my gaze in front of me and continued forward.

Back in my car, I tilted my head against the headrest. What had my Hardy Boys expedition dug up? Nothing. And I didn't even get to see the log book. My restlessness had gotten the better of me, and I botched it. As painful as it was to admit, Tom was right. I shouldn't have shown up unannounced outside of working hours.

I smacked the car window with my elbow as my cell phone rang. I fished the phone from my pocket.

"Hello?"

"Bryce, it's Larry. I just got a call from the night supervisor. Were you up on one of the units?"

"Yeah, I was. With all that's been going on, I felt like an impromptu visit was in order. Is there some concern?"

"The night supervisor had the impression you were disrupting the unit and disturbing the patients. So I got the call."

"You're joking! That's crazy! No one was disturbed unless it was the staff members who'd left the desk unattended."

"Stop by my office when you get in tomorrow, would you? We'll discuss this more then."

I dropped the phone on my lap. I stared out at the dark sky, where images waited.

* * *

Junior high school. It's a fall day. The previous summer, I had been diagnosed with asthma. Lots of early morning attacks, waking up gasping and wheezing. The maddening sensation that the next breath might not come. I couldn't walk a block without hitting the verge of collapse. The sports I loved so much and was so good at became more of a memory.

A new school with new kids, and I began the year with a deficit for any young man — I couldn't take gym class. I was "medically excused."

And then a routine gym class became monumental.

"Davison! Why aren't you dressed?"

"What?"

"Are you deaf, boy? Why aren't you in your gym clothes?"

"I have a doctor's excuse. I've had it for weeks."

"That's for sissies. Are you a sissy, Davison? Come to think of it, you've got the name for it. Right, Brycey?"

Some guys snickered. My face felt hot.

"No, I — "

"I want to see you dressed and out on the football field in five minutes."

I didn't know what to do.

I slipped into a too-large T-shirt and a pair of shorts stored in the locker room, available for kids who'd conveniently forgotten their gym clothes.

I walked out to the football field.

Mr. Scissa rallied the troops. "Today, we are going to run cross-country. The course starts and ends here. Follow the path and try and keep up with the lead runner. Everybody finishes. No excuses!"

The group took off into the brush, an area choked with ragweed and other pollens. I ran into trouble almost immediately. My lungs felt like they were going to explode. I started wheezing. My breath came in gasps. I tried to pump my legs, but they felt like cement pillars. I slowed to a walk but still couldn't regulate my breathing. I was afraid I might lose consciousness. The slowest, fattest guys in my gym class had each passed me long before.

Somehow, I made it to within fifty yards of the finish line. I fell to the ground and vomited while the entire class watched.

Mr. Scissa shook his head as he considered my quaking body. He turned to the class. "A real man," he said, "would have finished."

I was in a heap on the ground. A couple of stragglers looked in my direction momentarily before following the crowd to the gym. It took about fifteen minutes before I felt well enough to move, and a few minutes more of concerted effort before my breathing improved.

CHAPTER FORTY-TWO

THE ALARM CHASTISED ME. I looked at it with one eye. It probably had been going off for forty minutes, and I slept right through it. Why had I bothered to crawl into bed at all?

Larry's secretary bristled when I entered his outer office. My presence seemed to be irritating all kinds of folks these days.

Larry and I sat at his conference table.

"I'm concerned about you."

"Why?"

"Well, for one thing, you look like you haven't slept in days. And you've seem pretty uptight to me. Then you make a middle-of-the-night visit to one of our units."

"I'm concerned about what's happening," I replied "The safety of the unit seems to be in jeopardy. Is there a problem with me checking things out after hours?"

"I would have preferred to know about it first, rather than get a call after the fact from the night supervisor. Makes it hard for me to back you up."

"Back me up?"

"The unit staff report from last night indicates you were...confrontational, and the commotion woke up some of the kids."

"Never happened! What a crock! Who wrote that up? Tom?"

"It doesn't matter who wrote up the incident. It's still something I need to deal with."

"This is all a fabrication! Those two are just trying to cover for themselves because no one was at the desk."

"I'll look into it. However, in the meantime, what I need you to do is take the rest of the day off. Go home, get some sleep. And for the time being, restrict your contact with patients to your normal work hours only."

I started to leave, then turned back to Larry.

"You heard about Dr. Raphael, right?"

"I did. Senseless. That kind of incident should make us all question our safety standards. Of course, sometimes we have to worry as much about people *inside* the building as we do thoughts from the outside."

He froze me in my tracks. After what felt like eternity, I turned to face him.

"Are we talking about the patients or the staff?"

"Just a rhetorical statement." He paused and stared at me. "I think you've been working too hard. You seem a bit, um, oversensitive. Go home."

A million thoughts ran through my mind. Larry watched me, a half-smile on his face. It was if he was daring me to say something.

I kept my mouth shut and walked away.

CHAPTER FORTY-THREE

I STOPPED AT THE FRONT desk on my way out. "Marge, I'm going home. Not feeling well. I hope to be back in tomorrow."

"Oh, my. I'm sorry to hear it. You do look a bit pale. You rest up and drink some juice. We'll take care of things here for you."

As I started to leave the building, I heard Marge call after me. I turned back.

"Oh, I forgot to give you this before you left. It was faxed to you earlier this morning."

She handed me a folder with a few sheets of paper in it. I found myself looking at a copy of my contract. Everything was intact, except for the part where my Social Security number would have been. That area was blacked out in a weak attempt to suggest privacy protection.

I held the page up to the light. I could pretty much make out most of the numbers. The page headers indicated they were faxed from a local office supply store.

"Marge, what happens when people call here and ask for our fax number?"

"Well, I give it to them, of course. Is anything wrong?"

"No, thanks. Just wondering."

Of course, *plenty* was wrong. I understood the intention of this message. More malevolent posturing. Someone was continuing to prove to me that he or she could access private areas of my life.

I could feel a little bit more of my psychic glue softening.

I steamed across the street. Got in my car. Pondered what to do next.

On an impulse, I drove the short trip to the courthouse and parked in the diamond. I checked the directory and headed for the clerk's office.

The receptionist didn't bother looking up at me but let me stand at the window. I glanced around and saw a little bell on the counter. I tapped it three times.

Even then, the young woman didn't put her magazine aside but continued to look at it as she stood. Finally, she approached the window.

"Yes?"

"These papers. Do you recognize them?" I held them close to the window.

"Well, they appear to be a contract for a Dr. Bryce Davison. Does that help?"

"No, as a matter of fact, it doesn't. *I'm* Dr. Bryce Davison, and someone just faxed this to me from a local business. How in the world could someone get a copy of this?"

She sighed. "Technically, since it is a county contract, it is a public record. Any taxpayer could get a copy of it."

"Can anyone just walk in here and get my contract, or do you at least ask people to sign in?"

She spoke as if she had gone through this very conversation a dozen times earlier. "Of course. We have them sign a register."

"Great. Can I see the register for today?"

"Sorry, that's classified."

I was speechless. I would have at least sputtered something if the woman hadn't flipped a sign over and walked away:

Please have a seat. Someone will be with you shortly.

I smacked the counter with my hand and cursed. I stomped out of the building, planning to return at some point and take up my complaint with someone other than an entry-level receptionist who didn't want to deal with me in the first place.

The contract in my hand taunted me. My feelings were all jumbled together. I didn't know whether to fight or flee. I seethed but felt ashamed.

A piece of paper fluttered beneath my driver's side windshield wiper. I unfolded the paper and saw a crudely printed note:

You're going to lose so much more than you ever dreamed possible.

I crumpled the note, shoved it in my pocket, and sped home.

CHAPTER FORTY-FOUR

I WAS HALFWAY DOWN THE sidewalk toward my front door when I heard footsteps. Someone closing in at a quick pace.

I turned around. Nancy ran toward me. "Dr. D, I've been waiting for you. I need to talk to you." She put her hands on her knees and tried to catch her breath.

"What's going on?" I asked, looking around.

"Just…a…minute."

I waited for her to gather herself.

"I need to talk to you. About last night. Do you mind if I come in?"

I wasn't feeling very receptive at the moment. But then I recalled Nancy asking Tom not to call about me being on the unit.

"Sure. C'mon in.

I was within a foot of the door when the smell of floral perfume hit me. I turned to Nancy.

"What is it?" she asked. "You look surprised."

"The scent. Do you smell it?"

She stepped closer. "Yeah. Flowers. Where's it coming from?"

I tried the door. It was locked. But the smell was stronger. I sniffed my fingers.

Nancy stepped past me and bent down toward the door knob.

"It's all over the knob," she said.

I turned the key in the lock and opened the door. There was a flurry of movement as Max shot out the door, ran right past us. She ran to the lawn and started rolling.

"That's not her usual routine. Something's wrong."

I walked over to Max, who was squirming in one direction and then another.

She reeked of perfume.

"Someone doused her in the stuff. What the hell? Can you watch her for a minute?"

Nancy stepped toward Max, and I moved away, phone in hand. "Hello?"

"Vicki, it's Bryce. I need to know when you dropped Max off."

"A couple hours ago. Why?"

"She was drenched with perfume. The same damn perfume I first noticed in my bedroom."

"You're kidding! No, I swear, I just opened the door, let Max inside, and I left."

"That's it? You didn't come in the house?"

"No reason to. I let her in and made sure the door was locked. I know how fussy you've been lately about strange things going on."

"Strange things? Like stuff from my own imagination? Let's cut to the chase. Do you have anything to do with this perfume? With what's been going on?"

"What are you accusing me of? Why would I do something like that? To Max *or you*, for that matter!"

It hadn't escaped me — she put Max before me.

"I don't know. But this is getting out of hand. And you were the last one here today."

"No. Not the last one. Obviously not the last one," she snapped. "And, much as I would love to have another paranoid conversation with you and listen to you accuse me of ridiculous things, I'm hanging up now. Don't bother calling back."

That sure went well. I rubbed my face and looked over at Nancy. She was kneeling on the grass, rubbing one of Max's ears. As I walked over to them, she gave no indication that she had heard my conversation.

"Your dog is great," Nancy said. "I always thought basset hounds were kind of sluggish, but she is very energetic. What did you say her name was?"

"Her name is Max."

"As in Max-imum overdrive? That would fit."

"She's not usually in overdrive. She was trying to rub the smell off, I think. It probably was pretty strong to her hound nose."

"Aw, poor thing," Nancy said, rubbing Max's belly.

"I should probably call the cops."

"For somebody assaulting your dog?" Nancy asked.

"That would be enough for me. But it means somebody was in my house. Someone that I didn't invite."

"Right. The door was locked."

I lucked out: Office Reiss was in the general vicinity. He arrived about ten minutes later. At least I wouldn't have to catch him up too much.

"Ah, you again," Reiss said.

"Yes. We met at the Cracker Barrel."

"So...your dog got perfumed?"

"Yes. And that means someone was in my house."

"You came home and the door was locked. What else?"

"Well, I noticed the smell right away. It wasn't until I turned the handle to make sure that the door was locked that I found the perfume all over the knob. So, once I opened the door, my dog ran out, and that's where we are now."

"Who else has a key?" Reiss asked.

"My...Vicki. My wife. We're separated. But she has a key for picking up Max and dropping her off. It's an arrangement that we have."

"Did you check with her?"

"I called her right before I called 911. She said she had dropped Max off about two hours ago, but she hadn't entered the house."

"That sound right to you?"

"It's not typical, but she might do that if she was in a hurry."

"Okay. And I'm sure the superintendent has a key."

"Yes. And the maintenance guy. I even called the manager recently to check the log to see who has been in my house. It showed only a couple of entries in the last six months. Both of which I knew about or had notice of."

"Have you been inside?"

"No. I...we were waiting for you. Uh, this is Nancy, um Rogers. She works with me. She had stopped by to talk about work."

Reiss looked at Nancy. "Rogers, you say?"

"Yes, Officer."

Reiss made a note.

"Well, let's have a look."

Nancy waited in the living room while I took Reiss through the house. Nothing else seemed to be disturbed.

"I wish I had an answer for you, sir. You seem to be having a string of bad luck. Odd things happening to you. Did you follow up with a detective like I suggested?"

"I was at the station recently about something else. I asked right then about seeing a detective, but no one was available. I've been expecting a call back."

"Good to know. I'll get in touch with those guys and let them know I've been involved with you now a couple of times. I'm sure you'll hear from someone soon."

I said good-bye to Officer Reiss and then joined Nance in the living room.

"I gather that you've had some shit happen, I mean, besides the perfume on Max?"

I guess she had been listening after all.

"Yes. Nothing that I want to get into right now, though."

Nancy shook her head. "I'm sorry to hear about that. I feel bad enough about the whole Flick situation. Some sort of bad karma or something..."

"Maybe. So what brought you here. You said you needed to talk about something."

"I need to talk about Tom. Something is going on with him."

"Why are you telling me? Why not go to the administrative director?"

"Yeah, I should do that. But it has to do with you."

Now she had my full attention.

"Go on."

"Well, Tom has always been a bit of a, I don't know, a blowhard."

"That's a word I haven't heard in a while. What does he do that makes him a blowhard?"

"Maybe I'm using the word wrong. What I mean is, he likes to talk. He likes to talk *big*. Likes he's a big shot. A know-it-all. I think he tries to sound important. He butts in on conversations he's really not a part of."

"I see. Like a blowhard."

Nancy smiled. "Well, it's taken a strange turn. Lately, when I work the same shifts with him, he seems preoccupied with you. He brings up your name under his breath. How you "think you know so much," how it's all bogus. How *he* could have gotten his PhD, but it would have been a waste of time because he would be out of direct service, and that wouldn't be good for the kids."

"So, he thinks I know less than I do and that I'm full of it. Is that right?"

"Yes. But last night. When you showed up, that *really* got him going. You left before he got into it. When he called the on-call supervisor, he was spouting off about procedures and protocol and ethics. I don't think the supervisor could get a word in edgewise. And after he hung up, he got nasty. Said you should be taken down a peg or two. It started scaring me."

"What did you do?"

"I told him to shut up, for one thing. A couple kids even came out of their rooms to look at us. And after that, I told him to just do his job and stop worrying about you, let you do your job."

She paused to catch her breath. I waited.

"Then he looked at me in a way that scared me. Like he was looking through me. He said something like, 'So you're not going to help me?' And I'm like, 'Damn straight I'm not,' and I told him if I caught wind of anything going down, I was going to go right to the director or Dr. Jones."

"What did Tom do?"

"He *smiled.* And just nodded and walked away. We didn't really talk the rest of the shift until it was time to give report to the day shift this morning."

"I'm glad you came to talk to me. I've seen you guys together at different points. Do you know Tom well?"

"Working on the same unit, even though we rotate shifts, you're going to work with people a lot. For whatever reason, he's gravitated toward me. And because he likes to talk so much, I know a good deal about what he thinks about things — from politics to popular literature."

"Have you ever seen anything inappropriate from him?"

Nancy froze mid-gesture.

"Inappropriate how?"

"Well, you've worked with him a lot. Have you seen him do anything that would be considered out of bounds for a staff member?"

"He's kind of a flirt. And I think he fancies himself a smooth talker."

"Are you talking about his behavior toward other employees…or toward girls on the unit?"

"I feel like you know something. I've told you what brought me here. Maybe you should tell me what you're looking for."

"Fair enough. Someone saw Tom staring at a girl's ass on the unit."

"I haven't seen that, but it wouldn't surprise me."

"Why not?"

"He probably thinks he's smooth enough to get away with it. Mr. Cool. But if it was something that he did often or was that obvious about it, I would have noticed it."

"Thanks. So you plan on talking to administration about your observations?" I asked.

"I think so. Even though it sounds kind of iffy to me as I talked to you. Tom could deny any of it if he was asked. I wouldn't want it getting back to him, though. That evil smile." She shuddered.

"I'd encourage you to discuss it and share your concerns about things getting back to Tom. I'm sure it could be handled discreetly."

I hooked Max up to her leash. and we walked Nancy to her car. When Nancy was on her way, I invited Max to do one lap around the development. I could use the release, and Max could use the fresh air.

We stuck to the parking lots and sidewalks on this trip. As we made our way around the townhomes in a semi-circular loop, I saw a figure ahead. It was a young woman, probably college age. She was struggling to open a plastic bag that was in her left hand. Her right hand had a tight grip on a leash, on the end of which strained a large bulldog. As Max and I approached, she pulled harder on the leash to move her dog out of our way.

"Watch out for that," she said, gesturing with her head toward a solitary dog turd in the middle of the sidewalk.

"Will do. We just made the rounds ourselves."

As we moved past the dog, he lunged toward Max, more playful and eager than aggressive. However, it caught both Max and the young woman off guard. Max leaped off the sidewalk as if she was on hot sand. The woman stumbled to the cement, appearing horrified and trying to maintain her hold on the leash.

"Jackson, no! What the hell are you doing?"

I stepped in to hold Jackson's collar and offered my hand to the woman. She had a little difficulty extracting herself from the leash. Jackson panted as if nothing had happened.

"You lost some skin in that fall," I said. "Are you okay?"

"Yes, yes. God, I'm so sorry. This isn't even my dog. I didn't realize how strong he is. I'm just dog-sitting. I'm so, so sorry."

I bent over and picked up her key chain from the ground and handed it to her.

"No problem at all. Max and I have been through worse. And it's been a while since a woman has thrown herself at me."

The woman laughed, and her facial muscles relaxed. She brushed off her shins and we parted company.

"Your dad is a witty man, Max," I said, patting her head when we put some distance between Jackson and us.

Max, her dignity tested, did not appear so easily amused. "Don't be so concerned. You're still the coolest dog in the development."

As we returned to our street, I looked toward our townhome. Someone was standing at my front door, hunched over, looking at the knob. He jiggled the handle. What was going on?

"C'mon, Max, let's hustle."

When we were halfway up the block, I yelled, "Hey!"

The person turned my way. It was Scooch.

CHAPTER FORTY-FIVE

"WHAT ARE YOU DOING?" I asked.

Scooch took a half-step back and glanced around. He rubbed his face. "Oh, I was knocking at your door. I was gonna talk to you. That's all."

"It looked more like you were messing with the doorknob."

"Oh, yeah. It's really smelly. I was trying to see what that was about."

"Someone put perfume on it."

"Never heard of doing that," Scooch said.

"It was a new one for me, too."

Scooch didn't seem shifty at the moment. His eye contact was decent, and he didn't fidget. But my canine barometer was still off kilter — Max kept my body between her and Scooch.

I trusted her instincts.

"What did you want to talk to me about?"

"My boss was talking to me about something you had called about. I'm supposed to check with you about changing your lock. Is that something you want me to do? No charge or anything."

"It's a good idea." I started to mention about the incident today, but I didn't need Scooch knowing my business. "When can you do it?"

"I'm off for two days. Kind of my weekend off. I can do it in three."

"Do it. How do I get my keys?"

"Stop by the front office after noon that day. They'll get you taken care of."

Scooch headed off into the night.

"One more thing before we turn in, Max. I have to give you a bath."

I hooked Max up on the patio and got the hose out. In a few minutes, she was cleaned and dripping wet, finishing with a towel wrap.

While Max finished air-drying, I sat on the patio and maneuvered mental puzzle pieces around. Nancy had described some disturbing behavior from Tom. The increase in stalker activity suggested potential escalation. Was Tom my stalker — and becoming more unglued? That would mean that he had been in my house and perfumed Max, wouldn't it? I couldn't make those pieces fit.

Max sat down at my feet and looked at me.

"Is that my cue? Time to go in?"

I yawned. She was right. I was guessing that I would need my energy for tomorrow.

CHAPTER FORTY-SIX

"GOOD MORNING, MARGE."

"Good morning, Dr. Bryce. Are you feeling better?"

"I am, thanks. Anything new for me since I was last here?"

"No, you are up to date."

I unlocked my office and glanced at my phone. No red lights blinking. I blew out a breath and rolled my shoulder muscles. Time for a cup of tea.

I had just taken my first sip when someone knocked at my door.

"Dr. D?"

"Oh, hi, Wendy, come on in. What's up?"

"It's Maegan," she said. "I was having a session with her, and in the middle of it, she totally shut down. I didn't know what to do. I was hoping you were here."

"What do you mean, she shut down? She stopped talking?"

"She stopped talking, she got all flat. She stopped responding at all. I couldn't get anything from her."

"Where is she now?"

Wendy blanched. "I left her in the therapy rooms. I closed the door and ran down here."

"Let's go."

Wendy and I jogged up the back hallways and up the stairs to the western unit. I unlocked the door.

"In here," Wendy said. "Room One."

She opened the door and I entered. Maegan was sitting in a beanbag chair, a seat often selected by adolescent girls. Her eyes were open, but she had a faraway look in her eyes.

"Maegan, can you hear me?"

No response.

"Maegan, I'm going to touch your hand." I took her hand in mine and lifted it a few inches. I let it go and it dropped to her lap.

I turned to Wendy. "Tell me what happened right before Maegan stopped responding."

"We were really just getting started. She told me how her week was going, and we talked about a TV show she had seen. I asked her what was happening on the unit. That's all it took."

"Did you ask how she was *doing* on the unit or what was *happening* on the unit?"

"I'm pretty sure I asked her what was happening. Why, was that bad?"

"No, no. But the wording — it's what she was responding to. You wouldn't have had any idea. It was a question that would typically be innocuous. But it may help us here, now that we know that."

I turned back to Maegan. I sat down on the floor in front of her.

"Maegan, it's Dr. Davison. Wendy's here with me. Maegan, I need you to focus on me. Listen to my voice. You may hear it as if it is coming from a distance. That's okay. I'm here with you. I'm going to touch your hand again."

I lightly touched two fingers to the back of her right hand and rested them there.

"You can feel my fingers on your right hand. Listen to my voice, feel my fingers on your hand. Feel the cooler air that you're breathing in, the warmer air that you're breathing out...I'm right in front of you, looking at you — you can see my eyes."

Maegan's glassy stare began to shift.

"That's right. Here with you. Right here with you."

She began so stir.

"Maegan, Wendy and I are here with you in the therapy room. You may feel a need to stretch in a few moments, just take your time and reconnect here, in the room, with us."

Maegan looked at me.

"Hi. Wendy and I have been hanging out with you."

Maegan blinked, took a deep breath, and then stretched her arms and arched her back. She looked from me to Wendy, furrowed her brow, and finally spoke.

What the fuck?"

"Not a typical hello, but we'll work with it," I said.

I moved perpendicular to her and rested my back against the wall.

"What are you doing here?" Maegan asked. "This is supposed to be my therapy session with Wendy. I can't handle both of you being here. It makes me feel like a whack job."

"I'm just visiting," I said. "Wendy asked me to join. She ran into difficulty and I came with her to help, if I could. That's all."

Tears welled in her eyes. "I disappeared, didn't I?"

"Yeah, you did. Does that happen a lot?"

"Sometimes. Usually when I'm outside."

"Outside the building or outside of a placement?" I asked.

"Outside of a placement. In the real world."

"Gotcha. The main thing is, you're back now. And you've shown us how we can help you better. So disappearing was actually a good thing."

"I'm glad you think so. It's ain't real good from where I'm sitting."

"I hear you. But would it be okay if Wendy helps you with getting through the rough spots so you can disappear less? Would that be good?"

"Yeah, if you think I can."

"Great. I think you can. I think you're capable of a lot of good stuff, Maegan. So I'm going to leave you guys to get back to your therapy session."

I got to my feet with difficulty, wobbling a bit as I got balanced.

Maegan smirked. I smiled at her, then turned to Wendy.

"We can catch up later if you like. Thanks for asking me to join your session."

I left the room and closed the door.

CHAPTER FORTY-SEVEN

WHEN I RETURNED TO MY office, this time the red light was blinking. I shut the door, settled in at the desk, took a breath, and hit the message button.

"Dr. Davison, it's Lieutenant Dean from the New Alex Regional Police. We met recently. I'm calling to follow up on a message from Officer Reiss. It seems that you've been looking for a call back. I want to apologize for the delay. The message actually went to my colleague, but he's been quite ill. So I'm your follow-up guy. I'm sorry I missed you, but I have to leave here in a few minutes. I expect to be tied up most of the day. But tomorrow is Saturday. Give me a call on my cell. The number's on the card I gave you. Have a good day."

That was a message I didn't mind hearing. Actual police follow-up. It made me wonder, though, how things had gone for the detective when he left my townhouse the other day. Was he able to corroborate my story?

I marveled at my ability to move from positive to negative. I was perfecting it. I didn't want to. I could remember times when I was more carefree.

Or could I?

"Dr. D?"

"Wendy, come on in. How did things go with Maegan after I left?"

"I'm not sure. I mean, I can tell you what she said and what I saw, but I think I need to go back in time first."

"Have a seat in my time-machine," I said. "Where would you like to go?"

Wendy sat in the chair nearest me. She chose connection.

"I'd like to go back to the point where you and I first walked back into the therapy room. What was all that?"

She started to cry.

"I wanted to be a therapist for so long. It meant everything for me to go to grad school in counseling psychology. I graduated at the top of my class. I had a great internship! And then, today, I felt like I didn't know a thing, hadn't learned a thing. I felt like a stranger in a place where people were speaking a language I didn't know."

She hunched over, elbows on her knees. The tears flowed down her face and onto her slacks.

"Maybe I...shouldn't be a therapist. Maybe I don't have what it takes."

I handed her a box of tissues. She blew her nose and dabbed at her eyes.

I sat with her, silent, waiting until she made eye contact with me.

"Can you help me?" she asked.

I nodded. "Yes, I can help you. And you need to know one thing right off the bat. There is not a therapist alive who hasn't sat where you are now. You can have great training. You can be at the top of your class. But no program, no internship can teach you everything that you will need to know in the real world. You will continue to come up against things that you don't understand. Some days you'll just know — it's not that you don't know anything, it's that you don't know enough."

Wendy sat back in her chair. I sat back in mine.

"I want to ask you...if you've been where I am," Wendy said. "But maybe we can talk about that another time. I need to know what was going on with Maegan. I need to know what you saw, what you thought, and how you were able to intervene. Please help me understand."

"You're right. It's important. It's important for you as Maegan's therapist, and it's absolutely vital for Maegan's treatment, for her recovery."

Wendy sighed and nodded.

"Maegan was in a dissociative state," I said. "Like what we saw when she was being restrained on the unit that first day. Only this was more severe. It was like part of her was present in the room, but a bigger part of her was somewhere else."

"Where was that?"

"I don't know for sure. I have a hunch that it plays out a couple of ways for Maegan. At times, her dissociation takes her back to painful experiences. That's when we'd be likely to see symptoms like depression and cutting. The pain begets more pain."

"And the other?"

"The other is an *escape* from pain. It's like going away to somewhere far enough that the pain can't get to her. It's like psychic insulation. And that's a powerful draw."

"I think I see. So why did you talk to her like you did?"

"I was trying to make contact with her. I wanted her to know that I was there. And then I wanted to draw her senses into the experience in the room. Like the sound of my voice. Like my words. Like me sitting in front of her. Each of those comments was like a breadcrumb…a trail back to the present. I needed her to go one breadcrumb at a time until she was back and oriented in the present."

"That makes sense. You were helping to ground her, right?"

"Yes, grounding her experiences in the present. By offering her truths that she could acknowledge. I didn't tell her to remember anything or forget anything. I didn't promise her anything."

"You told her that she was showing us what she needed. Was that to make her feel better?" Wendy asked.

"Not at all. In therapy, people will show us what they need from us. Where they need to go. I believe that Maegan was showing us that she needs some respite from what she is dealing with. I have concerns about that. She was also showing us that she needs some help with coping skills, because what she is dealing with is overwhelming. Terrifying."

"Dr. D, what's your concern?"

"Something is going on up there. Something on her unit. She's a barometer for the pathology of her group."

I paused and took a breath.

"And that scares the hell out of me."

CHAPTER FORTY-EIGHT

BEFORE I LEFT FOR THE day, Wendy and I developed a plan for Maegan, at least with respect to Maegan's therapy and support. Wendy was scheduled to work the weekend, which was helpful. There is a psychiatrist on-call, but the only clinicians around are the therapists in my department. Wendy would check in regularly with Maegan and keep an eye on her when she makes her rounds. I asked her to double the frequency of her trips to each unit.

I continued to be needled by uncertainty. I was on edge. Uptight.

My interaction with Maegan had scared me. To me, it was a sign that something sinister was in play. Like an unseen fog had swept in and created a cascade of negative energy.

Time to go. I left later than intended. The parking lot had lots of open spaces. It made it easier for me to give the area a once-over before I got in my car.

I knew there wasn't a lot in my fridge. I either had to get some groceries or pick up dinner on my way home.

As I drove home, fatigue pulled at my body. I felt heavy, sluggish. No way did I want to go through a grocery store and then take time to prepare something.

I stopped at a Mexican restaurant a few minutes from home. The place was busy. The bar was packed with patrons, and I didn't see a single empty booth.

"Takeout menu, please?" I said.

I ordered a taco platter with refried beans and rice. I leaned against the wall by the entrance and watched the behavior of the patrons. Some looked to be on dates. Couples with kids at other tables. No solo diners in booths, but it looked like a couple men at the bar were on their own. Not too long ago, this would have been a place that Vicki and I would have enjoyed.

I was tired enough that I couldn't remember when I had last talked with my wife. Oh, yeah. The case of the perfumed dog. My heart sank when I recalled how I had confronted Vicki. She had every right to hang up on me. I would have hung up, too.

I paid for my meal and headed out to the car. As I opened the door, my cell phone rang. I put my dinner on the passenger seat and pulled the phone out of my pocket. Vicki.

"Oh, hi, Vi—"

"*You piece of shit*, where do you get off sending me email like that? I should never talk to you again, and maybe I won't. I thought I knew you. And then you do this!"

"Wait. Wait a second. What happened?"

"Really? *That's* your response? If you think so little of me, why have you bothered talking to me at all. I should pick up Max and never give her back to you."

"I didn't send you an email."

"You son of a bitch. You're a liar."

"Vicki, I swear I had nothing to do with this. But I don't want to argue with you. Just forward the message to me. Let me look at it."

"Just go to your outbox, you asshole."

"Send it. Please. I need to see it. I'll get back to you."

I closed out the call. Saying good-bye in a civil way wasn't possible.

I looked out the window. My stomach rumbled, but not with hunger. I swallowed some spit and tried to keep from vomiting. I reached in the backseat for a water bottle and found one on the floor mat. With trembling hands I opened the cap and took a sip just to get the foul taste from my mouth.

Deep breaths, Bryce, slow this down. I closed my eyes and leaned my head against the headrest.

CHAPTER FORTY-NINE

WHEN I FELT LIKE I could sit up without heaving, I headed home. What happened? What email had Vicki received? I sure didn't send her anything. It was like I was having an out-of-body experience.

I grabbed my dinner and jogged to my front door. Max greeted me as the door swung open.

"Max, just a minute. I need to put this food in the fridge, then I'll take you outside."

Max followed me to the kitchen. I put the container away and headed toward the door. I stopped and looked up the stairs. Should I go and read the email?

Max's tail thumped against the floor.

"Sorry, Max. Let's go and take care of you first. You've waited all day."

I grabbed her leash, snapped it on, and we headed out toward the trail. My skin crawled, and the tightness in my back ratcheted up. I felt eyes on me, but I saw nothing when I looked around. I couldn't tell whether I was spooking myself or if my instincts were accurate.

Max finished her duties, and I bagged her muffins. We walked back toward the development. I pitched the bag in a trash bin.

Inside, I gave Max some fresh water and a treat, then hit the stairs two at a time. I landed in the chair hard enough to slide it into my desk with a crash. I pushed back on the desk to move the chair back and then straightened the desk. Powered up the computer.

Vicki's email message was the most recent of several. I clicked it open.

When I married you I didn't know you were a whore But that's all you are. You think you're so hot, but that's just a cover for being frigid. So don't go thinking that you're making Tony happy in bed. For him to get any pleasure, he'd have to thaw you out in the microwave first. I don't miss sex with you. I do better on my own.... After Tony leaves you don't come crawling to me.

My stomach gurgled and my throat burned. I ran to the bathroom and dropped to the floor in front of the toilet. My stomach emptied, and I braced my hands against the back of the toilet seat until the spasms stopped. I leaned back on my feet and tried to catch my breath. My whole body was shaking.

I pulled myself up by leaning against the sink. I splashed water on my face and cupped my hands to draw some water to my mouth. In the mirror, I saw Max watching me from the doorway. Her tail was not thumping. She knew something was wrong.

"I'm okay, Max. Just sick to my stomach." I patted her head as I walked by. She followed me into my office. When I sat down, she dropped her front legs to the floor and watched to see what would happen next.

"You look like a Sphinx."

Max panted lightly.

I moved the computer mouse to wake the computer. Vicki's email appeared. I read through it several times.

Vicki was right. It *was* nasty....

I checked my outbox. No recent sent messages to Vicki. I stood up and looked at the back of the computer. I didn't see anything amiss.

Puling up messages I had sent Vicki, I saw the one where she had said that Bathrobe Guy, aka Tony, was angry at me. So his name could have been pulled from that message. What else would someone need to have known to send the new message? That Vick and I were married, but separated. My stalker knew that. The only other part that was added was the comment about Vicki thinking she was hot. I never typed *that* in an email message, and it wasn't an adjective that I use in conversation. It was an assumption and a way to contrast with the sexual frigidity that "I" mentioned. The latter description was designed to hurt Vicki and inflame her reaction — which it had.

I sat back in my chair. At no point in our marriage would I have considered Vicki frigid. And never did I ever imply anything like that, not even during an ugly argument.

The waves of sickness had passed, and my body no longer trembled. I took a deep breath. My muscles were pretty tense, but I could deal with that. But I was ready to step away from the stress. Time to get into a pair of shorts and a T-shirt and cool off.

When I entered my bedroom, my knees buckled. My bathrobe was on the bed, tattered and practically shredded. A knife pierced the chest pocket of the robe — right where my heart would be. And the blade of the knife was covered in blood.

CHAPTER FIFTY

I SAT ON MY COUCH in the living room, trying not to tremble as various members from the regional police office combed through my bedroom. Lieutenant Dean was back for a second visit. He told me to sit tight and that he would be back to ask me some questions. Sitting, yes, but I was well beyond tight. I felt like my mind and body were stretching beyond their limits. Anxiety was piloting the ship. I struggled to stay on board, but a part of me was searching for the lifeboats. And poor Max was tied up on the patio to keep her out of the commotion.

"Dr. Davison, are you up for some questions?"

I hadn't heard the detective sit down in the chair opposite me. The big cop was light on his feet.

"Should I have an attorney present?"

The cop smiled and said, "Not unless you have something to hide. Do you have something to hide, Doctor?"

"Fire away." I forced myself to look him in the eye.

"Here's what we have. Or, more accurately, what we *don't* have. No evidence of forced entry through either of your doors, and no ground-level windows have been pried open. No fingerprints on the knife or the railing going up the stairs — or any other place we can find. As for the blood, we'll have to wait for the lab results. Oh, and we found this in what was left of the chest pocket of the robe."

He held up a plastic bag. There was a note inside. One word printed on it. *Closest.*

"Doc, here's what I'm wondering. Why the robe, and what does the note mean?"

"I don't have a clue about the robe. As for the note, someone has been threatening me."

"Threatening you? Tell me about that," the detective said as he sat forward in the chair.

I went through the chronology from the scent in the bedroom to the present, trying to state the facts simply. Lieutenant Dean took notes.

"Some of what you've said is consistent with what I've been told. I know you talked a couple of times with Officer Reiss. Did you get my voicemail at work?"

"Yes. I was glad to get it. I felt like maybe I could get some help."

"If I understand what you've said, the initial pieces — the perfume and the email — were enough to unsettle you but not enough to report, right?"

"It seemed surreal. I told Vickie — my wife — about it right away. Her reaction was that I was making too much of it. She thinks I have a tendency of doing that."

"I grant you that your early experiences could seem just shy of dangerous, even the panties on your car door. But that whole tone changed when your windshield was broken. That moved the line from 'peculiar' to 'violent.'"

"Yes, and that's when I talked with Office Reiss. I wanted to sit down with a detective to get at this stuff."

"And we have Dr. Raphael's murder in there, too."

"That threw me off at first."

"What do you mean?" asked the detective.

"Well, the other stuff centered around me. I knew it was about me. Raphael's murder seemed more random. It could have happened without any connection to me. Except the circumstantial part about my name in his appointment log," I said.

"But it's reasonable to assume someone tried to set you up for that. If it wasn't for your alibi checking out, I would have paid closer attention to you." Dean sat back in his chair and reviewed his notes. "Let's do this. You tell me what you make of this situation from a psychological perspective, and I'll tell you what my cop thinking suggests."

I figured the detective wasn't really looking for my insights. He wanted to see if I would trip myself up somehow.

"There is a parallel piece that I think is important. It's too unusual for it not to be connected. But I don't know how. But with my psychologist hat on, I have to mention it."

"Go."

"There's an adolescent on one of the residential units who is showing signs of serious disturbance. Her difficulties ramped up at the same time this stalking stuff escalated."

Lieutenant Dean's brow furrowed. "Interesting, but why are you telling me this?"

"I guess I'm reaching. But every part of my life is in play here. My wife, my dog, my mother, my work contacts. My contract. And this patient is a big focus on my job recently. I'm inclined to think that none of this is random. It all fits somehow."

Lieutenant Dean shook his head. "Nah, sorry. I'm not seeing it. It may be a random piece in the midst of other events that are actually directed toward you. Parts of your life have been exposed. You're being threatened. But not so directly that you can hold up one act that says 'I'm going to kill you.'"

"That's the part I've been trying to explain. I'm being manipulated. I have been from the get-go. Someone is gaslighting me."

"Explain."

"It's when someone toys with you in little ways to make you think that you're losing your mind. And when you talk about the things to someone, they don't get it. And you start doubting your own experience. Like with the email. I had to go and check my out box to make sure I hadn't sent it. I *knew* I hadn't, but I couldn't trust myself."

"It's good that other people have been around for some of these things, like the rock and the perfume on your dog. It's hard to doubt your sanity when someone else has the same experience."

That was the first time I felt like I wasn't making the whole thing up. Even if he hadn't used those specific words.

"Let me tell you what I think. You've wronged someone, or someone thinks that you have. Someone is tormenting you. He wants to make you feel powerless. It started with that, but it's ramped up since then. I think your life is in danger. Your mother's life, too. And your wife's. You're going to have to find a way to let them know. That won't be easy."

I felt the blood drain from my face. My heart raced.

"This is so bad," I said.

The detective nodded. "It's bad. But you're not alone. You've got people helping you now. We'll figure something out."

"There's one more thing," I said. "What you said about the ramping up. That's what I've been sensing. That this person is becoming unhinged. Their anger is seeping through. That makes it hard to predict what might happen next. The field is wide open..."

"Your job is to keep moving. Don't sit back and wait for something to happen. Be on guard and on your toes. And stay in touch."

Lieutenant Dean left to chat with one of the evidence techs who was carting off the robe, knife, and comforter in several large clear plastic bags. He appeared satisfied with their conversation as he nodded my way and exited with the remaining cops.

CHAPTER FIFTY-ONE

I STOOD UP AND LOOKED around. The place was a mess. Stuff was out of place, fingerprint dust was everywhere, and there was a scent of fear.

Or was that just me?

I gathered up some clothes from the laundry room and grabbed an overnight bag from the closet. I didn't want to even go upstairs, nor did I want to bring Max through the house. I went out the back door with her leash, and we headed to the Prius. I knew from word of mouth that one of the motels out by the interstate was pet-friendly.

I drove there and paid for a room., and after Max was situated, I walked next door to a burger joint and picked up some dinner. In the hotel room, I took the food out and put it on a table. I used the plastic food container for water for Max, which she downed in about twenty seconds. I refilled the container.

I shared bites of my cheeseburger and fries with Max. I tried not to overdo fried food with her, but she seemed to like a couple pieces occasionally.

With dinner done, I moved on to the first task on my list. I called my mother.

"Hello?"

"Hi mom, it's Bryce. How are you doing?"

"Oh, hi. Nice to hear your voice. I was watching Wheel of Fortune or something and I must have dozed off. I just wanted to close my eyes for a minute, but you know how that goes."

"Yes, I do. Well, I don't mean to interrupt, I just wanted to check in. Have you been feeling good? How have your blood sugars been?"

"No problems. A little tired, that's all. My blood sugar has been about average for me."

"That's good. Anything else going on?"

"I don't think so. Are you okay?"

"I am. But I was listening to the news. It sounds like there have been some...incidents near you."

"Incidents?"

"Yeah, some burglaries. Breaking and entering, things like that. Have you been locking your door like we talked about?"

"I have. I keep the doors locked unless I am out on the porch. And when I'm out there, I keep the handset in the basket on my walker. So I think I have things covered. But I didn't hear about any burglaries in town."

"I think it was happening in the next town over. But I wanted to make sure that you were safe. And you know, if you ever have a situation, noises in the house or anything, you call the police first, and then me, okay?"

"You worry too much about me. I'll be fine. But come down soon. Bring Max. She makes me smile."

"I will, Mom. Love you."

I tried Vicki's number. No answer. She probably would ignore my number now. I called back and got her voicemail.

"Vicki, it's Bryce. I wanted to say again that I didn't send you that email message. Somebody spoofed my email address. But there's other stuff going on, too, that I need to tell you about. The police are involved now. Please give me a call as soon as you can."

I hung up. "Well, Max, there's nothing more to do tonight. Let's make a pit stop outside and then call it a night."

CHAPTER FIFTY-TWO

MY NIGHT WAS FILLED WITH bad dreams.

Someone chasing me. Large black dogs with bared teeth cornering me. Running down a road filled with huge potholes that seemed infinitely deep.

At six o'clock I got up and took a shower.

After a quick trip outside for Max and getting her breakfast, I drove to a nearby diner. I had just finished some pancakes and bacon and was contemplating a second cup of coffee when my phone buzzed. I figured Vicki was calling me back.

"Hello?"

"D-Dr. Davison, it's Wendy. I'm calling you from a therapy room. You need to get over here as soon as you can. Something's happened with Maegan."

"What is it?"

"I...I can't talk about it on the phone. Please get here."

I could tell she was crying.

"I'll be there soon."

I drove back to the motel, bagged my stuff, and hustled Max into the car.

Then I paused. I couldn't take her with me. I had to make an executive decision.

I drove to Vicki's and pulled into the driveway. Max trotted with me down the sidewalk. I sure hoped Vicki was home.

She opened the door after the second ring. She was wearing her workout clothes.

"You should know better than just showing up here," she said, "especially after the shit you pulled."

"I don't have time to talk. Something happening at work. I'm here to drop off Max. Not sure when I can get here. I'll call you. If you don't answer the phone, I'm not going to leave a message. I'll just show up."

Vicki stood there with her mouth open. I turned and jogged to the car and headed to work.

Wendy was waiting for me inside the administration wing.

"I'm so glad you're here. Can we go to your office?"

"Let's go."

I flipped on a couple light switches as we walked and unlocked my office. I turned on my desk lamp and sat down. Wendy sat in her usual spot.

"Now, what's happening?"

Wendy tried to take a breath, but she was having trouble expelling the air in there already. She couldn't speak and started hyperventilating.

"Wendy, breathe. Blow your breath out, then inhale slowly through your nose. Long exhale through your mouth."

She nodded and started to relax her death-grip on the arms of her chair.

"Oh my God, this is so hard. I don't even know how to say it."

"Just tell me, Wendy. I can't help unless you get it out."

"Maegan. She told me she had sex with Jimmy."

Pressure filled my chest. "Oh, man. How did that happen?"

Wendy's face was red. She took a breath, swallowed. My whole body tensed as I waited for her to continued.

"It's worse. She, um, she said Jimmy forced it. He forced her to have sex. With him."

My heart raced. It was hard to breathe. I searched for words.

"Oh, no. Oh, my God. Not *again*. Not to her."

Wendy nodded and started to cry. "I can't…believe it…either."

I handed Wendy a tissue. We sat together in silence until Wendy made eye contact with me.

"Is there more?" I asked.

Wendy nodded. "Maegan said...this happened several times. But it wasn't until today that she could bring it up."

"How did she tell you?"

"After breakfast. She came up to me. She looked all around before whispering. She said 'Miss Wendy, can I talk to you?' So I took her to a therapy room. Maegan looked drawn, worried. Like she hadn't slept. She talked slowly. I wasn't sure she could get it out. But like you showed me, I sat with her. I let her talk at her pace. But it was all hard to hear. How could such a thing happen here?"

That same question had been running through my mind while I was sitting with Wendy. I was sad about Maegan, but another feeling was bubbling up inside. Anger. How had this happened? I turned my attention back to Wendy.

"There will have to be an investigation. But we have to focus on Maegan and the other kids."

"Dr. D, there's something else. Maegan gave me the impression there was more to it. I don't know what that is."

"What did she say to give you that impression?"

"She either said 'There's *something* else or there's *someone* else.' But her voice was so soft, I couldn't make that part out. I asked to her say it again, but she withdrew. I didn't get any more out of her."

I licked my lips. My mouth was cotton. "You did well with her, Wendy. She trusts you enough to let you in."

"I feel so bad for her," Wendy said. "None of this feels real."

"Trauma can make us feel numb. It overwhelms us. Have you heard of vicarious traumatization?"

Wendy shook her head.

"When we sit with people, when we hear their pain, their stories, it affects us, too. If we care, if we have empathy, it will hit us hard, even though we realize the story is not about us. So we have to be mindful of our own reactions."

"I think that's what happened...what's happening to me." Tears filled Wendy's eyes. "Just these last few days, I feel like I've been stretched so much. Beyond what I know how to do."

"It's true. It stretches us," I said. "We need our own supports."

Wendy sighed. "Maegan said...this stuff happened after lights out, when staffing is lighter. All it would take is a distraction and one of the boys could cross the primary group areas and slip into the girls' wing. Plus, Maegan's roommate was discharged about ten days ago, so she was alone in the room."

Was this what I had tuned in to? Vibes from the unit?

No. It was more than that. This was a bottoming-out.

"Wendy, let's get a drink of water. I need to stand up. My muscles are all constricted. Do you feel anything like that?"

Wendy paused and closed her eyes. She opened them and nodded. "I feel like a rubber band that has been pulled as far as it can go. Like I'm ready to snap."

"A drink, then. And then you can tell me what steps you've already taken."

I got a glass of water and one for Wendy, who had excused herself to use the restroom. I sat her glass on the side of my desk near her chair. I stretched my legs out and then clenched every muscle in my body, head to toe. I held the tension until it started to hurt, and then released it all.

Better. A little looser. Like the rubber band had some give to it.

Wendy sat down. "I had to splash water on my face. I felt a little better just doing that." She sipped her water. "I called the administrator on-call right away. The police were called. Jimmy was on his way to the magistrate's office. I had a staff member from another unit come over and sit with Maegan so I could make those calls. When I left her, Maegan was curled up, knees to her chest and rocking."

"Has the psychiatrist on call been contacted?" I asked.

"Dr. Jules was on her way when I came down to meet you," Wendy said.

"Things may get harder for Maegan because the police will need to interview her. We have to plan out how to support her. But first, we should go up to the unit and see what's going on. It's going to be a madhouse up there. This will affect every single kid and every staff member."

I left my office lights on but turned off the hall lights on our way past. No one else would be in this area of the building other than me.

Neither Wendy nor I spoke as we traversed the back hallways. When we climbed the stairs to the western unit, I put the key in the lock.

"Ready for this?" I asked.

Wendy nodded. "Let's do this."

CHAPTER FIFTY-THREE

THINGS WERE BUZZING ON THE unit, no question.

When the police handcuffed Jimmy and carted him off to a juvenile facility, anxiety rumbled through all the units as if the molecules and atoms themselves had become energized, but the ages of the kids brought out all the fear and edginess of that energy.

Kids with hyperactivity followed staff around, asking questions. Depressed kids rocked or asked for headphones. Anxious kids cried. Some kids paced. Staff members had to deal with child after child.

I heard the pressure in the adults' voices. They made more eye contact with each other in attempts to quell their own anxiety. Extra staff had been called in—for reassurance as much as safety. In the time that Wendy had briefed me, Maegan had been taken off campus and interviewed by the police. After her return to the unit, she had deeply withdrawn; she was now sitting in a common area known as "the pit" because it offered seating below the floor level of the rest of the unit. A staff member sat within six feet of her, just close enough to let Maegan know someone was there. When I got closer, I saw Maegan rocking. Her eyes were glassy.

Dr. Jules was leaving an exam room. I caught up to her.

"Hi doc. What's your assessment?"

The physician nodded toward Maegan. "She's dissociative. Her vitals are normal, though, so that's good. I'm guessing she experienced trauma as early as elementary school age if not before.

She was curled in a fetal position at one point. Her language struck me as that of a six-year-old. I've seen her be more trusting of female staff. She'll be okay, but not without a lot of patience and support. I've already talked with her attending psychiatrist. He's agreed that I'll follow her from here on. Are you involved in her care?" Dr. Jules smiled. "Please tell me you are. I've heard such good things about you."

"Wendy is her therapist, but I've had a couple of occasions to deal with Maegan directly. She presents challenges that require more experience than most young therapists have."

"I agree. I'd encourage you to work with her as you can and support Wendy's work with her. There's no such thing as too many clinicians in cases like this, as long as there's coordination. Please keep me posted and let me know if you need anything from me."

"Certainly. Anything else with other kids here?"

"Anxiety is high. The sense of safety that normally exists here has been breached. We'll see more regression across the board. I'd expect a few of the kids to have soiling accidents and bedwetting."

"Thanks, Dr. Jules."

I found Wendy listening to a pair of staff members in conversation. I managed to catch her eye and motioned her toward me. We met in the middle.

"I'm going to provide triage," I said. "I'll act as a floater and go where I'm needed. Check in with each of the kids on your therapy roster. That's a good place to start."

Wendy nodded. "I saw Dr. Jones arrive a few minutes ago. Seems like it's all hands-on deck for this."

"For sure. It needs to be. Nobody is off today."

CHAPTER FIFTY-FOUR

I WALKED SLOWLY ALONG THE entire perimeter of the unit. On this first pass, I wanted to just observe and get a feel for what was happening. I was looking for significant reactions from any of the kids which might indicate a need for changes in treatment. I was also there to lend moral support to the staff. Trauma had occurred, and it would be hitting people in many ways.

There would more people than I had ever seen on the unit. The place felt like a crime scene.

Time for me to dive in.

I sat down near where a counselor was talking to a young man. I recognized the teen from the unit.

"I don't get it" the boy said. "Why would Jimmy do that to Maegan? What he did, he screwed it up for everybody. We have to deal with all this shit because of him."

"He hurt Maegan. And he hurt the kids on the unit," the counselor said. "Jimmy's gone, but you're still here and have to deal with the fallout."

"This sucks bad. Jimmy's a dick. I hope he gets prison for this."

"We'll pull together. We'll get through this. It's okay to be angry about it."

I moved on. Nancy was talking to another female staff member.

"We knew something was going on between those two. We saw it early. Wait, here's Dr. Davison. He knows about this."

I moved closer.

"Dr. D, we were just talking about Jimmy and Maegan. I was just saying that before Maegan ended up in that first restraint, we know something happened, but we were never able to piece together what."

"True. How about since that time? What do we know about how Jimmy managed to elude the staff?" I asked.

"We don't know exactly the dates we're talking about. The possible grouping of staff would include three-to-eleven workers, eleven-to-seven workers, and floaters. I'm sure administration is getting a list together," Nancy said. "I was here for several threes and a couple of elevens over the past two weeks. And I didn't work with the same people. Do you think someone *let* this happen?"

I looked at the two women. "Right now, it's hard to imagine that someone deliberately looked the other way, but we can't rule it out, either. I'm not sure how much will be shared with me about what administration comes up with. They'll probably share their decision with all of us at some point. How are you two dealing with this?"

"I'm in shock," Nancy said. "Maegan has enough to deal with. Now this. I'm so pissed at Jimmy. He was one of my kids, but he was a gamer."

"What do you mean?" I asked.

"Remember when I told you that he was being interviewed by the police?"

I nodded.

"He seemed to move between withdrawal and acting cocky. I wonder now if he was just playing me, playing us. Maybe one part was an act. Maybe it was all an act."

"So, shock and anger, and sadness for Maegan."

Nancy nodded.

"What about you..." I looked at the other woman's name tag. "Shawna?"

"I'm just really upset. I've worked in partial hospital programs before. Those are day programs, but teenagers still try to find clever ways of hooking up. Here you have the overnight element. I would think it would be tough to be aware of everything. But I'm new here. I've only worked a couple of threes so far."

"Thanks for sharing. If either of you hear or see anything that suggests anyone's struggling, please let me know."

I started to leave, but turned back. "Nancy, have you seen Tom around here?"

"I heard he was off. He got called, though. I think he was out of town. He should be on his way in. He'll be here before the late night shift starts, and probably sooner. There are a couple of other staff members who aren't here yet. People who were in earlier and left. They're getting called back in, too."

"Thanks."

In the next group of kids and staff, one girl was wailing and gasping for air between plaintive sobs. I moved closer. Her counselor was sitting beside her, a box of tissues on her lap and her arms around the girl, who was leaning against the woman for support.

"A resident with a sexual assault history," someone said.

I turned to find Dr. Jules beside me.

"I see you didn't get far," I said.

"No. But this is no longer on-call for me. I'm here for the duration. I've worked with this young lady, medication management. With her history, Jimmy's behavior would bring all of her stuff back up."

We compared notes on other kids and staff reactions.

"I think I can finish triage," Dr. Jules said. "Why don't you see if you can help Maegan? I think Wendy may need some assistance."

"I'll do that. Thanks, Dr. Jules. Holler if you need me."

I walked to the pit area. Wendy was sitting close to Maegan, who didn't react to me joining them.

"Any change in her status?" I asked.

"No. No change," Wendy said.

I looked around and considered the scene from Maegan's perspective.

"Let's move her away from here," I said to Wendy.

I stood in front of Maegan's gaze and spoke. "Maegan, it's Dr. Davison. We're going to take you to a therapy room. It'll be quieter there."

Wendy and I each took one of Maegan's arms and helped her stand up.

"Just walk with Wendy," I said. "I'll meet you two there in just a second. I'm going to get some bottled water for you."

I walked into the small kitchen area where there was a refrigerator and microwave. I nearly bumped into Larry and Tom, who were standing just inside the door. I heard Larry saying something about looking at staffing patterns.

"Excuse me, guys, sorry. I just need to get some water."

"You need anything else out there, Bryce?" Larry asked.

I stopped in the doorway, the bottle of water in one hand. "No, it looks like there's ample staff, and it seems under control. I'm going to support Wendy in working with Maegan."

Larry nodded. "Good. Catch up with me later if you can."

Tom watched me, but said nothing. I moved on.

I entered the therapy room. Maegan and Wendy were both sitting on chairs around a small table. I pulled a third chair up.

"Maegan, here's some water for you." I cracked the tab on the cap and unscrewed it. I set it in front of her.

I took a breath and watched Maegan for a minute. When I had a sense of her breathing pattern, I joined it. It wasn't rushed. We sat like that for a while longer. I glanced at Wendy and nodded. She nodded in return and breathed at the same pace. I turned back to Maegan.

"Maegan, I know some of what happened to you. I know that you were able to talk some to Wendy, and that's great. It took a lot of courage for you to do that. As I told you before, you are a strong young woman. We're going to help you get through this. With your help, we'll also make the unit safe for your peers as well. You can help us do that."

Maegan stirred for a moment. A slight shift in her posture.

"You'll help your peers," I continued, "particularly the other young women on the unit. You'll help us take care of them. But we won't forget you — we'll make sure you're okay."

Maegan took in a deep breath. She looked at me and then the bottle of water. I picked it up and held it out to her.

She took it from me, twisted the cap off, and took a long drink. When she put the bottle down, she looked at me again, and said, in a soft voice, "I ain't no ho."

CHAPTER FIFTY-FIVE

"NO ONE THINKS YOU'RE A ho, Maegan," I assured her. "There are people here that care about you. Who care about what happened to you. We won't judge you. We want to make things better. For you and your peers. We want to help you get through this, whatever rough spots there might be. Would you be okay with that?"

Maegan nodded.

"Great. Are you able to talk more right now, or do you need some time?"

"I think I can talk. But I'm not sure I remember everything."

She said these words with little affect. I figured she must be pretty worn out.

"We'll work at your pace, then. We'll follow your lead. Would that be good?"

Maegan nodded again. She had a little more color in her cheeks. "I'm starving."

"Have you eaten today?" Wendy asked.

Maegan shook her head.

I looked at my watch. It was after five.

"How about you and Wendy hang out here while I check on the plans for dinner. Be right back."

The crowd on the unit had thinned a bit. Nancy was standing near the staff desk reviewing some notes, so I approached her.

"Have decisions been made about how the kids' meals will be handled?" I asked.

"Oh, hey. Yes, we had an impromptu meeting about it. We're going to take a group over to the caf. Kids who want to get off the unit. There are probably a half-dozen kids who would prefer to stay here. We'll bring back trays for them."

"Let's add one more tray to the list. Maegan is in the first therapy room with Wendy. Let's have her tray brought in there, please. She's coming around a bit."

Nancy smiled. "Oh, that's great. People are pretty worried about her. I'll bring a tray in for her, for sure. Thanks for letting me know."

I turned to leave.

"Dr. D?"

"Yes?"

"I'm really glad you're here. I think your presence on the unit helps calm things down. Thanks for that."

"I appreciate that Nancy. No thanks needed, though. We're all pitching in here, yourself included. Each of us makes a difference."

CHAPTER FIFTY-SIX

I ENTERED THE THERAPY ROOM and sat down at the table. "Dinner is on in the cafeteria, but I asked that you get your tray here."

Maegan nodded.

"Where would you like to start?" I asked.

"You know, right? You know about what happened? To me?"

"I know a little. I was hoping maybe you could fill in the blanks for me. But please understand that if you share information with me that involves sexual abuse, I have to report it. The same goes for if I consider you to be a danger to yourself or others."

I expected Maegan to clam up. Instead, she lowered her head and nodded. She was no longer a tough street kid, but a vulnerable child.

She looked away for a few seconds and I thought she might disappear on me. But she looked back my way, although she did not meet my eyes.

"For the last couple of weeks Jimmy has been sneaking into my room at night and fu...having sex with me."

She looked directly at me, waiting for acknowledgment.

"When Jimmy sneaked in your room and had sex with you...did that happen with or without your consent?"

Deep breath. "Well, I know he can be a dick, but he was being extra-nice to me when no one else was around to see us. I was so lonely. I just wanted someone to hold me. I didn't want to have sex with him, but I didn't tell him no either."

That sounded right. She was vulnerable, seeking intimacy. Wanting to be held, but, perhaps fearing rejection, lacking the self-esteem to say no to the sex. Her sexual abuse patterns continued. There would be another time to deal with that later. Right now, I needed information.

"But the sex started getting rougher, to the point I would bleed. And no matter what I said, he wouldn't stop." Her eyes filled with tears. "I tried to push him off, but my arms were pinned behind me."

"Jimmy pinned your arms behind you?"

"No, not Jimmy. Someone else."

My heart pounded in my throat. This was new information. Maegan's comment had knocked the wind out of me. I fought to get a grip on my thoughts.

"Who?"

Maegan's eyes were as big as saucers. I waited.

"Shit, I don't know! When I think about it, I can...*feel* someone there, but it's like I can't see who it is. I swear to you, I don't know. I feel like I'm going crazy!"

"No, not crazy. Not crazy at all. Dealing with the Jimmy piece is hard enough. You're only remembering what you're capable of handling right now. Plus, you need to feel safe, and we need to find a way to make sure you are."

I paused for a moment. Maegan stared into space but looked at me when I spoke again.

"From all you've described and all I've observed, you've been pretty upset. So upset that you go away for a time. You know what I mean by that, right?"

Maegan nodded. "That's what it feels like. Like going into a room and closing the door. And then another door. And then everything else goes far away."

"And that feels crazy to you, right? But you need to know that you're not crazy. Going away is your mind's way of protecting you. We have to respect that, but we also have to find ways to help you move through this. The safer you feel, the easier it will be for you to stay here with us. Does that make sense?"

Maegan nodded again.

"You need to know the risk, though. If we don't identify the second individual, he or she remains free. Free to hurt you or someone else. And you don't want that, either. We need to nail the bastard — and we need your help to do that."

"So it's like I both want to remember and *not* remember at the same time. Is that it? That's so psycho!"

God, this girl was bright. And so brave.

"All you've told me, all you've had to deal with, all these things tell me how resourceful and courageous you are. Don't ever forget it! From this point forward, though, we need to set the conditions to make it easier for you to sort your experiences out. Are you willing to work toward that?"

"What do you mean by conditions? Work toward what?"

"It goes back to the safety thing. In order for you to go any further with remembering what happened to you, we have to show you we can look after you and protect you. We'll do that in a number of ways, but the most important way will be that there will be a staff member at your side at all times."

"Like I'm under arrest? Like I'm a criminal?"

"No, more like a bodyguard. Like you're a rock star."

Maegan considered this.

"Okay, what else?

"Well, your dinner will be here soon. Be sure and eat. Other than that, we'll talk frequently, and I'll make sure Wendy and I know what you've got going on inside. If we work together, you may find it's safe to remember what you've temporarily forgotten. And then we can...."

"Nail the bastard, right?

"You bet. Nail the bastard."

CHAPTER FIFTY-SEVEN

WENDY ARRANGED FOR GETTING MAEGAN one-on-one staff coverage while I tracked Larry down. He had set up shop in a small conference room. Although he was alone in the room when I knocked on the door, there was a suit jacket hanging over a chair across from him. Larry's own shirtsleeves were rolled up, his tie was mostly off, and he looked haggard.

"Mind if I come in?" I asked.

Larry nodded to a seat across the table.

"Quite a mess we have here," he said.

"It gets worse."

Larry took off his glasses and rubbed his eyes. "Tell me."

"Wendy and I just met with Maegan. She reports nonconsensual sex with Jimmy but added that someone else participated in the acts. She's blocked out who that person is."

"Holy Mother of God," Larry said. "A second attacker."

"We have to inform the police," I said.

"We have someone here already — oh, here he is. Lieutenant Dean, come on in. This is our psychologist, Dr. Bryce Davison."

The detective shook my hand. "Doctor," he said, and then picked up the jacket from the chair next to me and sat down. He gave no indication that we had met previously.

"Dr. Davison just told me that there is a second assailant. This changes things quite a bit."

Lieutenant Dean's face tightened. "That's awful. But also confusing. I interviewed the young woman myself after the assault was reported and Jimmy was hauled out of here. She didn't say anything about a second person."

"She's overwhelmed, Lieutenant. It's taken a lot of time with her to gather additional information."

"So, who is the second individual?"

"We don't know. Maegan is blocking out that person's identity," I said.

"Do you buy that?" the detective asked.

"I'm sorry...buy it? What are you suggesting?"

"Does Maegan want to cooperate with the investigation? It sounds like she's stonewalling."

I felt blood rush to my face. I tried to respond without sputtering. "It is my professional opinion that Maegan *is* cooperating. She's being as open as she can. This girl has a long history of trauma, much of it sexual in nature, and she's psychologically overwhelmed. We have to move at her pace."

"I agree," Dr. Jones said. "Repression isn't uncommon in acute trauma. Accusing the victim of deliberately interfering with an investigation is totally out of bounds."

"I'm not accusing her of anything" protested Lieutenant Dean. "I'm just saying what it looks like. It could be construed has defensive. But at this moment, I'm deferring to your professional opinions. We need to sort out our options." He stood. "Would you gentlemen excuse me for a couple minutes?"

Lieutenant Dean left the room, pulling out his cell phone as he walked.

I looked at Larry. "Was he really suggesting that Maegan was playing the system?"

Larry ran his fingers through his hair. "I don't think so. I think he's frustrated. I've dealt with the lieutenant a couple of other times. He's actually a reasonable guy. A straight-shooter. I think he has a degree in psychology, actually. Not your typical cop background."

"I know this is hard. But we have to get it right. I'll cut him some slack. But I appreciated what you said about him being out of line."

"Keep your head in the game, Bryce. No matter what other stuff is going on, I need you at your clinical best. I'll handle the administration, the outside agencies, and the media. Those are my headaches. I want to keep you free to focus on the really important parts—the kids."

As much as I agreed with Larry about putting the kids first, I was struck by his comment about "other stuff." What was he talking about? I was about to ask him when I heard movement from the doorway.

The detective returned to the room, shaking his head. "Sorry about that. I had to check on a couple things. We need to get a game plan in place to move things forward. And we need to find out who this other individual is ASAP. In a complicated situation like this one, we usually seek assistance from a forensic specialist—someone in the FBI. However, those resources are tied up elsewhere. No one available for the immediate future, I'm told."

He looked uncomfortable.

"I did manage to talk to one of our top mental health guys, and I ran our scenario by him. He suggested I check with your agency and see if I can locate someone with the appropriate, uh, skills."

"What kind of skills are you looking for, Lieutenant? If you need a forensic psychiatrist, we've got a doc from Erie who consults with our outpatient clinic from time to time. Dr. Jennifer Burrows."

"Does she work with hypnosis?"

"Well, no, I don't believe so."

"Well, that's what our guy recommended. I almost hesitated to bring it up. Seems like I should be out looking for a stage magician or something."

"Well, I wouldn't go that far. Hypnosis is widely recognized as a therapeutic tool and is no longer considered an act of sorcery. And you needn't look outside this room. Dr. Davison is certified in clinical hypnosis and is well-respected for his work in that area."

"That right, doc? You do this kind of thing?"

"It depends on what you mean by 'this kind of thing.' Dr. Jones is correct. I'm certified in clinical hypnosis and have been practicing for many years. And there's nothing magical about hypnosis. There is a great deal of research support for using hypnosis for a variety of conditions—from pain to warts."

"Well, doc, this isn't warts. I need to find someone who can hypnotize this girl and see if she can remember the identity of the alleged second perpetrator. Can it be done?"

"Sure, it can be done, Lieutenant, and it would be better for Dr. Davison to work with Maegan anyway," Larry said. "She's familiar with him and would be more likely to trust him than she would some outsider. Of course, we'd have to get consent from the patient, as well as from her guardian. In Maegan's case, that should be easy. The Office of Children, Youth, and Families has medical rights. We could get them to fax a release to us tomorrow. With that in hand, we could move forward, if Dr. Davison is willing to do this."

"What do you say, doc?" asked Lieutenant Dean. "You up for some investigative work?"

"I'd be comfortable working with Maegan using hypnosis. She told me she wants to nail the perpetrator. But hypnosis isn't a tool for psychic archeology."

"Psychic archeology?" Dean asked.

"Memory retrieval. It's not like the mind is a video camera that records everything just as it happens. Memory is highly influenced by perception, attitudes, motivation, and so on. But if anxiety is interfering with recalling a recent event, hypnosis may be helpful."

"Understood. We're not talking about going back to Maegan's early childhood. Will you help us?"

"I'll do it. I'll help Maegan but leave the investigative work to you and your colleagues. Who would be sitting in?"

"I would be there. Wouldn't miss it," Lieutenant Dean said.

"As medical director, I need to be there as well," Larry added. "In fact, if we use one of our one-way mirror rooms in the outpatient clinic, we could have folks observe without disturbing the patient. Maybe a few staff people could sit in since this would be a great teaching case. With Maegan's consent, of course."

"Okay by me, Dr. Jones. Just not too many people. I don't want information leaking out."

"Agreed. We'll have attendees sign confidentiality statements to make sure the point is well made. It's usually understood in medical care, anyhow. How about tomorrow?"

"Absolutely," said Lieutenant Dean. "We need to move on this."

"We'll move," I said, "at Maegan's pace. That's the key for me."

Lieutenant Dean looked from Larry to me. "This is in your wheelhouse, right?"

I smiled. "No worries, Lieutenant. Maegan's in good hands. No stage hypnosis. Serious work with major implications. But also unknowns. There's no script here. It goes where Maegan takes it. It could be a wild ride."

"Meaning?" Lieutenant Dean asked.

"Buckle your seatbelt, Lieutenant."

CHAPTER FIFTY-EIGHT

I FOUND WENDY SITTING WITH Maegan, who was on the last several bites of her dinner.

"Lasagna?" I asked.

"With salad and garlic bread," Wendy said. "It smelled so good I almost grabbed Maegan's tray."

"You two should go on the road together. What a team," Maegan said.

"First things first. I have an update on the safety front. I've been asked to use hypnosis with you."

Maegan snorted. "Say what? Like, bark-like-a-dog hypnosis?"

"No. Turns out, there are a lot of misconceptions about it. It's a tool that a therapist and patient agree to use with specific goals in mind. Like helping you reduce any anxiety or mental interference to help you remember what happened to you."

"What's mental interference?"

"Right. Ever hear a radio station with static?"

"Yeah. Pretty annoying."

"How did you deal with it?"

"Easy, you take the knob and try to turn it just a little bit to clear it up."

"Bingo."

"I get it. Mental interference is radio static. And hypnosis helps me to turn the dial."

"Perfect!"

Maegan smiled for the first time I'd seen in a while.

"So would you be willing to work with me? We would do this in a room with a one-way mirror. Wendy would be on the other side."

"It makes me feel like a carnival freak. Me on display, everyone watching me."

"It can be scary at first, but once we get going, you're more likely to feel relaxation than anything else. Besides, I bet you've had similar experiences that you're not thinking of right now."

"What do you mean?"

"Well, have you ever had to give a speech or presentation in front of a class?"

Maegan paused to consider this.

"I had a speech class in English once. I had to stand in front of the class every week."

"That's a great example. How did it go?"

"I hated it. Well, at least at first. I was really nervous. But then I saw that other kids were more nervous than I was."

"What we're doing is even a little easier. You won't even see your audience. It will be you and me, and the other stuff will fade into the background."

Tears formed in Maegan's eyes.

"You'll make sure I'm okay?"

"I will. You can even rate how well I do."

"I get to rate you? Like thumbs up or thumbs down?"

"Yep. Can we give it a go, then? See how we can do working together?"

"Yeah, I'll try. But if I get freaked out or something?"

"Then we'll end the session and talk about what's freaking you out."

Maegan sighed and nodded her head.

"Thanks, Maegan. We'll get started tomorrow. I'll fill you in more when we're together. In the meantime, get some rest. Someone will be outside your door throughout the night."

Maegan departed with Wendy. I left the unit through the back door. As I walked each step in the stairwell, my legs felt heavy. My muscles ached. My forehead felt tight and tingly, and I guessed a headache was starting. And no wonder — it had been an arduous day.

But we were making progress.

I made my way along the back corridors, low-level industrial lighting illuminating the hallway. No windows back here. The usual *tinking* of metal from a nearby boiler and the echo of my footsteps sounded like effects from a horror movie. It was something I experienced each time I walked these halls, but it never ceased to spook me.

Still, I was glad to reach the back door to my area of the building. I had my key ready to go, and it took me only a few seconds to locate the keyhole by touch. I closed the door, checked to see that the handle was locked, and turned the corner toward my office.

I heard the rustle of clothing behind me and turned my head. A sharp blow caught my right shoulder blade, sending searing pain shooting across my back. Before I could respond, something hard and sharp struck me across my shoulders, just under my neck. I pitched forward a couple steps until a blow to my left calf sent me tumbling to the floor. I turned on my side and looked back, trying to catch my breath and shake off the pain. In the soft light of an exit sign, my attacker came into view.

Mr. Stud, grimacing and carrying a baseball bat.

"I'm gonna cause you the same amount of pain you caused me" he snarled, glowering down at me. "You're gonna squirm with all the other worms down there in the dirt. You'll wish you never got between me and my woman. You're gonna wish you had never been born."

CHAPTER FIFTY-NINE

MR. STUD STOOD OVER ME, breathing heavily, his face getting redder with each second. He slapped the fat part of the bat against his palm. "What have you got to say for yourself, you piece of shit?"

Large muscles throbbed. I couldn't catch my breath. My heart raced.

But this was no panic attack. This was a combination of physical pain and fight-or-flight. I was in no position to flee.

I sat up and lifted one hand, palm out. "Wait. Wait a minute."

Mr. Stud smiled menacingly. He pointed the bat at me. "You don't get to tell me what to do. You're the one on the floor, smartass. What, nothing clever to say?"

He stepped closer and kicked my right calf, causing my body to turn toward him and sending a spasm up leg.

"Are you...are you out of your mind?"

He jabbed the bat into my abdomen. I doubled over, no air to breathe. My torso burned. I wrapped my arms across my stomach and felt tears in my eyes.

"You don't get to talk. Look at you. Shaking in your shoes. Who's your daddy, bitch?"

I couldn't slow my mind down. My thoughts were as rapid as my heart rate. Everything in my body pounded and pulsed. I tried to push through the pain. My breathing was out of control. I tried to slow the next breath. I had to do a crisis assessment. He's unstable.

He's *going to kill me*. He expects me to beg. No mercy coming, though. Do something different.

I forced a laugh. I wiped at the spit on my mouth and rubbed it on my pants. "Look. At. You."

Mr. Stud scowled and hesitated. "What did you say?"

I gulped some air. Tried to catch a deep breath. My body shook when I exhaled.

"You. You're doing this…because of a woman?"

He pointed the bat at me again. "She left me because of you. She said you're a better man." He spit on me. "Don't look like it to me, bitch."

"Wait. Wait." I touched one of my front pockets. "I have money. I can give it to you. It's yours."

Mr. Stud looked at my hand and went back to slapping his palm with the barrel of the bat.

"Yeah. I'll take that. But after I split your head open. It'll be mine anyway."

"Please, don't. No more. You've hurt me enough. Just walk away. I won't tell anyone."

More bat-slapping. "You? More of a man? You're just a pussy. Begging for your life. *'I won't tell. I won't tell.'* Shit, you'd call the cops faster than you pissed your pants."

If this doesn't work, I'm dead. I may be dead anyway. Nothing to lose.

"Real man. Yeah, that's you. You had to write it on your hand to remind yourself. But points to you…at least…you spelled it right."

"You son of a bitch!" He raised the bat over his head, cracking ceiling tiles. Dust fell on his face and into his eyes. He swiped at his eyes and stumbled toward me. I grabbed his belt and yanked him toward me, swinging my right leg against his. He toppled further and I pushed him away from me. His face smashed the wall beside him. His mouth left a trail of blood on the wall as he slid toward the floor.

I leaned against the wall by my office door, pushing his legs out of my way. His head was only a foot away from me, but he posed no threat. I gently moved my arms and straightened my legs. Leaned forward and arched my back in slow-motion. I was glad I could move. Nothing felt broken.

I had survived.

As I rotated my head and felt knots pop in my neck. Mr. Stud stirred a bit. I looked down at him. He started to lift his head, and he moved a hand toward the bat. When he turned to look at me, I leaned his way and drove my elbow into his forehead. His head dropped to the floor. He was out for the count.

"Bastard," I said, then pushed back against the wall and struggled to my feet.

I unlocked my office door, hit the lights, and fell into my desk chair. I pulled open a couple of drawers looking for ibuprofen. I took several and swallowed them with the remainder of a glass of water sitting on my desk. I hit the speaker button on my desk phone and punched the emergency button.

"Emergency operator, how may I direct your call?"

"Get me the police, please. I've been attacked."

"Do you need medical care, sir?"

"No, just police."

A moment's silence. Then:

"New Alex Regional Police, may I help you?"

I thought for a moment. "I've been attacked. Can you send over a squad car?" I gave him the address. "Is there any way you can patch me through to Lieutenant Dean?"

A moment later. "Dean."

"Lieutenant. Bryce Davison. Remember that guy I told you was hassling me? Flick what's-his-name? Well, he was waiting for me to get back to my office tonight. With a baseball bat."

"Jesus," Dean said. "I'm still at your place. Where are you now?" I told him. "I'll be right there."

I limped out to the front door. The squad car was already there. I saw the detective walking down the hill toward the administration wing. I opened the door for both officers.

"Back here." I led them toward the office.

The patrolman knelt beside Mr. Stud. "He's out cold. Did you use the bat on him?"

"No. He hit a wall." Dean looked around the space. I gestured to where Mr. Stud had approached me.

"He must have gotten in here earlier. He knows my car. So he knew I was still here. He made himself comfy somewhere and waited for me to get here."

"I radioed for an ambulance, Lieutenant" reported the other cop. "Should be here shortly." He looked at me as I was rubbing my shoulder. "Do we need one for you, too?"

"No. I took a beating, but I'm moving."

Dean smiled. "You may not be tomorrow."

"I'll deal with tomorrow when it gets here. Too much excitement left over from today, yet."

As the ambulance crew carted Mr. Stud away, I realized that the patrolman was the same guy I had talked to the first time I reported the situation. The cop was about to follow the stretcher out the door.

"Hey, officer."

The patrolman turned my way.

"I took your advice. I let him hit me first."

The cop smirked and nodded, once.

CHAPTER SIXTY

"YOU NEED ANY HELP GETTING to your car?" Dean asked.

"No, I'm good. I'm going to take my sweet time. This time I know for sure that guy isn't going to accost me in the middle of the road."

"Good point."

"Are you going back up top?" I asked.

"No. I'm done here. You were the icing on the cake."

We got to the sidewalk, and Lieutenant Dean turned to walk up the hill. I started to cross the street when I noticed the white pickup truck parked down the block.

"Lieutenant!"

The detective turned around, and I pointed toward the truck. I walked down to it, and the detective joined me a few seconds later.

"Is this Flick's?" he asked.

"Yep. He sure feels safe in your town. He left his windows open."

Dean poked his head in the window. There was a manila folder on the passenger seat. "Assault with a deadly weapon," he said, as if considering his options. *"Attempted murder."* He reached in and grabbed the folder.

"Well, well. Lookie here."

He handed me the open folder. My consulting contract was in it, along with a scratch pad listing Mr. Stud's efforts to decipher my social security number. He already had most of the numbers.

"Looks like you were close to having your identity stolen," Dean said.

"Lucky break for me, huh? The issue with my contract was one of bits of stalker intrigue I was trying to figure out. Now I know who was behind that."

"Do you think Mr. Stud was behind all the stuff that happened?"

"No, couldn't be. He was a late arrival. Things were already happening before I even met him."

"Damn, Dr. Davison. *Two* stalkers? That's uncommon."

I shook my head. "When it rains, it pours, Lieutenant."

CHAPTER SIXTY-ONE

I STARTED HOME AND WAS well on my way when I realized my place was still in disarray. I didn't have anywhere to go. I didn't have any clean clothes. I passed my exit and drove to Walmart. I bought some clothes and toiletries. I was good to go. I returned to the motel where I had stayed the night before and paid for a room. The same room, it turned out.

Although I was hungry, tired, and sore, food would have to wait. I stripped off my clothes and let the water run in the shower for a minute. I was tempted to look in the mirror, but I decided to not be a glutton for punishment. I stepped into the hot water, and the pressure hit my sore spots. I swore a blue streak and rotated in a slow circle. New sensations emerged — the hot water coaxed relaxation from my skin. I washed up as best I could and then just stood in the steam.

I pulled on a pair of shorts and a plain white t-shirt, slipped on sneakers, and drove to a twenty-four-hour market where I bought a couple slices of pepperoni pizza, some iced coffee, and a large bottle of extra-strength pain killer.

I half-watched some comedy reruns while I ate my food. Then I switched off the television and finished the coffee in silence. Small movements made me wince, and I hoped that Mr. Stud was uncomfortable in his cell — once he gets out of the hospital. I swallowed some pain pills, slipped off my clothes, and crawled into bed.

Staring up at the ceiling, my mind was numb from the medication. But even the numbness couldn't keep the memories from emerging.

* * *

Mr. Scissa and the guys left me on the football field. No one came to offer a hand or a friendly word.

By the time I got to the locker area, almost everyone had cleaned up and moved on to the next class. I was alone in the shower until Mr. Scissa made his presence known with a smack to the back of my head. I turned and cowered, shivering and contorting, trying to keep my body covered.

"Quite a display you put on out there today, Davison. Last one through the course, and you never did finish. I could flunk you because you didn't complete your assignment. Or maybe you want to go out there now and finish it?"

"No. Don't make me go out there. Please."

He stepped closer, well within my personal space. "If you were one of my football players, I would go one-on-one with you on the field. Maybe I could knock some manhood into you."

He stepped aside and gathered up a towel. I reached out my hand for it.

Scissa let the towel dangle, but instead of handing it to me, he twirled the end and folded down the top third.

"You're not worth my time."

He snapped the towel against one of my wet thighs. It stung like mad. I tried to stand on my other leg. I covered my body with my arm. He snapped me again. I wanted to cry out. I didn't.

But I couldn't stop the tears.

"Big baby. Get out of my gym."

He dropped the towel in a puddle of water and walked away.

I rubbed the glowing welt on my leg and tried not to make a sound that might cause Mr. Scissa to return. I didn't want to touch the towel. I pretty much dried myself with my clothes, which clung to my skin in wet pockets. I finger-combed my hair as best I could and hurried to biology class. I didn't want added further embarrassment because of tardiness.

I could have spared myself the hustle. Even though the principal didn't catch me in the hallway, I wasn't even close to being on time. Still, shame was waiting for me.

"…threw up on himself."

"…couldn't run the mile."

"…the other boys think he's a fag."
"…everybody passed him."
"…didn't finish the course."
"…Mr. Scissa is going to make his life hell."

Soft fragments of conversation filtered through ambient noise. I was infamous — all through the world of seventh grade. Snickers and glances followed me as I walked the hallways between classes. Even though I made it to the end of the day, there was no relief on the school bus. Each seat had two kids before I even climbed up the bus steps. No one scrunched over to offer me a seat. Every pair of eyes watched me. I turned toward the front and stood in the aisle, choking to hold back the tears.

"We're not moving till you sit down," the driver said.

Kids taunted me. Someone pushed me from behind. I turned to see who it was, and an older student glared and me and faked a step toward me. I moved slowly forward until a girl in my glass sighed and moved over, turning her head away from me as I sat down.

With half my body in the aisle, the bus pulled out. From then on I was only safe when I was alone.

CHAPTER SIXTY-TWO

I BEGAN THE MORNING PREPARING for the work ahead of me. I needed to be ready to work effectively with Maegan. I didn't want anything in my head except the task at hand.

So no email checking.

I showered and ate some scrambled eggs and toast. I was ready to go.

I met Maegan outside the observation room in the outpatient clinic. She was rocking back and forth and chewing a fingernail.

"You ready for this, Maegan?"

Maegan pulled the finger away from her mouth but kept rocking.

"I'm a little nervous. My mind is here but my body wants to run away."

"I see that. And that's just fine. Your mind is here and that's all we need to start. Your body will catch up to us soon."

Maegan stopped rocking. "You know, doc, you say some of the goofiest shit. But every time you do, I know exactly what you're saying. Is that weird or what?"

"No, not weird. It just means that you're good at understanding goofy shit."

As far as I knew, our viewers were already seated inside the adjoining room. I opened the door, and we sat down in a pair of comfortable chairs in an otherwise sparsely decorated room. Each of our chairs had an end table beside it.

"Would you like some water or something else to drink before we get started?"

Maegan stared at the mirror and bounced one leg like a jackhammer. But she looked at me before she responded.

"Nope. Nothing. I'm not a big drinker in the morning."

I had a bottle of water with me, which I opened and placed on the table. I was aware of my reflection in the mirror, which made it look like there were two of me in the room.

I was good with that. I could use the extra help.

All consent forms had been signed, but for the record, I reiterated the ground rules and received Maegan's verbal consent.

"Maegan, I appreciate your willingness to do this. And I want to remind you that while it is just you and me in the room, there are some people who will be observing us through the mirror. Is that okay?"

"Whatever. Who's over there?" She looked directly at the mirror.

"Lieutenant Dean, Dr. Jones, and a few other staff members." I wasn't sure, but I thought Tom, Wendy, and a psychologist from the outpatient clinic would be in attendance as well.

"Are you okay with that?"

Maegan looked bored, but I figured she was covering her anxiety.

"Yeah. I just want to get done with this. Can we get going?"

"One last thing. As we discussed, what we do here today will be videotaped. Do you consent to that?"

"Yes."

"Thank you. Just remember, anytime you feel too uncomfortable, you can simply open your eyes and become fully alert. We'll only work at whatever pace is comfortable for you."

Maegan nodded.

"I'd like to ask you to take a few slow, deep breaths. During that time, you can close your eyes whenever you like, if that's comfortable for you. Closing your eyes can help you focus on what's going on inside your mind."

I watched Maegan slow her breathing. She moved her hands from the arms of the chair to rest on her lap. The muscles in her forehead and around her mouth went slack. I didn't need to tell her to shut the other distractions—the different room, the people on the other side of the mirror, doing something new—out...she was already doing that.

"During our work, we'll remain connected. You've experienced that you can be thinking something else and still connected to me. Maegan nodded her head, an almost imperceptible movement, but I was watching her responses and commented on it. "That's right — and, still connected, you can let your mind drift, pulling your more deeply into comfort."

Maegan shifted again and seemed to sink into the chair. "Your body can feel both heavy in the chair but also lighter than air."

From time to time, I asked Maegan what she felt or noticed. She was an excellent hypnotic subject and appeared comfortable speaking without increasing her level of alertness. Often, when people begin to learn how to enter hypnosis, they re-alert a bit when asked to speak. More experienced subjects who dissociate are more adept at handling the task.

"Maegan, if it's okay with you, I'd like to ask your unconscious mind to signal me by lifting your right index finger if you begin to feel discomfort. That finger would mean discomfort or "no." Would that be all right?"

She nodded.

"Anytime you want to let me know you are in agreement with me, your right middle finger can just float up. That finger would be agreement or comfort or "yes.""

Another nod.

"Good. Just imagine you're in a private room, sitting in a comfortable chair, in front of a large-screen TV. Beside you is a remote control that allows you to change anything you want about what shows up on the screen, even turn it off. When you're ready, I'd like you to turn on the TV and just allow whatever images emerge to begin to fill the screen. Perhaps a pleasant scene from a place you've never seen before. Or maybe a place you've been to but would like to see again."

Maegan nodded.

"What are you experiencing?"

She spoke slowly. "I'm in a garden. It's full of beautiful flowers. I'm sitting on a bench. I think I'm waiting for someone."

"Who are you waiting for?"

Maegan adjusted her weight forward in her chair. Her brow furrowed. "I don't know. I'm supposed to be there. Someone told me to be there. Wait …there's…there's someone behind me…."

A shrill, ear-splitting sound filled the room: electronic feedback followed by a chorus of noise and voices. I turned to face the mirror, my pulse racing. As I turned back toward Maegan, the noise ceased.

I refocused my attention on Maegan, who remained in hypnosis, although her right index finger was skyward and she was frowning. She shifted in the chair.

"Maegan, you can turn the volume down on any distractions, and when you feel comfortable once more, your index finger can float back down, and you can feel the muscles in your body becoming smooth and relaxed once more."

Maegan's body quieted, and her brow smoothed out. I glanced at my watch. We were about thirty minutes in; I had a decision to make. We could continue as we had and move toward reviewing what had happened to her on the unit, or we could reinforce Maegan's willingness to use hypnosis and highlight her success.

I opted to close out the session. Maegan needed something to feel good about. We could follow up the next day and build on today's visit. I gave Maegan some buffer time, suggesting images of comfort her, and then guided her through the process of re-alerting. She stretched and opened her eyes simultaneously, and then blinked at me, curious.

"That was...cool. Like taking a trip through time."

"Were there any interesting or unusual experiences you'd like to share?"

"Oh, just one strange one. First I was floating in a swimming pool, like on an inner tube or some kind of floaty thing. Then I climbed out of the pool and walked to a bench in the middle of a huge garden at the end of a path. All of a sudden I was in the junior high library, and Mrs. Pellegrino, an old witch of a librarian, was shushing a group of boys to be quiet. I was irritated because I was right in the middle of a really good book.

"Another wacko thing was one of the kids in the library was out of place. I knew him, but not from school. The other ones were regular jerks from that dump."

"You saw someone that didn't belong in the group of kids in school?

"Yeah, but...have you ever been in a situation where you kind of knew someone, but you weren't sure who they were or where you knew them from?"

"Like might happen if you bump into one of your teachers from school inside a shopping mall?"

"Yeah, like that! Exactly! That's what was happening."

She yawned.

"I didn't get to figure it out, though. Don't know why, but I ended up floating in the pool again. That's where I was when I heard you telling me to open my eyes."

I smiled. "Nice job, Maegan. Really nice. This was a great, great start. Now that you know what the process is like, I'd like for us to meet again tomorrow. Sound okay?"

"Yeah. Whatever."

In a few moments, there was a soft knock on the door, and Wendy appeared. She avoided making eye contact with me.

"I'm here to take Maegan back to the unit," she said.

"Great. Maegan, your personal escort has arrived. Your rock star status must be preceding you."

Maegan walked to the door, shoulders slumped. Although her experience in the room had been positive, the stress of her experiences was weighing on her.

"Try and get some rest," I said. "You've earned it."

We could both use a heaped helping of resilience about now.

CHAPTER SIXTY-THREE

As I ENTERED THE OBSERVATION room, I caught the tail end of a discussion between Larry and Lieutenant Dean. The lieutenant was red-faced, and it was clear his fuse was lit. No one else remained in the room.

I approached the duo with caution. "What did I miss?" I asked.

"We had a bit more drama than we expected today," Larry said. "Things were going well. You were speaking softly, but I had no problem hearing you. However, there was some muttering about not being able to hear you, and the next thing I know, Tom is over at the control panel. Instead of increasing the volume from the interview room, he reversed it. The feedback fed right through your speakers."

"Damn fool nearly ruined everything," Dean said.

"Lieutenant, always expect the unexpected around here. Accidents happen. The staff member apologized. Besides, Dr. Davison handled it well. No harm done."

"It threw me off for a second," I said. "But Maegan was such a good subject, she stayed right with it. She tuned it out as if it didn't happen. In her mind, it was just an irritating incident in a library."

Lieutenant Dean sighed and nodded. "I have to say, that was pretty impressive. On the other hand, we're not any closer than we were, are we?"

"Sure we are. We know Maegan and I have a good working relationship and she's an excellent hypnotic subject. I could have extended the session, but I asked Maegan to put her trust in me. I'm not going to rush things. As long as I keep my word on that, we can take the next step."

"Which is?"

"To take the interview to the next level. What Maegan was telling me during the debriefing was there was someone in the room that didn't belong—someone that didn't fit the context. That person may very well be the second perpetrator."

"In the room? You mean in the library?"

"She was talking about the library in her school. But something was out of place. Someone was in the image that didn't fit. That would be a good place for us to continue."

I was going to say more but noticed Larry and the detective were looking behind me. I turned and saw Wendy standing near the door.

"Oh, I'm sorry. I didn't mean to interrupt. I dropped Maegan off on the unit and wanted to see if there was any more I needed to know or if you needed my help with anything."

I thought she was asking me, but she looked at Larry when she spoke.

"We're just wrapping up here," I said. "I'll catch up with you later if I need to fill you in."

CHAPTER SIXTY-FOUR

I HAD A PILE OF assessments to review, so I hunkered down in my office and worked through the pile. No phone calls or visitors, which was rare. I shut my lights off and grabbed my bag and figured I'd stop by the western unit before I left for the day. I started down my hallway and thought better of it. I didn't plan on walking the back corridors any time soon. Instead, I left through the main door and walked up the long, sloping sidewalk to the upper part of the complex.

Routine had been re-established. Kids were doing pre-dinner tasks, and voices were pleasant. I saw Wendy sitting with Maegan in the TV area. Maegan looked asleep.

"Wendy, can we talk for a minute?"

Wendy looked at Maegan and followed me a couple steps away.

"Did she say anything more about her experience?"

Wendy looked at her feet. "She said it was *fun*. That was her word. She was surprised at how easy it was. I think she saw it as a good start."

"Great. It seemed that way to me, too. I just wanted to make sure that she's doing okay. We'll be doing a follow-up session tomorrow."

Wendy nodded. I started to walk toward the exit when I heard Wendy's voice.

"Dr. Davison?"

Pretty formal for Wendy. "Yes?"

She stepped closer to me and whispered, "I'm pretty...upset. I'm, uh, uncomfortable, you know, just standing here with you. I get that you're attracted to me and, uh, some girls would be flattered by that. I just don't see you that way."

I felt my mouth drop open. I shook my head, as much to clear it as to redirect the conversation. "No.... What? What are you talking about?"

Wendy stepped back and looked around. "You sent me an email. You, uh, declared your...your *lust* for me."

My stomach fell. My heart followed. "Wendy, I never sent that. It wasn't from me. Someone is spoofing my email address."

Wendy looked at me, brow furrowed, and shook her head. "I don't believe you. And if you make me that uncomfortable again, I'm going to Dr. Jones." She turned and walked away.

It was my turn to look around. No one seemed to be paying attention. I walked toward the exit as fast as I could without running. I heard the door swing closed as I rushed down the stairs toward the entrance.

I didn't stop until I was outside. I bent over, hands on my knees, and tried to catch my breath. My bag strap slid from my shoulder, and the bag hit my sore leg.

I heard footsteps coming up the hill. I stood up and hoisted the bag back onto my shoulder.

"Are you okay, doc?"

I turned to see Nancy standing beside me.

I wet my lips. "Yeah. Or maybe more like 'no.' I'm a little queasy. I probably ate something that didn't agree with me. Are you headed to work?"

"No, I clocked out. But when I got to my car, I remembered I had a book that another staff member wanted to read." She showed me the paperback in her hand. "I was just going to go and drop it off."

"Nice of you to take the time."

"It's a very good book."

"Thanks for checking on me. Also nice of you."

"You bet. Have a good night."

Nancy started up the hill.

"Hey, Nancy?"

She turned.

"Do you have time for a cup of coffee?"

"That would be nice. I owe you some catching up, if I remember right."

CHAPTER SIXTY-FIVE

NANCY FOLLOWED IN HER CAR as I drove toward a bookstore/coffee shop. Maybe the comment about the book made me think about it.

We found a table and settled in. The large menu behind the counter was easy to read.

"You pick, my treat," Nancy said.

"Make mine a vanilla iced coffee, extra cream, please."

Nancy walked off to order. I looked around the store. I had only been in the place one other time, but I loved bookstores.

Nancy handed the coffee to me and sat down.

"What did you get?" I asked.

"A triple double shotta something," she said, laughing. "It was almost too complicated to say."

"Sounds like it. Thanks for mine. I was just remembering that I'd only been here once before. But I don't know why. I love books. And coffee."

"I've been here several times. It's a nice place. What kinds of books do you like?" Nancy asked.

"I got ahold of an Agatha Christie book in junior high. Some of the language was challenging — the English way of writing — but I really enjoyed the story. I read more of hers, plus some Sherlock Holmes stories, and broadened into other mysteries and thrillers. You?"

"I like romance novels. Not the ones with busty women and bare-chested men on the covers. The ones about relationships. Love and loss."

"That's a big market, I hear," I said.

"Tell me about it. I support it big-time."

We both laughed. Nancy's gaze moved somewhere over my right shoulder. My heart jumped. I figured Mr. Stud was standing behind me. Couldn't be. I turned my body in the chair.

Vicki was standing there behind me.

"You scared me," I said. "I didn't expect to see you here."

Vicki scowled. "I bet not."

Oh, shit. What now?

"Aren't you going to introduce me to your date?"

"No, no. She's not a date," I protested. "It was an impromptu thing. We just decided to get some coffee after work."

"So *this* is what you're busy with? Why you dropped Max off in such a hurry?"

"Hey, listen, what Bryce is telling you is right. That's all there is to it," Nancy said.

Vicki was standing beside our table now. She looked Nancy over. "Not quite your type, is she, dear?"

"Vicki, stop," I said. "Why are you acting like this? This has nothing to do with you. Some intense stuff has been happening at work. What I told you was true. It's been very stressful."

"It's funny that you call me a whore, and then you're out parading around with this slut."

Nancy stood up. "Now, wait a minute."

Vicki stood her ground. "Sit down, you little —"

"You say it, I'll kick your ass," Nancy said.

I stood up and somehow managed to get in the middle of them. Everyone in the place had stopped what they were doing to watch. I felt the heat in my face rise.

"Vicki, *back off*," I said. "I don't know what set you off, but you're overreacting. This is uncalled for. You need to leave."

"Didn't you hear what this bitch called me, *honey?*"

The way she said the word turned my stomach. I put my hands on her shoulders and moved her a step back. My heart pounded in my chest.

Vicki looked at one of my hands and then the other.

"You don't get to touch me like that. In fact, you don't get to touch me at all. Why don't you go back to your plaything?"

Nancy stepped closer. "Listen, you —"

I was still between them but Vicki moved to one side.

"Kick my ass, was that it? That's what you were going to do?"

I moved between them again. My experience with Vicki and her anger suggested two thing were going to happen.

Tears started to form in Vicki's eyes. That was the first thing. She also wasn't about to cry in front of a room full of strangers.

"You can both go to hell. I'm out of here."

She stormed off. I watched her barrel through several people who had just entered the store and push the glass door so hard it smacked against the outer wall.

I turned back to Nancy. "I'm really sorry. I don't even know what that was about."

"That was your wife? *That's* the woman you're concerned about leaving you?"

I flinched when she said it. "Uh, yeah, that was her. But I've never seen her act that way, ever. I mean, she can have a sharp tongue, but that's pretty much only with me. I can't imagine what got into her."

"No need for you to apologize. You didn't do anything except try to break up an ugly catfight."

Nancy started to sit, but then said, "Maybe I'd better go. I was really enjoying our talk. Perhaps another time. Enjoy your coffee."

"Wait, are you sure? Can't we pick up where we left off?"

Nancy looked around. Most people had gone back to their conversations. "That whole scene...my adrenaline is flowing overboard. I don't need to add caffeine fuel to the fire."

"Maybe just sit for a few minutes, then?"

"Listen," Nancy said, "don't worry about me. I feel worse for you. I probably shouldn't say that since you said it wasn't typical, but...."

I sighed. "I understand. Like you said, perhaps another time."

I watched Nancy leave the store. I straightened the table out and sat down, hard. I felt like I was starring in *The Twilight Zone*. First, my discussion with Wendy, now this scene with Vicki. I rolled my shoulders to release some tension.

There it was again. The *unreality.* Someone was pulling strings. I got up from the table and grabbed my coffee. I dropped it in the trash on the way out the door.

CHAPTER SIXTY-SIX

WHAT I NEEDED WAS A long, quiet walk. I needed to get some thoughts together. Maybe a run. I hadn't done that in years.

I decided I should grab a pair of sneakers, so I headed home. Once there, I killed the engine in the Prius and sat in the parking lot. Drops of rain began to tap the windshield and roof. I wasn't sure why I was sitting there. Someone had used the word "surreal" in a conversation recently. I didn't remember who had said it, but it sure felt appropriate for my world right now.

I walked down the sidewalk, feeling the rain on my face. It felt cool and refreshing. Maybe that's what I had been waiting for. I put the key in the lock.

My key didn't work.

"Damn it!" Scooch had changed the lock, and I forgot to pick up my key at the office. Too late now, it was closed. I checked my mailbox. There was an unmarked envelope along with some junk mail. I tore it open. There was a key and a short note.

> *Dr. Davison: I figured you forgot to stop by and get your key. I've stored it in one of the package boxes near the office. This key will give you access.*

Very thoughtful. I walked down the sidewalk and looped around a row of townhouses toward the circle at the front of the development. The rain changed to a light mist.

I located the box and inserted the key. My new house keys were inside a small bag. I attached one to my keychain and stuck the other in my pocket. I removed the old key and dropped it in a nearby garbage receptacle.

Tonight would have been a good night to walk Max. While she didn't like baths or thunderstorms, she didn't mind light rain. She enjoyed puddles like a little kid. I turned the corner to head down my street. Like the other night, someone was standing on my porch.

It was Vicki. And she looked pissed.

"What are you doing here?"

"I figured you might bring her here. I shouldn't have let her talk to me like that. I should have let her have it."

"Vicki, you can't be serious. You want to pick a fight with a woman you never met before? What sense does that make?"

Vicki looked away. "You've never said those things to me before."

"Which ones?"

"You said I could learn a lot from her. How she made you feel things you never felt before. How she made me look...frigid."

I stepped closer and put my hands on Vicki's arms. "I never said those things. I *wouldn't* say those things. Does that sound like something I would do?"

Vicki looked at me. "No...but you've been acting really strange lately. Stranger than usual. I figured you were getting back at me."

"For shacking up with what's-his-name?"

Vicki shrugged away from my hands. "Yeah, see? There it is. The hostility. You act all concerned, and then — *wham* — the sarcastic comments come out. You're a piece of work. And you wonder why I don't want to be around you."

She may as well have slapped me.

"I'm sorry to hear that. I didn't know your opinion of me had dropped so low. You'd probably better go before I really embarrass you."

Vicki scowled and pointed a finger at me. "You remember this, Bryce. I'm done being civil to you." She stormed off.

I watched her walk away.

I started to put the key in the lock but changed my mind. I no longer cared about my sneakers. Time to go to the hotel. I blew out a breath and headed to the parking lot, thinking.

If what I just experienced with Vicki was her idea of *civil*, I was in for a rough ride.

CHAPTER SIXTY-SEVEN

LARRY, WENDY, AND I MET in my office. Wendy shared an update on Maegan from the unit report, looking almost entirely at Larry. She noted that Maegan had a hard night. Difficulty falling asleep, nightmares when she did, and crashing with exhaustion very early in the morning.

"Do we want to go forward with the hypnosis today?" Larry asked.

"I think we should strongly consider it," I said. "Every day that goes by without progress, there is more opportunity for Maegan or someone else to get hurt. Or for the second attacker can escape."

"Will her mental state affect her ability to use the hypnosis, Dr. Davison?"

Larry glanced at Wendy with a puzzled expression. He knew she was speaking to me differently. I felt like I did when Vicki had dripped the word "honey" in an exaggerated fashion. I took a breath.

"Good question, Wendy. It might affect her level of guardedness, but that's not necessarily a bad thing. Ultimately, we should leave it up to her. If she is willing to do this, then we need to respect that."

"Same observers?" Larry asked.

"Seems reasonable. No new additions."

"I agree," Larry said. "Lieutenant Dean wants to meet with us right after this. Wendy, we'll see you over in the outpatient area in a bit."

"I'm on it. I need to make sure there is enough coverage upstairs. When I came down earlier, they were short. Nancy is out. Someone said her husband called her off. So a temp was filling in while calls were made to get backup."

"Nancy's not married, is she?" I said to Larry.

He scratched his head, his brow knit. "Maybe someone misunderstood. Main thing right now is coverage." He turned to Wendy. "Good idea. Go up there, make sure there are enough bodies. On my authority, pull from other units as needed."

Wendy nodded and left the room. Larry followed a moment later and returned with Lieutenant Dean.

"Doc. How are things looking for the second interview?"

"As long as Maegan gives us consent, we're good to go. Poor kid had a rough night, though. I would understand completely if she decided to forego the added stress."

"Not me. We need to bag this guy. And if she backs out today, it just leaves her out there as the number one target. I don't like it one bit, and I don't have the manpower to provide a one-on-one officer."

"We're short-staffed ourselves today," Larry said., "but Maegan doesn't need to know about police staffing shortages. We have her covered closely."

"The main thing is, I don't want her to feel pressured to perform," I said. "She has a deep survival instinct, though. She'll do whatever it is that she needs to do. Is there anything else we need to discuss before I prepare her for the session?"

"Not that I can think of. We'll talk afterward," Lieutenant Dean said.

I left Larry and the detective on the lower level and made my way outside and up the hill to Maegan's unit. She was out of bed and a bit disheveled, but otherwise, she seemed alert.

"Hi, Maegan. Can we talk for a few minutes?"

"Not sure how much talking I want to do." The skin under her eyes was darker and her affect was flat.

"Not a problem. Let's go into the small conference room." Although her body gave all outward appearance of lethargy, Maegan's eyes were bright. I sensed she was ready to go.

"The plan is to continue with the hypnosis from yesterday. You did such a great job with this, even when we were interrupted. That shouldn't be a problem today."

"I might fall asleep" Maegan replied. "I'm pretty beat."

"Well, that's possible, but not likely. There's only one question to answer. Do *you* feel up to doing this? There's nothing that can't wait until later."

"No. I want to get this over with. I'm crazy scared every day, but with this shit, it makes it even worse. Know what I mean?"

"I think I do. We can protect you better once we identify the other person involved...."

"Well, let's go, then. Before I change my mind."

CHAPTER SIXTY-EIGHT

MAEGAN AND I SETTLED INTO the same chairs in the outpatient consulting room.

"Just a reminder that there are people watching us through the mirror" I reminded her. "Do I have your permission to proceed?"

Maegan nodded.

"Great, thank you. I'd like to remind you that you're in charge of this process. If anything makes you uncomfortable, you can stop. Yesterday we established a couple of nonverbal signals. Lifting the index finger on your right hand indicates discomfort or 'no.' Lifting the middle finger on your right hand indicates agreement or comfort or yes. Are you okay with that?"

Maegan nodded again.

"When you're ready, just take in a slow, deep breath. As you begin to breathe out, just let your eyes close. When you begin to move into that place of internal calm and comfort, the middle finger on your right hand will float up."

I watched Maegan move through these preliminary steps. When she exhaled, her body visibly shifted lower in her chair, as if her body became heavier. Within a few moments, the middle finger on her right hand lifted in a jerky motion. Smooth movement is characterized as deliberate. Jerky movement is interpreted as involuntary or unconscious.

"Very good, Maegan. You may find it comfortable to return to the garden spot you recently visited. Sitting on the bench. When you're there, the middle finger can float up."

Maegan's middle finger lifted.

"Good. What's happening in the garden, on the bench?"

Maegan licked her lips. "Just...just sitting. Pretty flowers. Bees and butterflies."

"Very good. What are you doing there?"

"Just sitting. Looking. I'm...I'm waiting for someone." She tilted her head to the right. "I think someone's coming." I waited.

Maegan's breathing rate increased. Her facial muscles grew taut. Her hands squeezed her legs. She opened her eyes and started to sob.

I moved my chair closer to her. "Maegan, what is it?"

Maegan looked at me, tears streaming down her face. "It...was...Tom. *That sonofabitch Tom!*"

CHAPTER SIXTY-NINE

I WAS AWARE OF TWO things. Maegan crying and me moving beside her, handing her a tissue. And a commotion in the next room. I heard chairs moving, feet pounding on the floor, shouting. I stood up and locked the door.

Footsteps pounded down the hallway past it.

Maegan's eyes were wide. Tears continued to flow. She kicked her feet forward and pushed her chair back toward the corner. I stepped between her and her line of sight toward the door.

"It's okay, Maegan. I won't let anything happen to you. We're good here for the time being." Maegan looked at me. I thought I saw her eyes begin to glaze. "Right, Maegan?"

Her eyes cleared. She nodded yes. Then lowered her face and covered it with her hands. I pulled my chair closer and sat with her.

A few minutes later there was a soft knock on the door. I looked at Maegan, who was wiping her eyes and blowing her nose. "Be right back," I said.

"Who is it?" I asked through the crack between the door and the frame.

"It's Larry. Can you step out for a minute?"

I opened the door and closed it all but a crack.

"Tom's gone," Larry said. "He was sitting nearest the door. When Maegan identified him, he bolted. Pulled down a couple chairs in front of the door on his way out. He made it to the back corridor before any of us could get there. Dean and a couple of outpatient staff are still back there."

"Do you need me back there?"

"No, I need you where you are. How's Maegan?"

"She's doing okay. She's staying connected. But the emotion is hitting her hard. I expect it to get rougher. We're going to need to keep the staffing up."

"And we will. What's your immediate plan?"

"I'm going back in there with her. Debrief. Let her know what to expect. Then we should have Wendy take her up to the unit."

"I'll arrange it."

I closed the door behind me and sat back down in my chair.

"Did we nail the bastard?" Maegan asked, sniffling.

"Sounds like he got into the back hallways. No update after that."

"Should I be worried? I mean, *more* worried?"

"No. We'll keep someone with you. Tom won't be able to get to you or even on the unit. He'll be recognized too quickly to be anywhere near here."

"I never did anything like this before."

"The hypnosis?" I asked.

"Well, that. And I never ratted on someone before. Well, Jimmy. But not before that."

"Do you regret it?"

"No. What they did was wrong." She rubbed the scars on her forearm. "Thing is, other people have done bad stuff. I never ratted them out, though. Kept it inside. Even when I hurt myself."

"Something has changed, Maegan. You've drawn a line, and if people cross it, that's on them. Asking for help when someone hurts you isn't ratting on someone else. That's what people who bad things try to get you to think. But only those people — those perpetrators — are accountable for what they did to you. What they do to anybody."

"People have said shit like that to me before. Other shrinks. I never listened. Why should I listen now?"

"There are moments where change becomes possible. Maybe it's the right situation. The right time of your life. The right people around you. Something different inside you."

Maegan watched me while I answered her. I thought I saw a slight nod of her head.

"Maegan, can you tell me what else happened, please? Now that we know that Jimmy and Tom were involved. Would you tell me, or would you rather tell someone else?"

"Nah. I can try. To tell you, I mean. Am I going to still work with Wendy?"

"You can, yes. Do you want to?"

Maegan nodded. "She's nice enough. I think she cares about me. She hasn't said any therapy shit to me."

"She deals with you honestly."

"Yeah. Like that. But I don't want to go through this ten times. Can Wendy be here for this part?"

"Yes. There's a phone on the wall. Let me find her."

A few minutes later, there was a knock at the door.

"Who is it?" I asked.

"Wendy."

I opened the door. Wendy entered with several bottles of water. She handed one to Maegan and one to me.

"Great, thank you, Wendy. Pull up a chair. Maegan's going to tell us what happened. She wanted you here so she doesn't have to keep repeating it."

"I understand. Thanks for letting me be here, Maegan."

Maegan held up her bottle of water. "Got any Bud Light?"

Wendy looked at me. I smiled. She looked back at Maegan. "No Bud Light for you. Water is healthier."

Yeah, I figured. Can't blame me for trying." She took a swig of water, wiped her mouth with her sleeve, and sighed. "I'm really tired of this shit."

"Which shit?" I asked.

Maegan pushed back against her chair and blew out a breath. "All of it. My life since I was eight years old. Going from one shit-storm to another. Everyone taking advantage of me. Doing bad stuff to me. I'm tired of it all."

"I can't imagine that you wouldn't be tired of it all. You've had a lifetime of shit-storms so far. But I'm guessing this is different."

Maegan frowned. "Different how?"

"You're taking charge. You're in a position to get the people who did these things to you here. You're not shying away from it. What you're doing takes great courage."

Maegan looked from me to Wendy and then back again.

"You're not bullshitting me, are you?" she asked, more incredulous than confrontive.

"No, I'm not. I'm telling you how I see it."

Maegan took a deep breath.

"Okay. It would happen like this. First Jimmy would come into my room. He would talk to me, you know, like sweet talk. But I knew he wasn't being sweet. Because the last time. He was pulling at me. Pulling on my pants. I started hitting and kicking him. But he was too strong. Too strong for me. He pinned my arms down. I was on the bed. I kept trying to get him off me. Kicking at him. I tried to knee him in the balls."

Maegan's breath became erratic. Her shoulders heaved. She closed her eyes, tight.

"Just breathe, Maegan. Stay with it. Stay with us."

Maegan nodded. Wendy gripped the arms of her chair. I had crossed my legs and was holding onto my knee.

"Maegan, Wendy and I are breathing, too. We're staying with you. Go on when you're ready."

Maegan opened her eyes, but looked at her lap. "Tom came in. He got behind me. The fucker held my arms! The fucker!" Maegan spat these words and pounded the arms of the chair. She screamed.

My heart pounded. I wanted to comfort Maegan. I looked at Wendy, who sat with tears in her eyes. Maegan knew we were with her. We needed to sit tight and follow Maegan's lead.

Maegan sobbed. She looked at me through tears and said, "How could he do that to me?"

"What he did was the worst violation any human being could do. He should not have hurt you like he did. I am so sorry, Maegan. He'll get punished for what he did."

Wendy nodded. She leaned in and rubbed one of Maegan's arms. "You are so brave. So brave."

Maegan reached for Wendy, who leaned forward in her chair. The two held each other. I tried to gather myself, to sort the emotional intensity from the therapeutic direction.

This is the hardest work a therapist could ever do.

I kept breathing. Kept my eyes open. I watched Maegan.

After a few minutes, Maegan pulled back. Wendy let go of her and sat back in her chair.

"He would hold my arms down while Jimmy...Jimmy did the nasty."

She looked off in the distance and then added, "And then they both left me there."

I nodded. Waited.

"Tom told me...that son of a bitch told me...if I told anyone...he would kill me."

CHAPTER SEVENTY

I PACED AROUND LARRY'S OFFICE. Lieutenant Dean was on the hunt for Tom and had called for support to the residential facility.

"Larry, I'm so pissed. That twisted bastard was right under our noses. Who knows what else he's done? Shit!"

"We almost had him. I didn't see him in the mix. If he hadn't been so close to the door, he'd be in handcuffs by now."

Larry looked like he had aged beyond the last week of real time. He had circles under his eyes, and he looked gaunt.

"Run me through what you learned from Maegan."

"It was rough, Larry. Hard to listen to. That girl is so brave. She managed to tell Wendy and me how it happened." I paused to take a breath.

"Sometimes Tom would stand guard when Maegan and Jimmy had sex. He also restrained Maegan at least twice. And on one occasion, he had Maegan perform oral sex on him."

"Do you think any of the other kids on the unit knew what was going on? Staff?"

"I don't think so—no kids. That kind of secret doesn't stay quiet for long. It would slip out—someone blurting it out. If someone knew, he or she would try to use it for payback. To get back at Jimmy or Tom. Information leaks out unless there is significant threat associated with breaking the silence. As for the staff...God, I hope not. Do we know anything from staffing patterns yet?"

Larry shook his head. "We're still pulling it together. We need more time and more eyes."

"It's hard to deal with something when it keeps piling on," I said. "What's next from your perspective?"

"We're in crisis intervention mode as an agency, both with the kids and with outside agencies—the police; the Office of Children, Youth, and Families; and state personnel in Harrisburg. We're under the microscope."

"How are you doing, Larry?"

"This is the worst week ever for me as a medical director. But I'll deal with it. It's my job. As a physician, though, this cuts me to the core. How someone in a position to provide care can do something like that to a kid." He looked at me. "It's pure evil."

A phone call interrupted our discussion. While Larry talked, I turned my attention to Tom. Not the fact that he was on the loose, but that he had been among us during this whole time.

Larry's voice smacked me out of my trance. "That was Lieutenant. Dean. They looked for Tom at his house. No one was there, but the front door was wide open. From the looks of things, he was prepared for all this. He probably had a vehicle parked in the back in case he had to get out through the old loading dock." He stabbed at a pad with his pen. "I'll deal with the police. You'll be of more use on the unit. If the investigators need to talk to you, I'll know where to find you."

The air in the building went stale. I needed to step outside for a minute or two and collect myself. I noticed my hands were shaking. The tingling sensations told me a panic attack was imminent.

I pushed through the main entrance and stumbled toward the street. I sat on a low retaining wall and focused on diaphragmatic breathing. It was difficult at the moment, but I knew I wasn't alone. Everyone, from Maegan to the cafeteria staff, was dealing with the fallout.

I was tired, but I was needed. I stood up, dusted myself off, and headed up the hill.

CHAPTER SEVENTY-ONE

WE WERE BACK TO SQUARE one: extra staff and stressed-out kids. There were clusters of kids in various corners being brought up-to-date by team leaders. I moved from group to group to observe, listen, or answer questions if any were directed to me. Some kids were afraid of being harmed or abandoned. Others were more stoic and pointed out that recent events were just more evidence that life sucks.

I held several small group debriefing sessions for staff members. The most powerful tool available was information, along with shared common experiences and education about stress responses. People needed to know that their reactions were normal and not to expect things to change in a short time. I even shared my personal reaction—running outside to deal with a panic attack—and reminded staff to take care of the kids, themselves, and each other.

In between all that, I checked in with Maegan. Wendy had taken a bathroom and hydration break, so a staff member from another unit was sitting with Maegan.

"How are you doing, Maegan?"

She looked around the unit. "I feel like I did this to everyone."

"Nope, not you. *Tom* did. Jimmy did. What you did was protect people. If you hadn't spoken up, who knows what would have happened?"

"It still sucks."

"It does. And it probably will for quite a while. But there's other stuff going on. Good stuff."

"Yeah? Name one."

"First, a reminder about the obvious. Here I am sitting with you. A day or two ago, all this would have pushed you into a black hole big time. I wouldn't have been able to sit here and ask you even simple questions."

"I get it. You're going to say that I'm handling things better."

"I am saying it. Does it make it therapy shit?"

Maegan looked me over. "No. I think you're being straight with me."

"I am. Here's the other part. Do you know why you work with hypnosis so well?" I asked.

"Nope. At least I don't think so."

"It's something that you've been doing for a while now. You just never called it hypnosis."

Maegan sat, quiet, for a few moments. "Do you mean when I go away? When I go inside myself?"

"Exactly. You've had a lot of practice. We're just using your skill for a healthier outcome."

"You mean, for good and not evil? Like the Force or some shit like that?"

"Yes, like that. It's like one of your superpowers. You'll need more practice at figuring out how to use it for good."

"Damn," Maegan said, "A *superpower*. How about that."

CHAPTER SEVENTY-TWO

WHEN THE LATE-NIGHT SHIFT workers arrived, it was time to leave. The kids were in bed, Maegan had coverage, and most extraneous staff had already cleared out. I said goodnight to people at the desk and peeked into the conference room.

Larry was still there, an empty pot of coffee nearby.

"You spending the night?" I asked.

Larry jumped.

"Sorry. Didn't mean to spook you," I said. "I just wanted to let you know that I'm calling it a night."

Larry nodded. "Come on in for a minute."

I sat down across the table from him. He rubbed his eyes and looked at the coffee pot.

"Quite a day again," he said. "You and your therapists did yeoman work today."

"It was 'all hands' again. Lots of people pitching it. But I'm proud of my team, if that's an appropriate description."

"Yeah. It fits. I don't know how long it will take for this place to get on the other side of this. We have our work cut out for us."

"It would help if Tom's ass was in jail," I said.

"Out of our control, I'm afraid," Larry said. "We have to focus on what's here in front of us. Trust is broken. We have to repair it. Find a way past the violations, if we can."

Larry paused at that point and stared at me. The hair on the back of my neck stood up.

"What do you suggest?"

He broke eye contact and looked at the pile of paper in front of him.

"We come back tomorrow and keep chipping away."

I was about to ask him what he meant when a staff person I didn't recognize burst into the room.

"Dr. Jones, Dr. Davison, a message just came in...it's for Dr. Davison. It's from Tom."

CHAPTER SEVENTY-THREE

I SAT UP IN MY chair. Larry knocked over an empty paper cup.

"Here," the staff member said, "let me call it up on this phone." She punched in some buttons and then stood beside the table, waiting.

"This is your assistant unit director, Tom," said Tom's disembodied voice through the speaker. "I'm calling to leave a message for Bryce Davison. Bryce, if you're listening, I want you to know that I'm sorry I wasn't able to chat with you before I had to leave so abruptly. I've been watching you, you know, and I've come to appreciate that you've taken notice of Nancy. I think that's great. Has anyone noticed that Nancy hasn't been to work?

"Well, let me get to the point. I have her, and whether she lives or dies is up to you, doc. But it's going to be only you. No police. If I believe that you have involved the cops, that's the end of the story. And her blood will be on your hands. You'll get my next message on your cell phone. Tomorrow. To the rest of the staff, hey, nice knowing you. Sorry it had to come to this. I wasn't done doing my good work on the unit. Shit happens."

Larry picked up a pen and clicked it several times. The room felt small, like the walls were closing in. My mind was foggy. Pressure built in my chest. I stood up, started to pace.

"He's calling me out," I said. "He's accusing me of something, and no matter what I do, he's going to be in control."

"We've got a staff member in jeopardy," Larry said. "We have to be careful how we proceed."

"We have to call Lieutenant Dean. We need his guidance here."

"I have his number." Larry punched in the phone number on speakerphone.

"Dean."

"Lieutenant, it's Lawrence Jones. I have Dr. Davison here with me. We just got a phone message from Tom. He claims to have kidnapped another staff member. His message was directed at Bryce. He told him to involve no police and that his next message will be via Bryce's cell phone."

"He really wants to up the ante, doesn't he? That could mean he's desperate, volatile."

"It could also mean he's acting outside of reason," I added. "His logic is twisted by his anger. He's directing at me but I have to wonder how much I have to do with it."

"What do you mean?" Lieutenant Dean asked.

"I'm guessing he has other issues that are driving his behavior. Whatever his beef with me is, it's a surface thing. He has longstanding conflict or trauma pushing him."

"I'd have to agree," Larry said. "So he's desperate and unstable. That puts anyone who deals with him at risk, including Nancy *and* Bryce."

"What do you think, doc? Are you up to dealing with this guy? It's going to have to look like you're on your own, but we'll figure out a way to keep you covered. But it's a huge risk for you."

"I need to do this to help Nancy, if I can," I said. "I don't even know what the next step is, and I'm scared. But I have to do this."

"Well, let's see what tomorrow brings," Dean said. "I think it would be best if you get in touch with me through a phone other than your own. Can that be worked out?"

"We have extra cell phones that we make available to staff at different times. Bryce can use one of those. I'm not even sure Tom would know about those."

"Great. Get him one. Dr. Davison, we'll talk tomorrow."

CHAPTER SEVENTY-FOUR

I CHECKED INTO MY HOTEL room and dropped onto the bed. I was beat, but my mind and gut were in overdrive. The residue of the day seeped from my pores.

I stripped off my clothes, turned the shower on, and cranked up the temperature. I stepped into the water and stood with my palms against the shower wall, letting the water cascade over me. My back and neck muscles strained beneath my skin. I turned the showerhead to pulse and let the hot water pound a staccato beat against my body.

"Damn it!" I yelled, and slammed my fist on the shower wall.

What Tom did to Maegan was heinous. It was Tom whom I wanted to pound. For all the posturing he had done in the phone call, he was still a coward, as bullies often are. He had notches on his belt for a minor and a defenseless woman. I was determined to make the next step more difficult for him, whatever it was.

I soaped up and rinsed off. I toweled off and didn't bother with clothes. I turned down the bedcover, shut off the light, and crawled into bed.

CHAPTER SEVENTY-FIVE

THE SUN STREAMED THROUGH THE partially closed blinds. I swung my feet over the edge of the bed and sat for a few moments. *What day was it?* The last days were so long, one flowed into another.

But I had to keep going. People were counting on me.

I got dressed and headed out the door. I drove toward Cracker Barrel. At least I was going to start the day in a pleasant manner. I ordered a breakfast platter and some hot tea. As I sipped the tea, I wondered how long it would take before Tom contacted me. I had my phone in one pocket and the work phone in the other. I should have asked for a holster.

My left pocket vibrated. Personal cell. I pulled it out of my pocket and glanced at the screen. NARP. I thumbed the "answer" icon.

"Hello."

"Dr. Davison, Lieutenant Dean. How did you sleep?"

"On edge, I think. I had to take a hot shower before I crashed for the night to get some kinks out."

"You sound like a cop. Welcome to my world."

"Give me a badge and I'll see what I can do. What's up, Lieutenant?"

"Just getting my ducks in a row for the day. Do you have the spare phone with you?"

"Yep. Fully charged. I'm ready for whatever comes next."

"Good. Call me the second you hear something."

My food came, and I took my time with it. One more cup of tea.

I was paying the bill when my left pocket vibrated again.

"Hello?" I stepped out on the porch.

"Hey-ho, Bryce. You know who this is. Are you ready to follow my instructions?"

"How's Nancy?" I asked.

"She's fine. I haven't hurt her...too much."

"You'll answer for whatever you've done. You can't get away —"

"Oh, but I did get away. Ran right out of the building, even though there was a detective no more than fifteen feet away from me. Don't you remember that?"

"Yeah, I remember. I was getting evidence to put you away. Which is what's going to happen."

"Don't count on it. Who's going to put me away? You? But quit stalling. Here's what I want you to do. I want you to drive to Pinemist Park. Come to cabin six. Alone. I don't want to see anyone else. You don't do this right, Nancy dies. And you will, too. Understand?"

My hand was shaking. I pushed the phone against my ear to try and steady it.

"I got it. I'll see you at two."

I sat down on a rocking chair and called the lieutenant.

"Dean."

"It's Bryce. He called me. He wants me to go to one of the cabins in Pinemist Park at two."

"Interesting choice. That's outside the checkpoints we've set up. He knows his way around. So here's what we're going to do. I want you to meet me out by the abandoned office building on 711. You know where the veterinary hospital is?"

"I do. I've had my dog there for checkups."

"Be there at one. We'll get you fixed up. I want you wearing a transmitter so we can keep tabs on what goes on, and to record the conversation. I want you in a different vehicle, too, in case he's messed with yours — mechanically, or hiding a recording device, whatever."

"I still have a couple of hours. What do I do until then?"

"Just get ready. What you're about to do isn't a normal day at work."

"Those days are gone, Lieutenant. None of them have been normal lately."

CHAPTER SEVENTY-SIX

I SAT IN THE ROCKING chair for a half-hour, focusing on the rhythm of the movement and listening to the creak of the floor with each forward motion. I was going over scenarios in my head for what might go down. I may as well have spent my time picking lottery numbers.

I didn't know how things would unfold. I just knew I could get killed.

My gut rumbled and my palms were sweaty. I took some deep breaths to steady myself and decided it would be more helpful to consider how I might deal with Tom. I thought about what Larry and said. *Unstable and desperate.* If this was a crisis call, how would I deal with it?

Not the same, I reasoned. My goal in a crisis call was to assess and divert a negative response. I needed to get my patient to the other side of distress so that there could be a positive outcome. With Tom, I needed a positive outcome, but for *me*.

He would have a weapon. I would have only my wits.

I considered the two recent phone contacts. Tom sounded arrogant. Sure of himself. Invincible. I needed to attack his bravado and his narcissism. But that would enrage him. He could go off script, and that would be the end. If I did challenge him, it either needed to be a last resort, or he had to be in a position that I could overpower him. Could I even do that?

I had done it with Mr. Stud. I thought I was going to buy the farm that time, but I worked out of it. Could I do it again? If I failed, did I have my affairs in order? I had a will. Vicki was the beneficiary for whatever I had.

Did I need to say good-bye to people?

That brought tears to my eyes, which I wiped off. I pulled my cell out and called my mother.

I got her answering machine. That added tension to my neck and shoulders. I took a breath and left a message.

"Hi, Mom. Just checking in on you. Sorry I missed you. I…was thinking about what it was like growing up. Thanks for doing such a good job. That's all. A little nostalgic, I guess. I'll, uh…well, I'll talk to you soon. And Max and I will be down for a visit. Soon. I love you."

I tucked the phone away. I had chickened out with what I wanted to say, which only would have scared the poor woman. I said I loved her. That's mainly what I wanted her to know.

I pulled the phone out again. Called Vicki. No answer, but he voicemail kicked in.

"Hey, Vicki. I know you've had Max for longer than you probably figured. I hope to get her soon. Give her an ear rub for me. Hope you guys are okay…."

Was it sad that I only had two calls to make? Or was I doing better than average? I sighed and got up from the chair.

I drove to a place where I could wait until I met the lieutenant. I entered the bookstore and ordered an iced coffee. While it was being made, I walked to the magazine section and picked up a sports magazine and a science magazine. I took the back to a table and picked up my coffee at the counter.

By the time I had finished both magazines and my coffee, it was time to go.

There were a couple cars in the parking lot when I got there. A van and a sedan. Lieutenant Dean opened the sedan door and waved.

"We're going in here for a minute." He slid open the side door of the van and motioned for me to climb in.

"Dr. Davison, meet Smitty. Smitty's going to hook up a transmitter. While he sets you and tests the system, we're going to run through our game plan."

Smitty, a young cop in casual clothes, asked me to unbutton my shirt. As he did his thing, Lieutenant Dean told me what to expect.

"I've talked to people who know the park inside and out. There are a couple of old maintenance roads that aren't on the map. They have gates, but it wouldn't take much time to disable them. They're more to remind people to keep out. Smitty and I are going to come in via those roads. Cabin six sits at the end of a cul-de-sac. We should be able to get in tight to keep an eye on you. I need you to get Tom to talk. Any information that we get would be great. He might divulge something important."

I rolled my head and tried to flex my shoulders. "And if he decides he's done talking?"

"Yeah, that's the difficult piece. If you can bolt for the door, do it. If he's in close, try and hit him in the Adam's apple, like this," he said, miming a knuckle punch. "The element of surprise also works in your favor. You've done suicide prevention, right?"

"Yes. Lot of hours on the phone late at night."

"That gives you an advantage. You have experience talking people off the ledge. I need you to fall back on your instincts." Lieutenant Dean paused, and then put a hand on my shoulder. "I've noticed something about you. Something you probably already know, but, if not, I need you to think about. Got it?"

"Got it. What is it?"

"In your personal life, you're a bit of a mess. Your emotions work against you. Anxiety, fear, depression."

"It's been stressful lately, Lieutenant."

"I know. Everything you've told me is turning out accurate. But here's the other part of the equation. When you've got your shrink hat on, you're a different guy. You're in control, you make good decisions, and you don't shy from difficult situations. I've met bunch of shrinks over the years, and I'd put you at the top. I need that guy out there at the cabin. Can you make that happen?"

Deep breath. "I hear you. I think you're right. I've usually put personal stuff aside when the shit hits the fan."

"Good, doc. Because the fan is running."

266

CHAPTER SEVENTY-SEVEN

I LEFT LIEUTENANT DEAN AND Smitty and drove the unmarked sedan toward Pinemist Park. I tried to focus on a mantra along the way.

I can handle this. I've been through worse.

I can handle this, I've been through worse.

It did help me focus, although I also felt the muscle tension and increased heart rate that accompanied me on the trip.

I had only been to Pinemist Park once before. I had rented a cabin with Vicki for a weekend a few years back when we wanted to get away for just a couple of days relaxation.

Now another woman was bringing me back.

I nearly jammed the brake pedal when I rounded a bend toward the park entrance. Blocking the road, right at the entrance to the park, was a police cruiser with lights flashing. Not state cops, though. Locals. Had I been set up? Would this cost Nancy her life?

The officer nodded at me as I rolled down my window.

"Afternoon, Officer. What can I do for you?"

"Turn off the car, please, sir. I'd like to see your license and registration."

"My license is in my wallet, but this isn't my car. I'm not sure where the owner keeps the registration card."

I handed over my wallet. The cop studied it.

"Step out of the car, please."

The cop motioned for me to stand at the side of the road. He spoke into a radio transmitter as he walked beside the car. He glanced at the license plate. A minute or two later, a second squad car pulled up. Out stepped another officer, who joined Cop Number One for a chat. Periodic glances in my direction ratcheted up my muscle tension.

Cop Number One wandered over, handed me my driver's license. "Sir, I would like to request your permission to search your vehicle."

"Like I said, it's not my vehicle." Was I stammering?

He nodded. "Sir, I'd like you to walk over to the vehicle with me and open the trunk."

"And if I refuse?"

The cop smirked. "Well, *sir,* I guess we'd have to make ourselves comfortable until the search warrant arrives."

I glanced at my watch. I popped the trunk, hoping that the police didn't store shotguns and ammo in there. The trunk was pristine. Not one speck of dirt. No weapons or ammo or surveillance equipment. Nothing Puzzled, the officer closed the trunk.

Cop Number Two approached.

"I tracked down the owner of the vehicle. You're going to love this. It belongs to the regional police. They tell me it's on loan to this guy. I don't know. It's what they said."

The first cop turned toward me.

"We received an anonymous tip that a man matching your general description would be entering the park carrying drugs and other contraband in the trunk of his vehicle. Although the car was totally wrong. Our caller said you would be driving a Prius. Sorry to have troubled you, sir."

He wished me a good day and moved his car aside so I could pass. I drove on through, my entire body trembling. In my rear-view mirror, the cops were talking again, watching me disappear down the lane.

Obviously Tom made the call. Was he just trying to slow me down? What would be the point? Trying to discredit me? Just playing with me? More blasted games.

Whatever it was, I had been saved—by Lieutenant Dean's cop instincts. I was certain, though, there were drugs in the trunk of my Prius.

The payoffs of paranoia. I would have the lieutenant take care of that.

As I approached the cabin area, I looked for cars. There was at least one vehicle parked near each cabin, so not much help there. Cars meant people. Potential witnesses. That wasn't a good sign. It seemed like poor planning, and I doubted Tom was doing any of this on impulse.

Rather than drive right up to the cabin area, I parked the car in a small lot reserved for visitors. That was me. I slid my work phone under the seat and closed the car door. It was a short stroll to the cabin. I stepped onto the porch and rapped on the screen door.

No answer. I knocked again. Silence. I tried the knob. It turned.

I stepped inside the cabin. It seemed clean. Lots of pine and oak. A breeze floated in through the screened side windows. I flashed back to my previous stay at the park—the getaway with Vicki. Right now those memories were just distractions.

I glanced in at one of the bedrooms, which looked to be the only room occupied. Was this for Tom, or had Nancy been in here?

"Well, Dr. Davison, so nice of you to pay me a visit."

I jumped at the sound of his voice.

Tom closed the door behind him and locked the handle. He showed me the key and smiled as he made a show of putting it in his pocket.

"You seem jumpy, doc. Not so cool in a crisis after all?"

"Yeah, you startled me. I'm pretty wound up right now." I spoke the truth. I hoped it helped. "Were the cops your idea?"

Tom smirked. "Yeah it was a test. I wanted to see what you would do. But I didn't think you'd get through it so easily. If you hadn't, I would have gone to Plan B. So no matter what you were able to do, I was ready for it."

"Weren't you concerned I'd get them to help me?"

Tom shook his head. "I've known guys like you all my life. You're stuck inside this goody-goody box. You always do what someone in charge tells you to do. I knew you wouldn't ignore my instructions."

Tom was following his playbook. "Where's Nancy?"

Tom pulled a gun from the back of his pants. He motioned me toward the couch.

My heart pounded. My legs felt like cement. But I managed to shuffle toward the couch and sit down. I squeezed the arm of the couch to steady myself. It was hard not to look at the gun, but this was a crisis situation. I forced myself to make eye contact.

Tom was watching every movement.

"Nancy. Are you really here to talk about Nancy?"

"It's why I'm here, right? I'm following your instructions. So you can let her go. I expected her to be here with you."

"Yeah, I figured you would think that. No, she's safe…elsewhere. If I need a hostage for a bargaining chip, I can still get her."

"What do you need a hostage for? You've got me."

"Just covering all the angles. Right now, you're the one I want here. I've got a small window of time before I'm out of here. So we only have a little uninterrupted time together. Won't that be cozy? We can have, um, closure. You shrinks love closure, right?"

"Closure is good. I have some unanswered questions."

"I figured you might. Well, ask. I'll answer until I get tired of looking at you. But all fun and games aside, you're not leaving this cabin. There's no hero act for you. I didn't think you had the guts to sacrifice your life for someone. I figure it must be the hero angle, then. Being a hero *would* get you off. But we're not in Hollywood, doc."

He'll kill me, I realized. And I'm not going up against someone with a bat this time. My legs were trembling, and I pressed them together to try and stifle it. Words weren't coming. *Think*, damn it. I needed to be a shrink.

"All along. The calls. The emails. The perfume. The panties. All your doing?"

Tom dragged a side chair over near me and sat down. He kept the gun aimed at me.

"Everything that happened to you. *My* doing. Part of the plan. Toy with you. Push your doubts and fears. Drive you crazy. So fun to watch."

"But kidnapping? This? Those things aren't 'toying with me.' This is big-time sociopath behavior."

Tom stepped out of the chair toward me and back-handed the side of my face so hard my body lurched and the couch slid a few inches. I felt the blood rush to my face, and the stinging pain followed it.

"Don't label me. I'm beyond anything you could come up with."

I straightened and rubbed my face. I struggled to come up with something to say, but was interrupted by my cell phone buzzing in my pants.

"Let me see that," Tom ordered.

I pulled the phone from my pocket and saw "Mom" on the phone display. I handed it to him.

"It's your mother. Here, put it on speaker."

"What?"

He raised the gun. "Answer the phone on speaker."

What the hell?

"Mom?"

"Hi, Bryce. I got your message from earlier. I thought you sounded worked up. Everything okay?"

"Yeah...I was just thinking about the past, I guess. Mainly, I was just checking in. I was surprised not to reach you."

"I must have been in the bathroom at the time. I should have called you back right away. But it slipped my mind. I was thinking about other things and the time got away from me."

"No, that's fine. That happens to everybody."

"I know it does. But before I forget everything, I wanted to tell you someone was here to see you."

"Oh? Who? When?"

"A couple of days ago. Out of the blue."

"Who was it?"

"He said he was an old friend of yours. I think he said his name was John. No, Tom, was it? I should have written it down. He said that the two of you go way back together. It's funny, though, I don't remember hearing about him before."

"What did he want?"

"Well, he was disappointed you weren't here. He left something for you."

Chills cascaded down my spine.

"What is it?"

"Some lovely perfume. I asked him why he would be leaving perfume for you, but he said you would understand. Do you?"

I looked at Tom. He had a wicked grin on his face.

"It's an old joke between us. Back from our college days. Why don't you keep it?"

"Why, thank you. It has a nice, flowery smell to it. He and I chatted for a bit. He admired the atomic clock you got for me. I told him it was a godsend not to have to worry about climbing a chair to change the time."

Atomic clock? Tom had been in my mother's dining room?

"That's great, Mom. Sounds like you had a nice visit. Everything else okay?"

"Everything's fine. Come down and see me when you can. Love you."

"Bye. Love you, too."

"Touching, doc. So, your mother liked the perfume? It was a delivery I had looked forward to. Gave me more of a chance to see where the great doctor grew up." He pretended to blow smoke from the barrel of the gun. "Think I'll visit your mother again soon."

"You're a sick son of a bitch. If you harm her in any way, I'll—"

"Save your energy, asshole. You don't tell me what to do, and I don't care what you do. I could have killed her right then, but I didn't. Maybe that was bad on my part. I should have shot her. By the sounds of it, she's a little…forgetful. It would have been mercy killing, right?"

Arrogant son of a bitch.

"Truth? That visit was just part of the head games. It was before things went bad at work for me. Because of you. You've cost me so much. Today is payback. Don't worry about what I do afterwards. You won't be around to deal with it."

His words reflected increased intensity. I had to do something. I had no idea where my backup was.

"You've overestimated yourself, Tom. Assault and kidnapping aren't murder. Killing someone requires a different mindset."

"Again, *no*. You've *under*estimated me—like you have all along. I've already killed someone. Remember your buddy Raphael?" The gun no longer pointing at me. He rested his gun hand on the arm of the chair.

"*Y-You?* Why?"

"Yes, m-me," he said mockingly. "Because I hate shrinks, and I knew you were going to meet him. The suspicion would have been on you. But you ruined it. Like you've ruined things for me all along. *You're* the reason my life turned to shit. It's time for you to pay. I want you dead and I want your soul. And I'm tired of talking."

Tom stood up and lifted his weapon. I dove from the couch — and the front door seemed to explode from its hinges.

Someone's arm holding a gun appeared in the doorway. Tom looked at me, his face a mix of surprise and anger. I rolled to the side of his chair and watched from the floor. Tom turned his gun toward the door and fired. Two shots returned; each hit Tom in the chest. He spun toward me and collapsed on the floor.

Lieutenant Dean walked over, breathing hard, gun still trained on Tom. He kicked Tom's gun away and knelt to check for a pulse.

"He's dead."

He holstered his weapon and stepped over Tom's body to get to me. He offered a hand and helped haul me up from the floor.

I sat back on the couch and looked at Tom's body. Blood pooled on the floor around his chest.

"You okay?" Lieutenant Dean asked.

"I...think so. Hard to breathe."

"Give it a minute."

I scanned my body. "No damage. But I feel like the life was just sucked out of me."

Dean nodded. "I know that feeling. There's no easy way to go through something like this. But you'll get your breath and your senses back."

He looked at Tom's body and shook his head. "You handled it well. I was on my way in after he copped to the murder. I'm glad there weren't two."

"You and me both. Thanks, Lieutenant."

CHAPTER SEVENTY-EIGHT

SEVERAL ADDITIONAL POLICE CARS HAD arrived, lights flashing. Lieutenant Dean stood with me outside the cabin.

"How do we find Nancy now that Tom is dead?" I asked.

"It may take some time. I'm guessing that she's alive from what Tom was saying. We have no reason to believe anything he was saying, but at the same time, he had no reason to lie about that particular point."

"Now I know who was behind all of this crazy stuff happening to me. The strange thing is, I think Tom was blaming me for more than what happened at the residential unit. It was like he blamed his shitty lot in life on me. I don't get that."

"And what was that stuff about your soul?" Dean asked. "That seemed over the top, even for him."

"I'm sure it means something. I don't know that I have any brain cells left to figure it out, though. Although I hated every second of it, I was hoping he would tell me more about his thought process. Turns out he wasn't into sharing. I really don't think he had planned any other outcome than killing me."

"Things may make more sense in a few days as we gather more information. We'll run his prints, check for matches, see what our detective work gets us. We've got every cop in the adjoining counties and into Ohio looking for Nancy. Not your worry now. Maybe you should go home."

"It's been a while since I've been there. It's still a mess from when you guys were there and dusted up the place."

"You haven't been home since then? I'm sure your life didn't get any better in a hotel. Besides, it's not like you're going to move out, right? I mean, you have to clean it sometime."

"Yeah, maybe I will. I think I need some pet therapy. I'll see about picking Max up."

"Now you're talking. Give me a call tomorrow, and I'll fill you in on what I know. Oh, and I called Dr. Jones earlier to let him know you might miss a day or two of work. He asked me to let him know what happened out here. I'm going to tell him you were a hero after all. Anything else I should tell him?"

"Yeah, tell him my consulting fee is going up."

Lieutenant Dean laughed. "I'll have one of my guys give you a ride to your car. If you ask nicely, maybe he'll run the siren for you."

CHAPTER SEVENTY-NINE

MY POLICE ESCORT DROPPED ME at the office building. Before he pulled away, he rolled down the window and motioned me over.

"The lieutenant wanted me to let you know that he had someone clean out the coke and pot from your hatchback area. So you're good to go."

"Tell him thanks for me. I didn't need the hassle of having drugs in the car."

"Have a good rest of your day, sir."

I opened the car door but stopped to lean on it. The tension started to leak out. My eyes teared up, and I gasped for a breath. I sat down and hunched over, elbows on my thighs. *Just breathe.* It took six or seven slow breaths, but things started to stabilize after a moment. The calm after the storm.

And then something else enveloped me. Something similar to what I'd felt after Larry's picnic. Tom was dead. Mr. Stud was in jail. I was alive, and I was free of my stalker burdens. I called Vicki.

"Oh, it's you. I got your message. I'm good with watching Max. She can stay forever as far as I'm concerned."

"That's why I'm calling. How about if I come and get her? Is now a good time?"

"Well, no, I don't think so. Wait...is something happening? You sound...different."

"Like what?" I asked.

"Like you're *excited* or something. I haven't heard you like this in ages."

"You won't believe what just happened to me. I just—"

"Spare me. I don't care what it was. If you got laid, fine by me. You don't have to brag."

"No, you don't understand, I just—"

"Listen. I'm on my way out. Meet me at your place. I'll drop off Max."

She hung up.

I had done better with Tom. What was it with Vicki and being civil?

I drove home. I didn't bother going in. I leaned against the wall by my front door and waited. I saw Vicki pull up a minute later. The next thing I heard was a deep "woof" as Max barreled up the sidewalk. She bowled into me as I bent down to greet her.

"Hi, Max, good to see you! It's been a while."

Max did a circle around me, sniffing.

"Who knows what smells are on there today, girl. But let's say good-bye to Mom."

I started toward the parking lot when I realized that Vicki was gone. She hadn't even bothered to say a word. I felt like shaking my fist at the parking lot and cursing, but it would have been lost with no audience.

Instead, I waved. "Forget her, Max. Let's go inside. I should warn you, though, it's still a mess. But I'll get you some fresh water and a couple treats. But in return, you have to help me clean the place up."

I opened the door and Max went in ahead. She looked up the stairs but then followed me into the laundry room. I filled her water bowl and dropped a couple dog biscuits in her dish.

"I'm going to check my email. It's been a while. And then I'll get us some dinner, and we'll figure out which room to clean first."

Max was about done with the entire bowl of water when I headed upstairs to my office. I was guessing it was probably the least messed up room in the place, but things were still in disarray. I booted up the computer and looked around. I couldn't suppress a smile. My house was messed up, but I was here, *alive*. And that felt good.

One message jumped out at me from a greeting card company: *Tom has sent you an e-card.* A message from the dead. Tom had made no attempt to hide his identity. He knew he had been discovered by then. And apparently his grandiosity was such that he had needed to heighten my anxiety another notch.

I clicked on it. It was a clown releasing a bunch of balloons.

Have you talked to your mother lately? the caption read.

"I have, as a matter of fact."

I forwarded the message to Lieutenant Dean.

The rest of the messages were run-of-the-mill. Not even a message from Vicki or anyone else. A slow week without stalker mail. I was going to go and change my clothes, but I lingered at the computer. I did something that I hadn't done in months. I opened up a chess game that I liked to play.

I played the computer. It was getting dark by the time I finished. I lost, but I didn't care.

"C'mon, Max," I said, looking toward her usual spot. She wasn't there or anywhere else in the room.

CHAPTER EIGHTY

I FOUND MAX DOWNSTAIRS ON her bed in the laundry room. I sat down beside her.

"What's the matter, girl? I asked.

She looked at me and lifted one of her front paws.

"What? You want to shake hands?" I took her paw and shook it. After I let go, she lifted it again.

"Not feeling well?"

I sat back against the washing machine and rubbed Max's belly.

"It's this place, isn't it? It doesn't smell like home right now. It smells like evil has been in here. Maybe tonight isn't the time to deal with it."

I got up and looked around the laundry room. There were some shirts hanging on a rack and some folded shorts and underwear in a basket that I hadn't carried upstairs yet. I got the overnight bag back out and started putting some clothes in it. I grabbed the handset from the table in the foyer, punched the speakerphone, and speed-dialed my mother.

"Hello?"

"Hey, Mom. What's going on tonight?"

"I just had the game show channel on. I was thinking about turning in. What's happening there?"

"Max and I were just talking. She suggested a visit. How about if we come down tomorrow morning?"

"That would be great. If I'm not on the porch, I may be watching TV. I'll see you two then."

It was a good plan. Max and I would get out of the house a while longer.

Max stood in the doorway, watching, tail wagging.

"Did you get all of that?"

I knew she was responding to the overnight bag. She knew that meant travel.

"Just a couple more things. I need your water bowl, your stuffed yellow doll, and some treats."

I put those items in a restaurant take-out bag that I found on a shelf, and we headed out the door.

On the way to the car, I said to Max, "Don't think you're going to get out of house cleaning so easily. We're just going to delay the inevitable a little while longer."

CHAPTER EIGHTY-ONE

MAX AND I WENT THROUGH a drive-through for breakfast. A sausage patty on a biscuit for me and a sausage patty for Max. I threw a mix CD in the changer, and we hit the interstate.

Traffic was brisk, but we made good time. As we drove up the street toward my mother's house, I craned my neck to see if she was on the porch. I didn't see her.

I hit the release button near the front seat for the hatch. I was going to go around and open Max's door, but she was already climbing onto my seat.

"In a hurry, are we?"

Max jumped down and then raced up the steps. She would have opened the door if she were able.

"Hey, don't worry, I'll get our stuff."

I grabbed the bags and walked up the stairs and onto the porch. Max moved up to the door so she could nose through it once there was an opening.

I turned the knob. It was unlocked. Did she forget again? I opened the door, and Max started down the hall.

"We're here!" I said, closing the door. I was about to follow Max down the hall, but there was no reason to. My mother was sitting on the loveseat in the living room.

"Hey, this is unusual," I said, walking through the doorway, "why —"

I stopped. Nancy was sitting across the room. She had a gun on her lap.

CHAPTER EIGHTY-TWO

"What's going on?"

"Have a seat," Nancy said. "I'll bring you up to speed."

Max peered in from the opposite doorway, then walked past Nancy, keeping her distance. When she had clearance, she took two running steps and jumped on the loveseat beside my mother. My mother's hand was shaking as she put it on Max's back. She touched the handle of her cane, which was leaning against the loveseat. Odd, because she almost always used her walker.

"Mom?" I asked, my voice cracking.

When she looked at me, I saw her cheeks were tear-streaked.

"I'm sorry, honey," she said. "She said she was from the church."

My chest felt tight.

"That's okay. I would have done the same thing. Don't worry. We'll be fine."

"Will we?" Nancy said.

"Nancy, what are you doing? Why are you here?"

"Things have gotten way off track. I'm improvising, big-time."

"My mother has nothing to do with whatever you're doing. Just let her go."

"I think it's too late for that. She knows too much."

"What could she possibly know?"

Nancy looked at my mother, who was focused on the carpet.

"Your mother and I have been having a chat while we waited for you. I figured she needed to know how you had turned out as an adult. Things that you wouldn't have told her."

My thoughts raced, but I couldn't corral them.

"I told her she probably thought you were a big-shot psychologist, but she was mistaken."

My mother looked at Nancy. "Bryce was never a big-shot about anything. Even when he won tournaments, he was a sportsman. He doesn't brag."

"Touching," Nancy said. But tell your son what I told you."

My mother turned toward me. "She said...you had failed her and her family. And because of you, bad things happened to her. I said that couldn't be true."

"It's not true," I said. "Ever since I've known Nancy I've tried to be kind to her. You even stayed overnight with me when you had nowhere else to go."

"Yeah, I stayed with him, but he couldn't keep his eyes off my ass the whole time."

"What? That never happened. I didn't do that."

"Liar!" Nancy hissed, thrusting the gun at me. My mother gasped. Max sat up, and I felt like I would collapse in my chair. My legs felt like rubber.

"Your son is a liar and a fraud," Nancy said.

My mother said nothing.

"How did I ruin your life, Nancy? Tell me that."

"That's easy. It all started with my mother."

"What about her?"

"You should know, *Doctor* Davison. You killed her."

CHAPTER EIGHTY-THREE

I STOOD. NANCY STOOD AS well, keeping her weapon pointed at me.

"Sit your ass down. And don't move again."

I hesitated.

"Bryce, please sit down," my mother said.

I sat, but I couldn't slow my pulse or my breathing. My body was in fight-or flight-mode, but I could do neither.

"You see, Mrs. Davison, my mother was a patient of your son. When I was a girl, Mommy killed herself. And your son did nothing to stop it."

Oh, shit. My suicide.

"She was your mother?"

Nancy nodded.

"Oh, Jesus, Nancy. I'm so sorry. I didn't realize. If I could have stopped that, I would have."

"Shut up! Shut up! You did nothing. *Nothing!*" The gun shook with each word.

I waited until I saw Nancy's breathing slow down before I spoke again.

"I'm sorry that I failed you. That must have been awful for you."

"Apology *not* accepted. And spare me the shrink talk."

"So you're here because your mother died and you blame me for it."

Nancy nodded. "The moment she died started me on this path. I've been planning my revenge ever since."

"Then let my mother go. I'm the one that failed you. She has nothing to do with it."

"You're missing the whole point. It's an eye for an eye. You killed my mother, I'm going to kill yours. You'll have to watch. But compared to me, your suffering will be brief, because you'll be next."

I tried but couldn't swallow.

My mother looked at me. "Don't worry about me, Bryce. I've lived a long life. You're the best. The joy of my life. And Max, too."

I couldn't stop my tears. "I'm sorry, Mom. It should never have come to this."

"He's right, Mrs. Davison. It *shouldn't* have come to this. Do you remember Tom?"

My mother nodded.

"Your son killed him, too."

My mother's eyes widened.

"You're twisting things, Nancy. Tom was killed by the police."

"You were there! It was all over the police band. It was on the news."

"Tom was going to kill me. He shot at Lieutenant Dean. That's why he's dead."

Nancy sprung from the couch and slapped the side of my face. My head snapped to the side, my ear ringing. Max jumped from the couch. When Nancy backed off, Max crept to my side and leaned against my legs. I pushed back against her.

I tried to take a breath.

"I'm sorry about Tom. It was a tragedy. You're upset. You lost a coworker."

"Coworker? *You killed my fucking brother.*"

CHAPTER EIGHTY-FOUR

I COULDN'T BREATHE. THIS COULDN'T be true. I didn't know how to respond.

"Oh my god, Nancy. I didn't know."

"Tom and I plotted and planned all these years," she said, laughing. "Tom, he wanted to just kill you right away. But I said no. I said we needed to ruin your life first. Like you ruined ours. Start with little things eating at you. Making you more anxious and paranoid. And you...you responded even better than I would have imagined. By the time I got done sending lewd emails to Dr. Jones, Wendy, and your so-called wife, you were going out of your mind. I did that. I wish I would have been there to see when they realized how sleazy you are. Of course, I *was* there when your wife stopped by to visit in the bookstore."

"How did you —?"

"Do you know how to work a smartphone?"

"You...all of that was you. Even the perfume?"

"*Especially* the perfume," she said. "It was my mother's favorite. She wore it all the time, probably even to therapy sessions. I bet you even remembered it when you first smelled it."

I recalled the confusion of that night. The odd feeling of recognition that I couldn't quite put my finger on.

"You were in my house."

"Many times. You were so easy to hack. You keep your freaking passwords under your mousepad!"

"How?"

"That brainless maintenance guy. I didn't have to do much. Just flash some skin. He was almost as easy as Flick."

My heart sank. "You set that up, too."

"Flick was a moron. But he took one for the team. It was worth it to get him on your trail. He latched on to you like a pit bull on a bone. That guy has...*serious* issues."

"How did you know Max and I were coming here?"

"I heard you call your mother. I was there, in your bedroom, waiting for you. But you never came in. That fucked up all my plans."

My stomach churned. Bile burned the back of my throat.

"Why Maegan?"

"Oh, *that*. Very unfortunate. Even though that bitch set him up, she should have been off-limits. Tom kept doing things outside the plan. He thought being spontaneous made things more dangerous. Like killing Dr. Raphael. I wouldn't have done that, either. The stupid shit. Maegan was another detour."

"She's just a kid."

Nancy picked up the gun again. "Oh, boo-hoo. So what? I know all about it. I lived that life."

And then mental puzzle pieces began to fall into place.

"How long?" I asked.

"Not much longer, I think. I want to be out of here once it gets dark. It will be easier to slip away."

"No...*how long did Tom abuse you?*"

Nancy looked as if I had smacked her.

"Wh—how...did you know?"

"What you just said. It struck a chord in me." A pause. "Tell me."

"After Mom died, Daddy started drinking. It was bad. So bad. Everything changed at home. Terrible things."

"Did Tom know your father was touching you?"

Nancy's arm with the gun dropped to her lap.

"I never told anyone any of this. How could you know?"

"You told me. Your words, your face...What you didn't say. It all came together. I'm a shrink, remember? I've seen that family dynamic before."

Nancy looked like a little lost girl.

"Did your therapist know?" I asked.

"I only went a couple times. Daddy didn't let me go after that."

"I'm sorry, Nancy. No one deserves what you went through."

Nancy looked at me. "That's how I created ribschild. I took a phrase I had heard and put a twist on it. Revenge Is Best Served CHILLED. I changed it to 'child' since I was Mom's daughter. Double meaning. Tom never appreciated it, but I thought it was pretty creative."

I was sitting with ribschild. Chills cascaded down my back.

Nancy lifted the gun and put it against her temple. "Now you know the whole story."

CHAPTER EIGHTY-FIVE

I SCRAMBLED TO MY FEET, almost falling over Max, who grunted and moved to my left. "Nancy, no! Put the gun down."

"Don't come any closer," Nancy said, not moving the gun.

"Okay," I said, raising my hands. "I'm sitting down."

Tears ran down Nancy's face unabated. "My own brother. My father." She locked eyes with me. "Where do you go when there's no place left for you? No place on earth for you?"

My heart pounded in my chest. I knew those feelings.

"I know, Nancy. I know what that means. I've been haunted by those same thoughts. I know what it's like to sit with them—to not know if the next moment will be your last."

"It would be easy to…give in. So easy. No more worry, no more pain, no more abuse. No more anything."

"It would be easy. It's hard to walk away from the cliff. But when you do, you have something that you didn't have a couple moments before."

"What's that?" Nancy said.

"*Opportunities.* For something different. A smile. A laugh. A connection with someone. The chance to do something good for someone. All of those things."

"What if I can't?"

"But you *can.* I sat with you in a coffee shop not long ago. You were relaxed, we had a good time. You may have been faking the whole thing, but I enjoyed it."

"I didn't fake it. Part of me was playing out my role, but there was a part of me that felt...normal."

Nancy moved the gun away from her head and sighed. I sat back and blew out a breath. Until Nancy raised the gun and pointed at me. She moved toward me, stopping when the gun reached my forehead. My guts clenched.

"But I still have to do what I came here for. I owe it to my mother." She turned the gun toward my mother.

I yelled and pushed Nancy's arm as she pulled the trigger. The bullet shattered the window behind the loveseat. Max lunged at Nancy and sunk her teeth into Nancy's calf. Nancy screamed and pointed the gun toward Max, who was trying to shake Nancy's leg like a rag doll. I lunged from my chair, hitting Nancy with my shoulder and wrapping my right arm around her waist. I was sprawling on top of Max when I heard the second gunshot and felt searing metal punch into my left shoulder. Max yelped and flailed. I cried out, and Nancy screamed again as we all toppled to the floor. Max squirmed to free herself. I tried to hold Nancy down. I felt her crawling away from me. I knew the gun had dislodged and she was reaching for it. I reached blindly....

Then I heard a sharp crack as everything went black.

CHAPTER EIGHTY-SIX

MY FACE FELT SLICK. I heard sounds that seemed far away. My head was fuzzy, like I was trying to wake up from a long nap.

I opened my eyes. Max was licking my face.

I started to move, and the pain in my shoulder made me stop. I rolled right rather than left and felt Nancy's body beneath me. As I tried to clear my head, Max turned her attention to my wound and started sniffing and licking. It felt like my whole body was throbbing.

"I'm good, Max. Going to live. Thanks for...reviving me."

Shit. *My mother!* I looked up at the loveseat. She wasn't there.

The curtains moved from the breeze created by the gaping hole in the window. I struggled to my feet and, once I was up, tried to put pressure on my wound. I didn't know about my back, but I was bleeding from under my collarbone.

Nancy wasn't moving. I could see from the rise and fall of her back that she was still breathing.

My mother appeared in the doorway, hobbling into the room with her cane, wet paper towels in her free hand.

"We need to...to call for police and an ambulance," I said, cringing from the pain.

"They're on their way," she said. "Here, sit down."

I sat on the loveseat while my mother tried to clean my wound.

"I think...I think I'm going to need...to get sewn up for this. It feels like...an explosion went off in me. Hard...to breathe."

"What do we do with her?" she asked.

I turned my head to look. "She's...down...for the count." I looked back to my mother. "What the hell...happened?"

"It was like watching a crime show," my mother said. "Max chomped on that Nancy's leg like it was a steak. Then you tackled her, and all three of you landed in a heap. Nancy's gun was on the floor. She was trying to find it. But she was right on the floor in front of me, so I rapped her on the head with my cane."

CHAPTER EIGHTY-SEVEN

I LEANED AGAINST THE WALL outside the emergency room. I was stitched, bandaged, and medicated. I pulled my cell out to call Lieutenant Dean. This was going to be good.

"Dean."

"Lieutenant, it's Bryce. You're not going to believe this."

"I heard. You found Nancy."

"The locals called you already? I thought they'd let me break the news to you."

"Sorry, doc. Active case. But I want to hear from you how it went down."

"Did you hear that Tom and Nancy were siblings?"

"Shit, no. I didn't get that part. You've got to be kidding me."

"No. No joke. Turns out I knew Nancy and Tom's mother. She was a patient of mine years ago who killed herself during an argument with the father. Bad things happened in the family after that. Substance abuse. Incest dynamics. The two set their sights on revenge. And I was in the crosshairs."

"So let me get this part straight. You had *three* stalkers. Three. That's got to be some kind of record. So, like Tom, Nancy paid your mother a visit. Go on."

"Yep. Nancy reasoned that I had killed her mother, so she was going to kill mine. But Max intervened. That hound can move when she's motivated. She took a chunk out of Nancy, who was going to shoot *her*. But I got in the way and we all went down. Get this—I got shot trying to keep hold of Nancy, who was reaching for her gun again. I felt her moving away. But my mother—my eighty-year-old mother clubbed her with her cane!"

Lieutenant Dean laughed. "Wow, that took spunk! That's an amazing story."

I told him about Nancy and Scooch and Nancy's incendiary email messages.

"That's twisted. I'll pass that on to Dr. Jones when I update him on Nancy. How's your arm?"

"The bullet went right through me. It's stitched up, and I'm in a sling for a while. But it's not my driving arm."

"You were lucky." Lieutenant Dean paused for a few moments. I heard his chair creak. "You know, what you went through. All the psychological distress. Three people gunning for you. You had more assailants in a week than most small-town cops face in a lifetime of duty. What I said to you before was only partially true."

"What do you mean?"

"When I told you that you were pretty much a mess except in the trenches, when you acted as a psychologist. It's more than that, though. It took guts for you to face what you did. Flick, Tom, *and* Nancy. And in critical conditions. Man, you can come and work for me anytime."

"I appreciate that, Lieutenant. But I think I'll stick to shrinking. It might be safer that way."

"Well, how about this, then. We need someone to evaluate bad guys from time to time. And more importantly, cops. Line-of-duty reactions, fitness for work, PTSD, those sorts of things. You interested?"

"Now you're talking my language. I've actually been thinking about setting up a private practice. But putting way too much thought into it. Dragging the whole thing out. You may have just given me the motivation."

I hung up and went inside the lobby to sit down. A local cop had promised me a ride to my mother's house once he got done with transfer paperwork. Nancy had been treated for a concussion and a Max-brand dog bite, and was going to be picked up by New Alex Regional Police.

I looked around. This was the ER where my parents had taken me years before. The same hospital.

* * *

Thick black sutures in my belly. A drain in my side. Some warm, sticky looking discharge in the drainage bag.

* * *

The sledding incident made me miss a lot of school that year. In a way, that was helpful. No more gym class. No more cross-country running. No more bullies. My self-esteem had taken a big hit, though. Further development of my social skills was on hiatus. And no one ever knew, nor probably even suspected, that my sled-versus-tree incident was anything other than an accident. And the sutures—just like the long, pink scar that followed—reminded me that I had cheated death. Just as I had a short time ago.

Things had come full circle.

There was one more conversation I needed to have. I'd been avoiding it for years. But after what had happened today, there was no better time than the present.

CHAPTER EIGHTY-EIGHT

MAX, MY MOTHER, AND I sat on the porch. My mother was rocking, I was sitting on a glider, and Max was pretending to ignore her stuffed yellow doll. We were quite the crew.

"What kind of grip was that you used on the cane?" I asked, breaking the silence. "Better yet, let me back up a minute. Why did you have your cane with you?"

"Oh, that part. We never did talk about that. I told the police about it but not you. Nancy showed up early this morning. I went to the door and talked to her through the screen. She said she was from the church, and could she come in and visit with me. She seemed nice enough, so I let her in.

"We went in to the living room. I was using my walker. I asked if she wanted some water or coffee or something. She said she would get it, so I sat down. She took my walker with her! Carried it right out into the kitchen. I couldn't imagine why she did that. But I keep a cane under the loveseat. I worked it out with my foot and leaned it against the arm of the loveseat. I didn't want to be without support in case I had to go to the door from there or I needed to go and get my walker."

"Did you ask her why she took it?"

"I did. She said she didn't want it to be in the way and that I wasn't going to need it anytime soon. Then she showed me the gun."

"Wow. I'm sure glad you had it."

"Didn't know I would need it for something other than walking. And your other question. I used both hands on the cane. I hit her like I was pounding a nail. I was afraid if I used one hand I would drop the cane—or break my wrist."

I laughed.

"That was pretty frightening in there," she said. "And hard to listen to. Life isn't always easy. I was sitting in there, wondering what to do, what I *could* do. And then I was thinking about what it was like when your dad died. Those last days with him here, they were really difficult. Not just taking care of him, but watching him slowly fade away. I reminded myself if I could get through that, I could handle what was happening today, live or die."

"I'm glad you—we—made it through. You saved us there at the end. I wasn't able to hold Nancy down."

"I was lucky you knocked her so close to my loveseat."

She rocked a few times, then paused. "And I know something else that's true. You saved that girl's life. I was sure she was going to pull that trigger. You brought her back from the brink. That was a very brave thing to do. You could have let her do it. But that's not how you are. I'm proud of you."

I felt the tears well up. "Thanks, Mom. My upbringing wouldn't let me do otherwise."

My mother nodded. "Bryce, those things you were saying to her...."

"Yeah, I was thinking about those things just a little bit ago, myself. Things I never told you about."

"I know you had a hard time in seventh grade. Your asthma, the change in schools, the whole thing with the gym teacher."

"You remember those things?"

"Remember them? I've never forgotten them. Your dad and I drove to the school and met with the principal. These days, parents would just sue the school district. Back then, it was different. But your dad and I were hopping mad. That school knew they were in the wrong. They said they would take care of things."

"I didn't know that. I was so mired in everything happening. I didn't have any friends. Like Nancy said, it was like there was no place on Earth for me. That day, that winter day. I got on my sled and tried to kill myself."

"Oh, Bryce," my mother said, "you nearly did."

CHAPTER EIGHTY-NINE

"I KNOW. I'VE THOUGHT A lot about it. If Dad hadn't stopped to get me. If we had gotten to the hospital a few minutes later. I didn't know any other way. I had reached my end."

"But you hadn't. You had major surgery. They took out your spleen. You went on to do so many wonderful things. You became a psychologist. You met Vicki. Things you never would have done otherwise."

"I know, now. But I haven't fully escaped from those days, though. At least, not unscathed. I'm sorry that I couldn't find a way to tell you without crashing my sled into a tree."

"Maybe you did. Maybe I wasn't able to hear it. Maybe I let you down."

I knelt beside her rocker and hugged her. "I couldn't have asked for more than you gave me," I said. "I'm sorry."

"Me, too," she said.

We sat side by side for a few minutes until it was time to go. Max and I said goodbye to my mother and climbed into the Prius. When I reached the stop sign at the top of Church Hill, I pulled through the intersection and over to the curb.

I got out and opened Max's door. She hopped out. We walked to the top of the hill. The grass had been mowed recently. There was a smell of summer about it. I looked down at the bottom of the hill. I studied the two broad branches of land that formed a Y. I had chosen neither the right or the left arm, but went right down the middle. The tree that I had smashed into was no longer there. I doubted I had destroyed it with my Flexible Flyer. It was probably cut down at some point to create the garden area that took its place.

We walked back to the car. I knew that there was more to the story than the hill and the sled. There were demons that were trying to get out. That's what the flashbacks have been about.

But for today, I had held the demons at bay.

CHAPTER NINETY

IT HAD BEEN OVER A week since I had been at work. As I walked from the parking lot, I found myself watching the wind ripple through the trees.

"The winds of change," I murmured.

I stepped into the residential unit—and a loud *pop* jolted me. Fortunately, this was followed by streamers and a throng of staff members welcoming me back.

Larry smiled from the front of the pack.

"We all needed something to celebrate. Welcome back, Bryce."

The festivities were brief but enjoyable. Afterwards, I stopped in Larry's office for a conference. Loose ends to tie up.

"Sometime I'll catch you up on all the crap that went down. It's been a rough go for a while now. But I mainly wanted to let you know, Tom and Nancy hacked into my email. They sent messages from my account. I had nothing to do with those messages."

Larry blinked a couple of times.

"Lieutenant Dean was kind enough to fill me in about the messages. I told Wendy as well. She was quite relieved, by the way. She said they seemed totally out of character for you." He shook his head. "With all the professional and administrative issues I've ever had to deal with, the situation between Joan and me about those email messages was the most difficult. Like Wendy said, it didn't seem like something you would do. And you seemed so shocked when I probed for a reaction out at my place. Now it all makes sense. What a wicked stunt."

"Yeah. They knew how to cause damage. Will you please explain things to Joan? I want to make sure things are set right. I've got other fences to mend."

"Already done. Do you need some time off?"

"I might. I just need to see what a normal routine brings for now. Plus, I want to make some changes."

"What kind of changes?"

"Lifestyle changes, mostly. You know—more exercise, eat better, have more fun."

"All good things."

"I'd like to make a change here, too. I'd like to see some select patients for individual psychotherapy. Starting with Maegan."

Larry stroked his chin.

"There are two issues. First, that activity falls outside the realm of typical consulting practices."

"Is that a liability concern?"

"It's more of a contractual thing. It would set a precedent."

"Well, let's *set* a precedent, then. I'm sure there will be complex cases that will require more expertise than our full-time clinicians possess."

"No question about that, as is the case with Maegan. Which brings up the next point. It's quite possible Maegan will be placed elsewhere."

"Oh? Why?"

"Well, the managed care organization is concerned about the abuse that occurred here. They're suspending new referrals to us and are sending a team over to conduct a significant member incident review. We'd have to provide evidence we're able to treat Maegan effectively despite what happened."

"Will patient choice play a role in this?"

"She's of age, so I'm sure they will take her preference into consideration. The MCO *would* probably also appreciate that an experienced consultant will be directly involved in Maegan's treatment."

"So, if Maegan stays...."

"You're the man. I'll let the board know. Thanks for offering your services. We need to focus as an agency on recovering from all this."

Larry and I shook hands. I started to leave.

"Bryce?"

"Yes?"

"Glad you're with us."

As I made my way up to the unit, I had a feeling. A *good* feeling. More winds of change. The unit seemed more vibrant. Music blared from a radio near the staff desk.

Nurse Ratched—I mean, Nurse Weiss—was jotting a note in a chart.

"Hey, Dr. D. Welcome back. Your appearance is very timely. I just met with Maegan."

"What's the scoop?"

"You may have heard that the MCO is considering moving her out of here. I explained the concerns to Maegan. Bottom line, with Jimmy and Tom no longer threats, she wants to stay here. She feels that she has moved too often and wants to make it work here. She's quite insightful."

"That she is. *Brave* and insightful. I'm glad she intends to stay. Now I can break the news that she has to continue to put up with me."

I was barely two steps from the staff desk when I received the summons.

"Doc!"

Maegan trotted across the hall.

"Just the person I wanted to see," I said.

"Me? *Now* what did I do?"

"Nothing I know of. The nurse just told me you plan on staying. That's quite a decision to make."

"I've had enough life experience to know shit can happen anywhere. I'm tired of being shipped from place to place. I think I can do okay here..." She tilted her head and blushed.

"What were you going to say?" I asked.

"Oh, uh, I was going to ask you if you've ever had the feeling that something is just...meant to be?"

"I think I had that feeling once. I still didn't win the lottery, though."

Maegan laughed. "Chris Rock strikes again. Do you stay up at night just coming up with this shit?"

"Nope. It just comes to me. But to give a serious question the serious answer that it deserves, yes, I have had those feelings. And it's often wise to follow your gut instincts."

Maegan nodded. "Yeah. I've done a good job of not listening to them for a while now."

"It's a human thing to do. But listen, I'm glad I caught you in a good mood. I have some news to share with you. You've been assigned a new therapist."

Maegan scowled. "I have to break in another frickin' shrink? That's not right! And it's not fair. It already sucks to be in this nut house. What happened to Wendy? Don't I get a say in this? Why am I the last to find out?"

"Let's take those one at a time. Yes, you have a say in this. Wendy's still here. And, no, you don't have to break in someone new. *I'm* going to be your *frickin' shrink.*"

Maegan took a step back. I watched a range of emotions cross her face. I gave her credit, though. She was quick to recover.

"You? That's great. Just great. The nut house committee thinks I'm so psycho they have to assign the head shrink to my case. Finally, something to write home about." But she was smiling.

"Actually, the nut house committee didn't even have to vote on this one. It was my idea. I was hoping that we could continue with the good hypnotic work we've started. Besides, I don't mind a challenge. So, I'm your new shrink. If it's okay with you."

Maegan sighed. "Doc, no matter what people say about you, I think there's hope for you yet. You just need more practice. But, yeah, you can be my therapist. Don't think I'm going to just open right up to you, though." She paused, blushing again. "So...when do we start?"

CHAPTER NINETY-ONE

I MADE AN UNPLANNED STOP in the center of town. There was a small furniture store that sold other household furnishings as well, including framed photography and artwork.

I found what I was seeking. A large, oak-framed picture of a single tree beside a fence against a wintry backdrop. I knew the print was entitled *Solitude*, but to me, the work symbolized peace, harmony, and balance. I bought it, and with the help of the store owner, slid it onto the back seat of the Prius. I looked forward to hanging it on my living room wall later in the day.

A lot had happened in my humble abode.

In the last day, my townhouse had been cleaned from stem to stern. Compliments of the management, who had been informed by the regional police that a key and other access had been inappropriately provided to a non-resident. I heard through the grapevine there was also an opening for a chief maintenance man. I decided not to feel guilty about it.

When I got home, I was surprised to see Vicki and Max waiting for me outside. I leaned the new print against the wall.

"Art for the walls?"

"It seemed about time," I said.

Vicki tilted her head and looked at the print.

"A little lonely, isn't it?"

"I like it. You know art…in the eyes of the beholder and all."

"True. Is that your tree?"

"I hadn't thought of it like that. But it could be. It could be a new rendering of it."

"Well, good, then. Do you mind if I come in for a few minutes?"

"Come on in. The place is cleaner than it was the day I moved in."

I pulled a couple bottles of iced tea from the fridge. Fresh water in the bowl for Max. Vicki and I assumed our usual positions.

"You're all over the news." Vicki said.

"I hope they're not using my driver's license photo."

"Oh, be serious. You've become a national story. Even Max has gotten press."

Max was sprawled on her side on the floor, but her tail thumped the carpet nevertheless.

"How did you get through all that? There were so many times you could have been killed."

"Probably more than you heard about."

"Why didn't you tell me?"

I set my tea down on a coaster. "Are you serious? The last time I tried to talk to you about something that had happened, you cut me off. You even let Max out from your car without coming to the house or saying goodbye."

Vicki hung her head.

"That was...awful. I've been so awful to you. I think I was so upset about the email I got and the bookstore incident."

"Do you believe me now that I wasn't the one sending you messages?"

"Yes. I even made it out to be like you were paranoid. You were just being honest."

"It's been a long road."

"I could have lost you."

"I didn't think you were concerned about that. The whole bathrobe incident and all."

"That was such a mistake. I've let my anger push me into doing things that weren't like me."

"That's the most I've ever heard you admit to."

"I'm not very good at it. Maybe I do need therapy."

"Wait a minute," I said. "I think I need to see some sort of ID."

Vicki smiled. "Is it that bad?"

"It's pretty different. It's hard to reconcile what you're saying with what I've seen and heard. And what about bathrobe guy?"

"Bathrobe guy is history."

"Fun while it lasted?"

Vicki's face reddened. "I...guess I deserve that."

"Vicki, I've not had a chance to express my feelings to you. I'm angry and hurt about things you said and did."

Vicki nodded. "So, where do we go from here?"

"Let's make a date. Something low-key. We could even do coffee at the bookstore so we can get that taste out of our mouths. And talk. But we'll have to set up some ground rules. Rules for communication. I know you don't like to make things formal, but we should do that."

Vicki stood up and offered her hand. I stood up and offered my arms for a hug. She pulled in close and whispered in my ear, "I'm so glad you're safe. I never stopped loving you."

Her whispered breath smelled like cinnamon; her hair smelled like flowers.

She kissed my cheek as she pulled back.

"Thanks for coming over. I'll call you about the coffee. Just give me a day or two to see what's on my schedule once the smoke clears."

Vicki smiled, patted Max on the head, and let herself out.

I sat down on the floor with Max and rubbed her belly. Tonight, I was going to take it easy.

No stalkers.

No would-be murderers.

And nobody in my bathrobe except for me.

ABOUT THE AUTHOR

LEE MAGUIRE has practiced as a psychotherapist, behavioral health consultant, and taught master's and doctoral level psychology students. Clinical hypnosis has been a significant focus of Lee's clinical practice. Lee resides in central Pennsylvania with his wife and basset hound, the latter an inspiration for Max's character. When not writing or otherwise working, Lee is challenged to improve his golf game.

Connect with Lee

Website:
www.leemaguire.ink

Facebook:
www.facebook.com/groups/DrBryceDavisonThrillers

www.facebook.com/Dr-Bryce-Davison-Thriller-Series-1497309670567574

GET BOOK DEALS AND DISCOUNTS

Get discounts and special deals on books at

www.TCKpublishing.com/bookdeals